# Obedience

'Quietly written but intensely imagined, a novel about one of the defining questions of the century just past: where and how we choose to draw the line between innocence and guilt, ignorance and complicity.'

Hilary Mantel

'A wise, mysterious, gravely compelling story… *Obedience* begins as a novel of slow, intense observation and opens out into a novel of huge scope and profound questioning.'

Alexandra Harris, *Sunday Times*

'*Obedience* should have been on the Booker shortlist: seriously intelligent (and serious), steeped in ambiguities and hugely readable. Can a novel do or be more?'

Julie Myerson, *New Statesman*, 'Books of the Year'

'A convent in rural France is the backdrop to Jacqueline Yallop's spellbinding tale of betrayal and illicit desire… It is the human experience of love, desire, guilt and loneliness that are at the heart of the novel. Yallop writes with real flair about these emotions, and it is some measure of her skill that she turns a nun's failed hopes into a compelling and quietly devastating story about a woman destroyed by her faith.'

Lucy Popescu, *Independent on Sunday*

'A work of great originality, devastating in its impact… Yallop is a writer of rare, fine judgement and delicacy – it's no surprise that *Obedience* come

D0265543

Hilary Mantel. Intensely compassionate in her depiction of old age and its attendant miseries – in particular loneliness – Yallop is also uncompromising, insistently raising questions of culpability and complicity that seem calculated to disturb… As powerful as it is subtle, a novel of gripping emotional and psychological intensity.'

Stephanie Cross, *Daily Mail*

'This is darkly shocking fiction… Yallop is a powerful and seductive writer, and accomplishes the tricky task of fixing her readers' attention on a protagonist who is slow-witted, possibly to the point of being devoid of moral sense, yet gripped by two passions – sacred and profane love… Yallop's fiction forces us into an intensely troubling moral voyeurism. There is a chilliness to her narrative: the worst of human nature, from indifference to brutality, is the fabric of her coolly elegant fiction. That detachment makes *Obedience* a disturbing read. If you think the purpose of fiction is to soothe or beguile, this probably isn't for you.'

Jane Shilling, *Sunday Telegraph*

'*Obedience* is a thought-provoking novel about collaboration and divided loyalties… While it is interesting enough to meet Sister Bernard in her old age it is the story of her past that has us gripped.'

Lianne Kolirin, *Daily Express*

'An intense and devastating novel'

Fanny Blake, *Women & Home*

# Obedience

## Jacqueline Yallop

Atlantic Books
London

First published in hardback and trade paperback in Great Britain in 2011
by Atlantic Books, an imprint of Atlantic Books Ltd.

This paperback edition published in Great Britain in 2012
by Atlantic Books.

1 3 5 7 9 10 8 6 4 2

A CIP catalogue record for this book is available from the British Library.

Paperback ISBN: 978 0 85789 103 7
E-book ISBN: 978 0 85789 575 2

Printed in Italy by Grafica Veneta

Atlantic Books
An Imprint of Atlantic Books Ltd
Ormond House
26–27 Boswell Street
London
WC1N 3JZ

www.atlantic-books.co.uk

*For Mum and Dad*

# Obedience

# One

Mother Catherine knew the devil. He was twisted and dwarfish; his clawed hands were gnarled. His neck was short and his legs bowed. He had a hump on his back, heavy like a sack of walnuts. He was crafty, she knew that; she had heard how cunning he could be. But surely he could never stretch over five shelves of jars, pickles and conserves to take down the coffee and tempt her nuns?

Sister Bernard, too, was a little under five foot tall, and of limited reach. She had to ask for help to take the packet down from its place at the top of the pantry, and this is how she met the young soldier. He stretched over her. She noticed how thin he was. As he reached up, his uniform jacket swung away from his shoulders, too large and loose for his frame, making him gawky, cartoonish. He smelt of damp cloth. He brushed the packet quickly with his open hand, in case there was dust perhaps, and he gave the coffee to Sister Bernard without looking at her. Then he went back to join the other soldiers bent over the refectory table and she listened to their guttural chatter as she lit the stove. She understood nothing. The smell of the coffee made her hungry and light-headed.

Looking out through the small window above the sink there was just the sweep of the convent drive and the village clustered beyond, cramped and low, the moss thick on the heavy stone roof tiles. The wash house, the well and the water fountain huddled together in the dip of land by the stream; the church tower stood high to one side, its spire uncertainly modelled against the trees, and the square in front of it hidden from Sister Bernard's view. Smoke rose in the cluster of stores and farm buildings packed in by the bakers, hanging in the airless day, misting the street. A dog ran. Women bent low over buckets and baskets, the ridged earth encircling them, their hats pale. On the slope that rose behind the houses, the new leaves of the vines shone and the gnarled old stems greened with the promise of early summer.

Sister Bernard hardly saw it. It was too ordinary, the way it had always been. She could not see that the occupation had made much difference. For the few weeks the German soldiers had been there, the days had passed unremarkably. The women and the old men seemed to be getting everything done. There was a silence settling, an unstirring quiet that perhaps stretched across the whole of this part of France, creasing up against the mountains to the south and north, and unfolding over the flat land on either side. But Bernard hardly noticed this, and God did not mention it.

She stirred the coffee in the pan, watching its thickness bubble. It had been many months since she had tasted coffee; it might have been years, she could not remember.

This same packet had been stored on the top shelf of the pantry since long before the previous winter, she was sure of that at least. There was the rationing brought about somehow by the war, which had reached them finally, stripping the shelves at the *alimentation* in the village. And there was Mother Catherine's unshakeable belief that coffee was a temptation from the devil. Both of these things had kept it from her, and she had not once thought of the pleasure of it until now.

Sister Bernard carefully folded the packet again, slipping a pin through to hold the loose paper. Then she dipped her finger very slowly into the pan, feeling the warmth of the steam on her hand and letting her finger linger in the coffee until she could not bear it any longer. When she put it to her mouth, she closed her eyes and felt a drip slide down her chin. It was the coolness of her lips she tasted, more than anything.

It was a surprise when one of the Germans spoke, in French, so that Bernard could understand him. She opened her eyes with a start and popped her finger from her closed lips. She could not think what he might want. Even at thirty, in her prime, she was not beautiful. Her hair was already thin and her skin faded, her hands were wretched. No one spoke to her much, except God.

'Come in, Sister, we will not disturb you,' said the German.

Bernard half-turned from the brewing coffee, beginning to smile. She twisted her wet finger in the folds of her habit and she tried to quieten the monotone rumble of God preaching in her head. She stepped through the doorway to the refectory where the soldiers were waiting.

It was like somewhere new, the sun coming in through the long windows and the table shrunk by the bulk of the men, their uniforms somehow exotic and the temptation still tingling on her tongue. Bernard gulped down a stuttered breath.

But he had not been speaking to her. They were all looking towards the back door, where Sister Jean had paused at the sight of them, unsure.

'*Entrez, entrez*,' he said again, his accent sharp.

'I have come for the pig scraps, *monsieur*,' she said, blinking at the unfamiliar need to explain her routine.

He got up and went to the door, pulling it more fully open and standing to one side, his arm outstretched into the refectory, inviting in the nun. He bowed, low and loose, grinning. One or two of the other soldiers applauded. Still Sister Jean stood outside.

'Come on then, come on,' he said again.

Sister Jean did not move. The German looked at her for a moment, no longer smiling, and shook his head. He stepped towards her and pulled at her arm, yanking her across the threshold. She stumbled. He slammed the door behind her and brushed his hands together, ignoring her now as he went back to his place at the table. Sister Jean winced, the idea of pain keeping her bent over for a moment. And then she passed through to the kitchen, her steps hurried and her eyes fixed on the floor, the empty sack slumped behind her like old skin. The soldier whistled quietly and somebody laughed.

'What are they doing?' Sister Jean stood close to Bernard and piled the leftovers from the bucket into the sack. It swelled on the floor between them. She watched exactly what she was doing, did not even glance at the men.

'They're having coffee, Sister. They're waiting for someone who is with Mother Catherine; it's their commandant, I think.' Bernard was embarrassed by the hiss of Jean's question. 'They've been very quiet – they've been no trouble.'

Sister Jean pulled tight the neck of the sack and kicked the bucket back towards the sink. It was noisy on the stone floor.

'They're drawing straws.'

Bernard could not see how she had known this. There was hardly a movement between the soldiers.

'Pigs,' spat Sister Jean, dragging the sack out into the refectory again. The men did not stir this time as she passed.

Bernard took the pan from the heat. The handle was insecure and her hand unsteady, and she walked slowly with it far in front of her as she took the coffee to them. Two of the soldiers parted, pushing back so that she could fill their glasses, and Bernard held the pan high over the table between them before pouring a measure evenly into each glass. She did not spill anything. Some of them thanked her, and though her hand trembled, God was silent.

Later, when the Germans were preparing to leave, the soldier who had helped Bernard with the coffee brought his empty glass to the sink where she was scraping carrots. He stood for a moment at her side, and she paused in her work. She turned towards him; she saw how young he was, perhaps only twenty, and she saw the perfect blueness

of his eyes, an intimation of divinity. Smiling, he pulled her
veil back from her face, as though to take a better look, and
then he leant towards her and whispered something softly
in her ear in German. She did not understand what he
said, but she blushed anyway, surprised at the intimacy of
the coffee on his breath. As he left her, he tossed away the
short end of matchstick; one of the other soldiers nudged
him.

Smoke hung low from the house fires and the air was
thick. The shutters were closed tightly, blinding the rough
walls, the warm ochre of the stone faded in the grey light.
The clumps of iris pressing against the buildings and along
the edges of the street seemed pallid, their reds and purples
already exhausted. The shuffle of the village could have
been silence, and when the two German soldiers passed
the wash house their shoes clicked incongruously on the
cobbles, the abrupt echoes spiking the quiet. The nuns were
folding heavy wet cloths into baskets; they did not look up.
Bernard was rinsing down the long rows of stone basins,
each one split open like a giant missal so that the linen
could be scrubbed against its sloping surfaces. Unthinking,
she watched the dribble of sudded water disappear into
the unmoving depths of the central wash pond, and she
heard the tap of the soldiers' footsteps as a counterpoint to
the grumble of God. She lifted her head, the heavy bucket
hanging still for a moment, as she watched the Germans
go round the corner towards the church.

Her soldier followed, alone. He paused in front of the
wash house, stepping carefully to one side to avoid the
puddle of spilt water leaking away towards the stream.

He wished the nuns good morning, his French careful and studded with accent. One of the sisters with the basket of washing, a pretty young girl, returned his greeting, half under her breath, dropping her eyes. The soldier looked at the nuns in turn, as though weighing something up. He came to Bernard last. She was half-hidden in the gloom of the interior, the slouch of her habit making her shape indistinct. She met his gaze for a moment, the water dripping fast onto the dark fabric. She saw him clearly, even in that instant, the slightness of him soft in the smoky damp, his hands held tight in front of him, his face already anciently known to her. She looked at the way he stood, at the defeated slump of his shoulders, and she knew she had been chosen for something.

For the rest of the day and into the night Sister Bernard thought about what this might be. She went through events, tremulous and expectant, ignoring as best she could the incessant complaints that God hammered into her head. She recalled everything about the soldier; she went over and over his incomprehensible code of broken-nailed hand signals and half-obscured facial gestures. The thought of him was irresistible, a mystery. It made her feel beautiful. And, while it lasted, it gave her a glimpse of paradise.

The following morning, weary, Bernard sat for a moment on the flat wall that ran out to the henhouse. The sun was low behind the convent, trapping her in shadow. She dipped her head into her hands, and her veil fell thickly about her. She sat very still, doing nothing. God railed.

Since she was a girl, for every waking minute of every day and throughout her dreams, Sister Bernard had been pestered by the voice of God. He commented on everything she did, from the most intimate of habits to the most routine of chores. He was often taxing and abusive, always uncompromising. He disliked sloppiness, and was particular about clean shoes, stockings without holes, and the quantity of toothpaste squeezed onto the brush. His vengeance was swift and loud and stupefying. In the terror of it, her head would fill with the roar of Him until her eyes smarted. Only many hours later would a note of birdsong or the purr of a car engine creep back to her, wary. She could never hear her own voice above the din.

'Sister Bernard?'

There was no sign that she had heard. The other nun leant forwards and gently touched the sway of her veil.

'Sister Bernard?'

Bernard lifted her head this time, blinking. She was surprised that the soldier was not there. She was not sure where she was. All she could be sure of was the smell of cut grass and frying garlic, and she put her hand to her mouth.

'Are you quite well?' The other nun leant forwards, her words slow. 'The girl is here – Severine.'

The woman was of Bernard's age. She held a bundle of baby and stared at Bernard from behind the other nun, her face stupid and blank. Bernard concentrated for a moment on the rise and fall of her nausea; she stood, shaking herself.

'Yes. Thank you,' she said, frowning at the way things were settling back to normal.

'I'll leave you then, shall I? For a moment.' The nun smiled. 'I'll leave you,' she said again.

It was against the rules. Given over to God, the nuns were supposed to have forgotten their families and their friends in the greater vocation of religious life. Earthly ties should have been broken. But there had been no way of keeping Severine from Bernard. She had come silently and irregularly, waiting for long hours on the convent steps or by the kitchen door. They had tried explaining things to her, or shouting; they had shooed her away with the stray cats and once Mother Catherine had brought a great flat dish of holy water to fling at her, an exorcism. But she had always come back, waiting for Bernard without a sound.

Bernard went slowly to Severine and kissed her in greeting, stepping beyond the shadow to where the grass lay in the sun.

'Come on.'

Severine looked long at the nun, expressionless. Then she held out her hand and Bernard took it. They went together up along the wall. Swallows looped out of the open-sided barn, cutting across the dark beams where the last trusses of onions were hung. A pair of fat ducks limped into the shade of the spreading fig tree. Where the path narrowed, the two women dropped hands, waddling instead in single file, their clogs clicking out of time as they slowly followed the track past the pigsties to the far vegetable garden. Lines of sticks cast criss-cross patterns on the flat earth. Shoots pressed upwards in exact rows. God's complaints were muted here, unalarming.

They looked down at the baby. Its head was small and its skin yellow, the lines around its mouth unfinished. It did not open its eyes.

'I have brought you something, Sister,' Severine said quietly, her words careful. She shifted the baby onto one arm and reached into a pocket. When she held it out to

Bernard her face was too expectant. 'I saved it for you, this time.'

It was the baby's umbilical cord, shrivelled now and dried out, twisted and brown, like a shaving of something.

'For luck,' she said, shifting the weight of the baby again.

Bernard took the cord carefully and turned it over in her hand.

'It's kind,' she said.

The baby stirred. Bernard watched as Severine pushed her finger at its mouth, quietening it. But when Severine began a moment later to unbutton the front of her blouse, Bernard turned away. She did not see the baby pushed against her friend's breast, its mouth slack on the red nipple. She looked out instead to where the white cattle were grazing, and she put the present into her pocket, letting it fall deep inside, feeling it, a talisman.

'You're well?' Bernard asked, still turned away. 'You're all well?'

There was no reply for a long while.

'Oh, he won't…' Severine said at last. 'He never,' she added, defeated.

Bernard heard the rustle of clothing. She turned back; the baby was lying flat again across Severine's arms.

'Busy – busy at the farm.' Severine looked hard at her baby, pulling it close. In the brightening light, Bernard noticed new patterns of lines creased into her friend's face, the girl she had always known disappearing. 'Couldn't come here, with it all. When there's no men. Couldn't come.'

'It doesn't matter,' Bernard said.

'No.'

Bernard thought about the soldier. 'Have you seen the Germans?'

Severine nodded.

'Have they come to the farm?'

'No – not yet. It's too far. Too dirty.' Severine grinned. 'Don't like the mud, do they? It keeps them away. Lets us get on with things, doesn't it?'

She seemed to want a particular kind of answer.

Bernard shrugged. 'They come here sometimes,' she said. 'They come to the convent.'

She wanted to say more; she thought she could find a way of describing her soldier. But Severine stepped across and put her hand firmly on Bernard's arm.

'I see you in church,' she said. 'On Sundays. Every Sunday. I wait for it.'

This did not seem new. Bernard hardly noticed what her friend had said; she did not see the way Severine's gaze seemed fixed on her, pleading.

'I suppose,' she said vaguely, not knowing how to begin again, the thought of him so pungent.

Their lives had always been the same, commonplace and familiar, known to them both without thought. It was too hard now to find the things to say. The war had somehow crept upon them, tangling them in change, confusing and disorientating them. Everything looked as it had always done. The new vegetables pushed through the dry layer of bronze soil; the animals shuffled across the yard, unhurried. In the clump of trees beyond the wall, the song of a nightingale trembled and tumbled, remembered from years past, filling the air with the sound of old summers. But still nothing was quite settled. There was a new strangeness to things, as though everything was a little brighter, sharper, louder. They had secrets, for the first time, and no way of telling them. So they stood together quietly at the edge of the ridged garden and the baby made soft noises. They bent their heads in the sun.

When the clock struck, Severine started.

'Have to go,' she said. 'Can't stay.'

Bernard nodded. 'I'm pleased you came. Thank you.'

She watched her friend pick her way along the path and down towards the village. God was scathing about the idiot girl who had always followed Bernard around, the ugly bent-backed peasant. But Severine had always been in Bernard's life, constant and unobtrusive, something of a blessing, and Bernard felt the tug of momentary loss as she disappeared in the dip of the land. She put her hand in her pocket and closed her fingers around the tough string of the umbilical cord. No one had ever given her such a thing before.

Over the following three days, the soldier met Bernard twice at the wash house, once in the open street and once in the convent corridor. Once she glimpsed him briefly at the top of the narrow stone steps that led down to the village well, three of his comrades alongside him and a line of cattle ambling down towards the long troughs, their tails heavy in the air. But by the time she had scrambled down the hill, slipping on the new grass, there was just an old farmer swinging his stick at the last of the cows, his beret pulled low over his brow and a torn sack slung across his shoulders as some kind of coat. The soldiers seemed to have disappeared, as though they had never been there. The farmer nodded at Bernard and moved on. Bernard looked around at the green snarl of hedges, the empty shadows of the sunken well and the closed houses at the edge of the village, and wondered for a moment if the soldiers and their war were nothing more than a mistake of hers, a bizarre dream conjured by her prayers, a mystical, unfathomable story like the ones they taught her at the convent.

But there were times when he took her hand, making everything suddenly real. The touch of him was unmistakable. When he reached towards her, Bernard could hear her heart pummel the woollen vest beneath her habit, and God was silent. It seemed miraculous. It astounded her that merely the sight of the soldier could somehow put an end to His ill-tempered prattle. Even the anticipation made Bernard's breath come quickly and in the ecstatic hours of the night, with God droning in her head, the thought heaved within her, making her hot and unsettled, flushing her cheeks with sudden excitement. By the end of the week, she could no longer still the tremble that was lodged around her heart and when she saw him turn the bend in the convent corridor, she found the rapturous words of the Gloria coming full chorus into her head as the clamour of God receded. She stopped, amazed that the skinny German could do this.

'Do you want to have sex with me, Sister Bernard?' he asked in French, in a low tone. It was a phrase that had been easy to perfect with a little practice, and his accent was good. Bernard had no difficulty in understanding him.

She could not look at him, she could not think of a reply. The sense of things shrank away from her. Not wanting to be delayed, the soldier put his request again, raising Bernard's chin with his forefinger so that she was forced to look at his smile.

'You know my name,' said Bernard at last, trying to swallow the panic of her delight.

'Yes.' He did not want to be tempted into trying out phrases he had not practised.

They both heard footsteps, further along the corridor; the soldier instinctively moved several paces away. Two nuns passed them, one fingering her rosary. Bernard could not be sure who they were; everything seemed unfamiliar, distorted. It could have been a reflection, warped somehow.

When the nuns had gone, he spoke urgently, with authority, knowing that he had a deadline looming.

'You will come tonight at ten to the top henhouse.'

'Oh no – it's too late.' Bernard pulled at the end of her veil with a frantic hand. 'We can't leave our cells at that time.'

The soldier sighed and Bernard felt the strange ache of disappointing him.

'You will not come?' Reworking the plan and afterwards learning the phrases to communicate it would mean an inevitable delay. He risked failing, and he had a sense of what the rest of the unit would say about him then and of how they would exclude him. He stepped towards Bernard. 'You must come.'

She shook her head. The colour had left her cheeks now.

There was the click of shoes on the tiles, and two more Germans strode briskly along the corridor, seeming to fill it, smiling broadly at the soldier from a distance.

'You must come,' he said again.

She fidgeted under his fierce gaze. 'I don't… I can't.'

One of the other Germans spoke, pushing forwards so that he was close to her, stocky and immovable.

'What do you think of him, Sister? What do you think of Schwanz?'

She was confused by the press of them around her, their unfamiliar smells pungent and their faces too large. But she caught the soldier's name, and she looked at him again, seeming to know him.

'That's… that's your—'

'Schwanz. He is Schwanz – that's his name,' the other German answered her, smiling. 'And he really wants to meet with you, Sister.'

Bernard hesitated. The young soldier dipped his head, no longer looking at her, and the other two Germans grinned. When one of the nuns rounded the corner of the corridor and saw Sister Bernard looking up, wide-eyed, at the lanky soldier between his comrades she felt that something might be amiss. She came up and slipped an arm around Bernard's waist, above the belt of her habit. There was a moment's vacancy; then the soldiers bowed together in brief salute and left.

The nun dropped her arm.

'He knew my name,' said Bernard very quietly, the marvel of it rooting in her.

'Is that all, Sister? Did they want something?'

Bernard hardly remembered. She would never think about the soldier's request or its implications. She shook her head.

'You should direct these soldiers to Mother Catherine.

They should not be alone here,' said the nun. She looked hard at Bernard, trying to make her words penetrate.

Bernard shook her head again. She could hear God coming back to her, protesting at a distance, and afterwards the bell for prayers. But nothing would quite settle and she did not know where she was.

Several days later, he tried again.

'You can meet me in church,' he said when he caught Bernard on the way to the woodshed with a bundle of kindling. The sun was hot already, sliding off the red-tiled roofs of the outbuildings and bouncing back from the mottled stones. He wiped his sleeve hard across his forehead, unused to the southern heat. 'Tonight. I will wait.'

Bernard could not think of a reason why she should go to church alone.

'I will arrange it,' was all he said, remembering to smile.

Bernard shuffled in front of him for the few yards to the lane. She puffed under the weight of the sticks. She expected him to laugh at how her feet turned out when she walked, the way the village children did, but he was silent and she took his reticence as a kindness.

Something was done and Bernard was told by Mother Catherine to collect the altar silver from the church for cleaning. She was given the key to the cupboard in the sacristy and told that she could be excused evening prayers if her errand took time. How this came about, she did not know. But on the way to the church in the late spring dusk she could hardly stop herself from running. The light seemed sharp around her, making everything crisp and memorable and somehow new. The sky bent to her, expectant, and even God could not muffle the melodies of the world. When she pushed open the leather door into the dim nave, she expected something glorious to happen. She would not have been surprised by choirs of golden angels.

The soldier was sitting in the pew furthest from the altar. His head was bowed; he might have been praying. Even with the thud of the door as it swung back, he did not move. Bernard stood at the far end of the aisle and waited. The church was unlit and the evening was darker there than it was outside, the smell of winter still trapped within. The arches of the roof stretched away into shadow; the side chapels were nothing but dark. Bernard shivered. She had never learnt to be comfortable here.

When he finally turned to her, his face was white in the gloom. Without speaking he left the pew and walked along the back of the church to where some old benches were pushed in against the pillars, creating an extra block of seating out of sight of the altar. It was hardly used; the benches were untidy. He pushed the back two or three more neatly into rows, the scrape of them sharp on the flagged floor, then he spread his pocket handkerchief across the wooden seating and looked at Bernard, for the first time.

The wager was safely settled. Bernard had her hips jammed uncomfortably against the bench and kept up an animal whimpering that echoed in the cavern of the side chapel, but the German soldier was efficient and intense; he let nothing distract him, not even the unremitting flap of his uniform jacket. For a moment afterwards he held his head in his hands, but as Bernard sat up, dazed, he straightened himself. He folded the handkerchief evenly. When he left, his footsteps loud, he did not look back at the immensity of the church behind him.

God returned to scold as soon as she was alone. His wrath was tangled; He pointed out the scuffs on her shoes and the slight filmy drip on the floor where she stood, but He had no words for what she had done. Stretching out the soreness in her joints, Bernard went through to the sacristy in the confusion of His disapproval. Trying to open the cupboard she dropped the key and had to kneel in the almost-dark to search for it among the books and boxes piled on the floor. She could not move quickly. It was a long time before her thick fingers found what they were looking for, and even then she stood for a long while looking at the cupboard door before she tried to open it again. The state of the sacred silverware within threw God into a paroxysm of rage.

# Two

The old war was there in the stones of the village, in the unnecessarily neat walls built by the prisoners and in the hidden corners where the blood of murdered soldiers had once flowed. But it was more or less invisible in a new century. Music drifted up from the old *charcuterie*, transformed now into a bar, with bright lights and a pool table and a succession of boys on noisy scooters; there was nothing left of the hung hams and the wooden counter piled high with flecked *saucisson* and *boudin*. Even the wide window had been pulled out and altered; the old flagged floor concreted over. In the years after the war, when the shop had been empty, there had still been a smell there, the rich odour of drying meat. But that, too, had finally gone and now there was only the tinny repetition of songs in strange languages. Bernard stretched through the open window and pulled the convent shutters tight. The sound of the music faded; she had it almost shut out.

She continued purposefully, closing each set of shutters, not pausing in any of the empty cells, her progress steady and unhurried, the fall of the heavy dusk already a defeat.

The processional squeal of the hinges filled the long corridor. She paused for a moment, while her breathing settled, and she offered something, the hint of a prayer, in return for a brief balm for some of her pains. She had never thought it would be like this, to be old. She had never imagined the inescapable monotony of her decrepitude. She raised her eyes to the convent ceiling, where long trails of damp cobwebs darkened the pocked plaster, and she sighed.

At seven she rang the gong, as she always did, its tones weaker now than they once were. Then she went to fetch Sister Marie and Sister Thérèse who would not have heard it. They were sitting where she had left them, in the little snug fashioned from a corner of the ground-floor passage. When the convent had been busy, this had been something of a bottleneck, an awkward crick in the smooth running of things, where the nuns were apt to bump into each other with their bundles of firewood or bed linen, and where the sound seemed to gather, drawing in the grumble of things all around. Now, with just the three of them remaining, it was the only space small enough to seem habitable, a retreat from the cold wide rooms in the rest of the building, a corner of comfortable armchairs and a heavy television. It was where they spent most of their time. It was possible to imagine here that they were filling things, keeping the emptiness of the convent at bay.

A faded blue and white Virgin gazed out placidly over their heads from her niche and the faint perfume of chrysanthemums drifted up from the burnt-orange bouquet at her feet. Sister Marie smiled at Bernard, too lavish a greeting, and Sister Thérèse put down her sewing with a sigh.

'Supper?' said Thérèse.

Bernard nodded. She leant forwards and rearranged the sloping wimple on Marie's head. Stepping back, she noticed a fallen chrysanthemum petal and she bent to pick it up, the gathered age in her bones breathing a slight moan. She could not think of anything to say; there was a response to everything that was happening, she guessed that, but it would not come to her. Nor, she knew, could it be shouted into the depths of Thérèse's deafness, histrionic. So she put the petal in her pocket and pulled herself straight, her face unchanging.

'Supper,' she said quietly.

Thérèse saw the familiar flap of the word. 'It's been a fine day, Sister Bernard,' she said, nudging herself out of her chair. She took Marie's right arm.

'It's going to rain,' said Bernard, taking Marie's left arm.

They pulled. Marie swayed gracefully upright until, her knees still half-bent, she was balanced against the strain exerted by Bernard and Thérèse, a masterful demonstration of a physical law none of them would ever know. They hung there for a moment, the three of them, old women playing ring-a-ring o' roses, and then, with a final tug, they brought Marie to a stand. She swayed precariously.

'That'll kill me one day,' said Thérèse. She did not mean it. She felt strong. She still had the straight limbs of youth that made her seem tall, a firm face drawn tight around her sharp nose, and smooth hair that could not quite be called grey.

'God sees our pain, Sister,' said Bernard, beginning to edge Marie along the corridor.

The refectory exuded the damp chill of breathing stone. The light through the long windows was flaccid, and the stained plaster browning the ceiling and the tops of the walls was somehow an accusation. At the far end of the heavy table two high-backed chairs were set close to each other, draped across with the peeled skins of wet stockings.

'Is it pasta, Sister?' asked Thérèse, without curiosity, as they manipulated Marie past the draped chairs.

'It is, Sister. With butter,' said Bernard.

But the sound of shuffling slippers on the stone floor, of water boiling on the hob, of the bench being scraped aside to make room for the three of them, meant that Thérèse was unable to hear. It did not matter.

'I thought so,' she said, knowing.

Marie burped.

They ate without speaking, and when they had finished Thérèse pushed her empty plate towards Bernard and opened a puzzle book in front of her, tracing with ease the word connections on the page. Bernard watched the sure swing of the pen. She took a paper handkerchief from her pocket, spat on it lightly, and leant across to wipe around Marie's mouth. She collected the plates and took them through to the sink. When she came back, she could smell the familiar stench of urine and saw the dark leak of it from where Marie was sitting.

'We should begin to pack our things,' she shouted at Thérèse across the table. 'We must be ready. And we'll have to make sure Sister Marie is ready, too, since they're coming for her first. They're sending the minibus, very soon; she'll have to be ready.'

'I'm not taking any things,' said Thérèse, looking up briefly from her puzzle and frowning because she had lost her place. In her quick movements and exaggerated expressions, there was still the authority of her teaching days, and Bernard was cowed for a moment.

'You're not taking anything?' she said, too quietly.

'What?'

'YOU ARE NOT TAKING ANYTHING?'

'I'm preparing my soul to meet God,' said Thérèse solemnly.

'God is good,' chimed in Marie, grinning. 'He makes good wine.'

'Then what are you going to do with your things?'

This time Thérèse did not look up from her puzzle. 'Burn them,' she said. 'Or give them away. I don't know – I'll not need them where I'm going.'

'No – I meant your special things. Your collection.'

'So did I.' Thérèse circled another set of letters. 'I don't need all that now.' Then, as though a decision had been made, she closed her puzzle book and leant back.

Bernard went through to the sink and washed the dishes, drying them carefully and stacking them in their place on the shelves. She wiped round meticulously, even though the surfaces were permanently soiled and grubby, clouded with the unshiftable deposits of ancient grease. She ran another cloth under the tap until the water ran hot enough to scald the thin skin on her old hands, and she went back to the refectory, kneeling behind Marie to wipe the pool of urine from the tiles. In the dense quiet of the vast convent, the noise of her movements was essential. Even Thérèse watched for signs of it.

'Do you think it will be better, like that, to start again? Without anything from before?' asked Bernard at last, when there was no more work to be done and the shuffle of her activity was fading.

'I need to scour my soul. I need to show God... to prove to God... I need to...' Thérèse still could not quite think how her future should be. 'I can't just go on, can I, the same? This is a chance, if I get rid of my stuff. They won't let me have anything at the home anyway.'

There was one small orange left in the otherwise empty fruit bowl. Bernard picked it out. She offered it to Thérèse who declined with a shake of the head. Bernard began to strip off the already baggy peel.

'So you're not going to take your things, then?' she asked again, still not believing.

'No.'

'Like the camel through the eye of the needle?'

'Yes. I suppose so.'

Bernard put the peel, a single piece, on the table.

'That's good.'

'It's a start,' said Thérèse, pushing at the orange peel.


After prayers, Bernard helped Sister Marie to her cell where she wiped her face with a flannel, took off her veil and brushed her limp hair, dressed her in her stained nightgown and handed her the rosary beads from the small table. The sickening smells, the feel of Marie's damp loose flesh, her infantile helplessness, pricked Bernard with a sting of sudden nostalgia. When the jobs were done, she perched on the end of the bed. She had never done this before. But it seemed an occasion that should be marked somehow, the last evening they would spend together. She doubted she would ever see Marie again.

'You remember the day you came here?' She pulled the blankets up to Marie's wet chin.

Marie nodded, but perhaps not in response to the question.

'We were so nervous – about you. You'd given up so much to be with us. We put flowers by your window. We'd never done that before. They were pink roses, from the bush at the entrance to the cemetery. Someone had said you'd be used to that sort of thing. It would help you settle in. So I picked them. Every rose I could find. I took one of the vases from the Lady chapel and rubbed it down and put the roses on your table. They were pretty.' Bernard took Marie's hand, much softer than her own. 'But I don't think you noticed them, did you?'

She looked at the slumped face of the woman she had instantly disliked all those years ago, seeing the memory there of the fluttering socialite who had arrived forty years earlier, fresh from having her photograph taken with a minor film star at Monte Carlo, her eyes radiant with fervour, her accent cultured.

'You threw them away before they died,' she added, recalling the sight of the unwithered blooms caught in the garden hedge, still lovely. 'It wasn't really what you wanted. You wanted—'

'God,' said Marie.

'Penance,' said Bernard, letting the hand drop. She stood up, tired suddenly by the effort of trying to reminisce with someone without memory. 'You were always very disciplined, Sister,' she said. 'Very devoted.'

It was the most they had ever spoken together. Marie nodded. She looked sleepy.

'Well then,' said Bernard. 'Goodnight.'

'God bless,' whispered Marie as Bernard turned out the light.

On the way to church for the feast of All Saints, the rain came sudden and heavy, chill with the intimation of winter. Bernard was hardly at the end of the drive, the clank of the bells trying to hurry her. In a moment her veil was heavy and wet, her face burning. Her feet slipped on the soft ground. She bent low and pushed on, turning past the old wash house, silted now. She tried to shelter under the low eaves of the buildings, but the water streamed into her eyes and she could not see. The bells stopped. Bernard edged into a doorway and stood for a while, panting. It was all familiar, from too long ago. She wrung out her veil and pulled the hem of her habit higher over her wet boots.

When she wiped her face she could see the end of the church steps and the wide porch, the doors already closed. She only had to cross the square. She looked around for something she could use to protect herself from the whipping rain, a carrier bag or some piece of cloth someone had left, even a piece of board. But there was nothing. And when she looked again, there were figures now at the top of the steps, pressed up against the wall of the church, one of them in a habit. Bernard stared through the haze of rain, sure for a moment that it was herself there under the porch, the young woman she had once been, but it was only Sister Thérèse and another woman, elongated in their wet clothes.

Bernard watched them. They stood together, almost touching, their intimacy everywhere in the flicker of their movements. Bernard saw the woman take Thérèse's hand and lift it in her own. She saw Thérèse dip forwards, perhaps laughing. It was nothing to do with her, she knew that, but nonetheless she took their closeness as some kind of insult. She shook herself down again and set off towards them, hurrying across the square, not noticing now the rain thrown at her by the gusts of wind.

'Sister Bernard.'

Bernard looked up. Thérèse had pulled away from the other woman and was coming down the steps, her hand outstretched, offering help.

'I thought you were already at Mass. Look at you. You're soaked through.'

Bernard could not speak. She let Thérèse take her hand and help her up the final steps, and she stood shivering alongside the other woman. Water dripped quickly from her habit onto the paving. From inside there was the rising voice of the congregation in prayer.

'This is Corinne Bousquet,' said Thérèse. But the introduction fell awkwardly and there was a long pause before she added, 'This is Sister Bernard. You remember? The other sister I was telling you about?'

Bernard looked at the woman called Corinne. There was nothing special about her. In her black woollen hat and heavy coat she hardly seemed there.

'What are you doing out here?' Bernard asked.

27

Corinne smiled. 'We were plotting. And now it has made us late.'

'We're going in. We saw you, just as we were going in,' added Thérèse.

Bernard felt the cold settle across her wet shoulders. 'Plotting,' she repeated, not understanding.

The other two women looked at each other.

'It's nothing, Sister Bernard. Nothing to worry about,' said Thérèse. 'I knew Corinne when we were both teaching. It was an old idea, nothing more.'

They heard the heave of the pews as the congregation rose to its feet.

'We should forget it,' said Thérèse, looking across at her friend.

But Corinne shook her head. 'We should think about it,' she said.

'We're missing the Mass,' said Bernard. She was surprised at how the other women looked straight into each other's faces.

'We are, Sister. I'm sorry.'

And Thérèse glanced only briefly at Corinne before taking Bernard's arm and walking with her into the porch.

The back rows of the congregation turned at the creak of the door, their faces unclear in the dim light. Bernard paused, half in and half out, and Thérèse had to push her gently forwards. Corinne closed the door as quietly as she could and the three women stood at the back of the church, behind the pews, seduced by the glitter of the altar, unexpectedly golden in the gloom.

'It's different, from back here,' Bernard said very quietly.

Thérèse nodded. But Corinne had already moved to one side and was making space on one of the back pews, getting the men sitting there to slide along. She beckoned towards Thérèse who reached again for Bernard's arm.

From here, the old-fashioned gilt and candlelight glowed distant, fixing the altar in the dark; it was a show, a spectacle, the priest tiny against the stretch of the arches behind and above him, and everything magnificent. Transfixed, Bernard failed to pay attention to where she was going. With her boots still wet and the floor slippery, she tripped on the kneeler upended along the length of the pew and fell forwards with a clatter, flailing out an arm that slapped the head of the man in front, and thudding her leg hard into the seat. The kneeler swung down onto the stone floor with a clank. The noise was enormous. It seemed everywhere.

Thérèse pulled Bernard down into the pew.

'Are you all right, Sister?'

But Bernard's hands were already sharply folded in prayer, her head bowed. It could have been that nothing had happened, except that she was trembling.

'Sister?' asked Thérèse again, too loudly, confused by the echoes of the church.

Bernard did not move. The pain swelled in her bruised leg.

'You see? God be my strength. You see what would happen if I went – if she were on her own?' said Thérèse, sliding onto her knees and looking at Corinne.

Corinne took her friend's hand. They bowed together, as though they were praying.

Bernard did not understand what had been said until towards the end of Mass. As the bell rang out she raised her eyes for the first time, seeing the priest on the golden stage, his arms raised, and then she realized. Thérèse was leaving her.

Thérèse was sitting at the table in the refectory. The collar of her cardigan was pulled up to her ears and she was completing another puzzle from her book, spinning the pen between her fingers as she considered the clues. She looked up as Bernard passed her; the pen dropped onto the table and rolled into the joint between two planks of oak.

'It's All Souls, Sister,' she said. 'It almost slipped my mind what with everything else.'

Bernard had not forgotten. 'I could make some coffee,' she suggested. She thought about the dark, perilous pit of purgatory. When He had still been speaking to her, God had threatened her with it, a place of obscurity and absence, incompleteness. She had tried to imagine how it might be, but nothing had come to her except a muddled sense of musty cellars and damp rock and indescribable suffering. She had taken a place at the front of the gathered nuns in the chapel, motionless through the desolate night, praying on her knees without ceasing for the terrified souls who were trapped there, the damp autumn chill, the dislodged fear and the intoned rites creating a kind of bleak ecstasy.

Thérèse picked up her pen. 'If you like,' she said.

'To warm us through the night. We usually have coffee.'

'If you like, Sister Bernard.'

But there was such unwillingness in her tone that Bernard did not move, and almost immediately Thérèse began again.

'Have you see it? Les Cèdres?'

Bernard looked across at Thérèse.

'What?' she said, the murky hollow cave of purgatory, its unfathomable loneliness, consuming her uncertain sense of Les Cèdres, the diocesan rest home for the elderly where they were being sent.

'Have you seen it? Have you been?' Thérèse glared, as though already Bernard was to blame.

Bernard blinked, the bare shadows of the refectory becoming clear again, familiar.

'No. I thought I'd wait,' she said. 'They provide everything, furniture and linen. I saw no reason to go.'

'You weren't even curious?'

'I've been very busy.'

Thérèse glared. 'You're ninety-something years old. You don't have to be busy. You could have found time to go. Someone would have taken you. I've been.'

Nothing Thérèse could have said would have surprised Bernard more.

'You've been to Les Cèdres?'

Thérèse nodded, thinking of the four magnificent cedars at the genteel religious retirement home and the room she had been allotted at the back, from which there was a view only of unkempt ground and the giant green gas cylinders for the heating and hot water.

'You've been to Les Cèdres?' Bernard had to ask again, unbelieving. 'You've seen it? Where we're going?'

Thérèse looked down at the word puzzle but her eyes slipped across the long table as she remembered.

'First I went to the nursing home for Sister Marie. I know she needs extra care, somewhere with medical staff, with facilities; I know she can't come with us – but still, it's a terrible place. It stinks. I thought at first it was, you know, urine, but it's not that. I think it's what they use to clean up the urine. It's not nice. It can't be necessary. It never smells like that here.'

Thérèse sniffed, as though to make sure.

'And of course there's men there, everywhere, in all the rooms. And brown linoleum. And it's too hot. It's very hot.'

She had hated the place so much, its inescapable heat scrubbing everything smooth, that she had left without seeing the room they were intending to give to Marie when the present occupant finally died.

'But afterwards I went where we're going – to Les Cèdres. And that's nicer. Really. I saw them getting lunch and it looked all right. And there's a pretty little chapel where you can stay all day if you like. It's peaceful. And they were quite friendly.'

Bernard nodded. She could not picture what Thérèse was describing. She rolled fragments of paper tissue between her thumb and forefinger, still anxious about the towering emptiness of purgatory and the unheard cries of the souls that were suffering there.

'Really. It's OK,' said Thérèse weakly.

Bernard heard the accusation in it. 'They thought you should come with me,' she said. 'They thought you needed some care.'

'Because I'm deaf? That makes no sense. It's not as though I'm sick or anything.'

'At our age…'

'At *our* age? Sister, I am twenty years younger than you.'

Bernard frowned. 'But living alone…'

'I live alone here. More or less. Perfectly well. I can manage perfectly well here. Why do they think…?' Thérèse slapped shut the cover of her book and looked straight at Bernard. 'Why do they think I can't manage just because you're old and she's senile?'

Bernard stood up, escaping the punched anger of Thérèse's questions. The cold had settled firmly in her legs. She went stiffly through to the kitchen to find a sponge and when she came back she wiped down the table. There were always crumbs from the bread stuck in the hollows and joints of the wood. She prised them up with her nail and put them aside in a small dish for the birds, knowing that when she scattered them outside nothing would come for them.

'I don't understand, Sister,' she said at last, but not loudly enough.

Thérèse leant forwards, frowning, trying to catch the words. Bernard sat down again.

'I don't quite understand,' she repeated, more loudly. 'What else can we do?'

Thérèse looked for a moment at the old nun. Then she pressed her hand hard against her forehead, steadying herself.

'I'm only seventy. I could live for years, sitting out my time in that place, with a chemical stink in my nose and nothing to look forward to except wet pasta.'

It did not seem to Bernard like an answer. She wrung the sponge in her hand and the crumbs fell to the floor.

'I thought you liked pasta,' she said.

Thérèse sprang from her chair. She thumped her hands down onto the puzzle book, sending the pen dancing along the table, and she set her gaze on a point through the window, above Bernard's head.

'Sister,' she said, the word snapping shut. 'Sister…' There was a moment when she could not think how to go on. 'How can you do it, Sister? You haven't even been there. You don't even care. You'll just do as they say. You'll just go along with it, with God's will, if that's what it is, and you'll never say a word, never even wonder.' She dropped her eyes for a moment and saw Bernard's unruffled face gazing at her. 'God have mercy, how can you be so… good?'

Thérèse pushed back from the table, and her chair clattered to the floor. Bernard could see pink spots spreading across her cheeks and tears gathering.

'I'll put the coffee on,' she said, as some kind of comfort. 'For All Souls.'

Thérèse shook her head. 'I can't,' she said. 'I can't do that tonight.'

'You're not coming to the chapel?'

'Is Sister Marie?'

Bernard was confused. 'No,' she said.

'No. Well then. We are not gathering in the chapel. Not this year.'

'No one will pray for us, Sister, when our time comes. We'll be trapped there, in purgatory, with our sins. We'll be lost. No one will think of us.'

Thérèse could not bear Bernard's panic. 'I'm sorry, Sister,' she said. 'It's too much. I can't do the vigil for All

Souls.' She gripped the edge of the table, startled at having said such a thing. She did not know what was happening.

Bernard sat for a long time in the refectory. Then she went to the chapel, lighting a single candle at the back, near the door, and sitting near its puttering glow. The shadows around her would not stay still. The altar loomed, undeniable, but the crucifix above was flat and unreal, disappearing into the gloom. Bernard did not kneel. She kept her hands gripped together, her fists tight. The words of the prayer would not come, just the thought of her soul, spinning in a dark place, cold and sick and in pain, entirely forgotten.

She blew out the candle and waited for the smell of the smoke to clear. Then she went back to her cell. The convent was closed in behind the shuttered windows, and the greyness within it hung steady. But Bernard could not sleep. She could hear rain starting and a car struggling up the hill out of the village. Somewhere downstairs something cracked.

She switched on the light by the side of her bed. The luminous yellow Christ which had glowed in the dark above her head went out, leaving only a badly modelled plastic blob, the colour of old bone. From the drawer in the bedside table she took out a thin leaflet, a photocopy folded clumsily where the binding would have been in the original. The front page displayed dark trees with something, impossible to pick out, in the smudgy ink beneath them. The words 'Les Cèdres', italicized, were draped above the trees, and beneath, in a smaller, plainer font, 'Diocesan rest home for the elderly.' It had been sent to her in the post, along with a list of the things she was permitted to take with her, which included medication, nightwear and items for individual prayer, but not soap or toothpaste, which would be provided communally. This would prevent, so the letter had suggested, unnecessary expenditure or 'personal hoarding'.

The photocopied leaflet offered little information. There was a photograph of the chapel, looking dingy, and another of the day room, at which Bernard peered long and hard. The description listed the 'public areas' as a refectory, television room, library and entrance hall, as well as the chapel and day room, but there were no photographs of these; there was nothing about the bedrooms. While it looked and sounded much like the convent in which Bernard had spent the last seventy-five years, it still terrified her. She wished she could have died earlier.

She thought of the kitchen knife she had stolen during the war, of another, earlier, autumn night, with the rain on the shutters and the luminous Christ extinguished in the early hours. She had turned the blade over in her palm, stroking it. It had taken the warmth from her flesh and, lodged between the creases on her palm, it was comforting. She had run her free hand over her stomach. She had been ready to die then. It would have been a consolation. But when God had caught her, He had raged and hollered, frightening her; she had leapt from the bed to her knees, the knife slipping from her hand and rattling across the wooden floor towards the window. Trembling, she had pleaded for mercy, begged the Virgin to intercede on her behalf; for the remainder of the night she had wept and moaned and pleaded, listening to the fury of God. At dawn she had had a nasty headache, but God had been calmer and she had eased herself from her knees to pick up the knife. She had taken it back to the kitchen before breakfast and washed it thoroughly in the sink, letting the tip of it cut her fingers and watching the blood run away, barely pink in the strong flow of water.

She knelt again now, placing the leaflet on the floor beside her. Through the long night of All Souls she prayed and wept, the years undefined and everything new, her fears fresh. The darkness in her cell was as it had always been. Only God was changed, silent now and unknowable. She could not tell if He was there. But still she knelt, her joints stiff and old, until the stippled light of dawn edged round the shutters and everything was past.

# Three

Although he had already won the bet, the soldier contrived several more meetings over the following days. It was as if he could not help it. Each time he looked hard at Bernard with something like wonder, nodded slightly and drew away.

While she waited for him, Bernard prayed. During morning prayers, she pressed the closed steeple of her hands hard against her face and was surprised to find them wet with tears. During the brittle spring dusk of the evening office she found herself flushed and breathless, tingling, the voices of the other nuns splaying from her, her hold on things precarious. In the long routine of the cold days, she floated; when God spluttered His fury in her ear, she did not mind Him, taking only to sleeping on the hard floor of her cell in an attempt to appease Him.

But when, finally, they talked again, coming together in the dip of land where the stream ran low behind the wash house, Bernard felt it only right to mention that God disapproved of what they were doing.

At first the soldier laughed. He put his sleeve across his face to muffle the noise and looked away towards the orchard where some of his unit were gathered, clustered together, sharing something. Beyond he could see the high blank walls of the convent, ugly and patched with cement, a blot on the honey tones of the village and its shabby French picturesqueness. Everything else was broken-down and decaying, unexpectedly pretty in the brilliant light; the convent's steadfast neatness was a blight.

Bernard thought that he had misunderstood and she explained again, more slowly, telling him how God pestered her about their wickedness. And when he looked back at her, the fear creased old and worn in her face, his laughter slipped away.

'What does He say?'

He was standing on a flat stone to keep his boots out of the thick wet vegetation that slid down to the water. He shuffled and Bernard, below him, already ankle deep in the marsh, reached out an arm as though to help him.

'He doesn't speak to you about it?'

She had not thought of this.

'*Nein.*'

'How come?'

He shrugged.

'Doesn't He speak to you about anything?'

'*Nein.*'

Bernard marvelled. 'Not even before you were a soldier?'

He stepped off the stone and pulled himself up the slope, turning to rest his elbows on the low wall of the wash house. Bernard tried to imagine the kind of silence he must live with; she did not dare approach the slouch of his thin back. Instead she bent and picked a thick round leaf from the stream's edge. She chewed it.

The soldier kicked the toe of his boot against the wall while he thought of the words. He did not face her, even when he spoke.

'Does He say anything about me?'

Bernard swallowed the leaf. 'All the time.'

'*Was?*'

He had not understood her. But Bernard answered with another question.

'Do you think it's right, what we do?'

She was beside him now, her head not even to the height of his shoulder and her hands pressed hard against the stone wall of the wash house to steady herself on the slippery ground.

He tried out the construction of his reply in his head. 'Does God think it is right?'

'Oh no.'

As he pulled abruptly away, pushing at her, making her fall back into the wet ground and threatening to go out into the open of the village lanes where she could not follow, Bernard tried to explain about the God she lived with.

'It doesn't matter. He thinks nothing is right. I can't please Him.' She heard the soldier say something in his own language but she went on speaking. 'He doesn't understand, that's all. It's not important, what He says.'

He could not make out the contortions of the strange language spoken so quickly. Looking back he saw the nun scrambling up the wet slope to meet him and he dipped back low behind the wall, hiding them again.

'You are crazy,' he said, when she was close.

'Because of what He says?'

'You think you hear God… you are crazy.'

And he stood tall, heading out from the wash house, passing the pillar into the street. As he walked away, a farmer on a cart slowly rounded the bend and rattled across to fill buckets from the water fountain. Bernard went behind the wash house and back along the track, unseen.

But the soldier could not settle. He did not join his colleagues in the orchard, and instead of taking the path to return to his quarters he walked on, a long way, following the lane as far as it would go, until it peeled out into a string of farm tracks and the daylight was fading. He watched flocks of small birds skitter along the hedges and dip into the fields. Walking too fast, he felt his legs strain and took off his uniform jacket, folding it neatly over one arm. And when he returned, coming into the village in the dark, he still could not understand. He could not believe that the moon-faced nun he had corrupted might be genuinely pious, chosen, blessed even by the voice of God. But her certainty was unnerving; it discomfited him. He could no longer pretend it was not serious in some way. It meant there would be consequences, in one life or the other.

The nuns filed into the pews at the front of the church. Bernard felt the cold through her shoes already; when she knelt, a draught from somewhere tugged at her habit. They prayed in neat rows, their heads bowed, as the congregation arrived around them. They were not allowed to talk. The church filled behind them and

Bernard could smell the warm damp of stored clothes and something in the common breath that reminded her of home. She bent further and the priest began the Mass.

She hardly moved. God spoke to her in a drone, weary and undemonstrative, barely audible above the sound of the priest, and the cold closed around her, fixing her stillness. Mostly her eyes were closed. She did not think about anything. Only when the bustle of communion finally broke the order of prayer, suddenly stirring the unlit dust, did Bernard shift, stretching her back and shoulders, as though emerging from sleep.

She took her own communion quickly, trying to hide her splayed gait as she approached the altar, and bowing her head so low that the priest, too, had to bend as he offered her the host. She slid back into her pew, knelt as she was meant to, and waited.

She knew most of the shoes. The scuffed toes and dented heels were learnt now and she watched them file slowly alongside, shuffling on the uneven stone of the floor. She did not look up, not until most of the line had passed and the movement around her was settling. Then, knowing it was time, she lifted her head so that the weight of the veil fell away from her face, and she watched the final communicants as they passed, the quick draw of her breath annoying God.

Her father walked slowly, leaning on her sister's arm, his face small and shrivelled, hardly a part of him. As they came by her pew they were, for a moment, a family, the three of them all that was left now. Bernard could have reached out and touched them, but her hands were clasped close in front of her, her rosary roped across her fingers, and they carried on without pause, moving up to the altar rail and taking their places there. Bernard watched until Severine came by, clogging the aisle with children, looking down at Bernard as she always did and smiling, their communion made. Then Bernard closed her eyes, drawing the rosary beads sharply into her skin. The rite was ending. The priest led the altar boys away and the congregation followed, beginning already to chatter. Then it was only the nuns left in their pews, swelling the gathering quiet with prayer, and God, abrasive, berating Bernard mercilessly.

Walking along the long corridor from the chapel after morning prayer, Mother Catherine warned Bernard.

'I want you to be circumspect,' she said, gripping her prayer book more tightly than was necessary.

Bernard did not understand the word. She tried to keep up with the Mother Superior's wide stride, but her feet slipped on the tiles, unbalancing her, and she stumbled into a chair. When she stopped, Mother Catherine spoke again.

'It's a difficult time, Sister. We need to have our wits about us.'

'Yes, Mother,' said Bernard, straightening her belt and skirt.

They came into the narrow bend in the corridor and were pushed together. Mother Catherine paused and spoke more quietly, turning to Bernard.

'It's a time of vigilance, Sister, and of wisdom. God has put us at the heart of the village here – at the heart of His community, to guide and to protect, to bear witness. We need to be circumspect.'

She raised her hands into a stiff steeple, as though she might be beginning a prayer. Bernard instinctively bowed her head. Then Mother Catherine turned out again into the wide straight of the corridor, her pace quickening.

'There are things you do not understand, Sister,' she said.

Bernard knew this.

Mother Catherine turned towards her study. She stopped again, waiting for Bernard to catch up with her, her hand already impatient on the door handle.

'You should let others guide you, Sister Bernard – you should be guided by those who *do* understand.' She was suddenly sharp. 'Consider, Sister, what you have to lose.'

Bernard saw something was demanded of her. She nodded.

'Good,' said Mother Catherine. 'Then we are agreed. I know I can rely on you, Sister.'

Mother Catherine went quickly into her study and shut Bernard out. The other nuns filed past, not seeming to notice. Bernard remained by the study door. She was not sure what had been said, but she did understand, vaguely, that it was about the soldier, and that she risked everything she knew if she continued to love him.

In time the bustle after prayers subsided and the convent was quiet again. Bernard moved away from Mother Catherine's door and went to sit on a stone ledge further along the corridor. She traced the pattern in the tiled floor with the toes of her boots. God pestered her sharply, pointing out patches where the skirting boards needed washing down. The sunlight from one of the square-paned windows swung towards her, finally settling across her knees. The anger growing in her made her tremble and when she finally went back to the kitchen to take up her chores, she surprised the other nuns with the sharpness of her movements, the way things clattered and rattled about her, the stomp of her feet on the cold floor.

She told the soldier what Mother Catherine had said but, struggling with the mechanics of upright sex, he only grunted. His breath was acid in the chilly air and as he pressed her further against the back wall of the barn, Bernard turned her face from him. Inside, heavy-footed animals – cows or horses – shuffled on the dry ground with a series of reverberating thuds, creating an odd arrhythmic accompaniment that made her nervous and watchful.

The effort left him panting, his thin cheeks flushed. Bernard's back was raw from the rubbing of the rough stone through her habit, and she wanted to feel inside her vest, to check for blood, but she did not dare; she thought he might be offended somehow. So she stood and rubbed her hands instead while he caught his breath.

'Do you think they understand?' he asked at last.

He had been trying to think of another, better, verb. He knew this was not quite right, but nothing else would come to him.

'I don't know.'

Bernard did not want to think about them. She looked for a moment at the narrow band of wrist that had slid out of his uniform cuff. She wanted more than anything to kiss it. The soft, childlike texture of his skin there, the way the blue veins rose up and faded, made her shiver. She forgot the pain of her scrubbed back, but she did not dare to bend and kiss it.

The soldier shivered too. 'It is cold.' He brushed stone dust from his arm and turned to Bernard; he placed a hand on each of her shoulders, weighting her, dipping his head. 'Be careful.' He spoke quietly. 'We don't want trouble. If it is trouble…'

He shook his head. He was weary and his articulation of the strange language was poor. But he left the threat hanging, and Bernard could not help but hear it.

'It'll be all right. I promise.' She pushed the words at him. 'It's… nothing. I shouldn't have said. It's just Mother Catherine – she's strict with us. It's nothing.'

He lifted his hands from her shoulders and pulled his jacket tight across him to keep out the cold. He thinned in front of her, disappearing.

'Please,' she said. 'You believe me, don't you?'

She could feel the sudden chill where his hands had been.

'I do not want them knowing. I do not want trouble.'

'There won't be trouble.'

'This is a war,' he said.

She had no answer to this and he left her, stuffing his hands into his pockets and whistling drily, hardly making a sound through his narrowed lips. She strained to hear him through the noise of the beasts and the shuddering leaves.

Bernard crept in through the back door of the convent, bringing a small handful of spring mushrooms as some kind of offering. Instinctively she turned for the kitchen, stealthy in the echoing cold of the corridors. She had her eyes to the floor, and almost bumped into Sister Jean emerging from the pantry with a covered plate. The two women stood together for a moment, uncertain. Bernard saw how heavy the plate must be. She saw creases of alarm fold around Sister Jean's wide eyes and the odd way in which the other nun suddenly looked at her, as though noticing her for the first time. Then Sister Jean nodded and moved on. God reminded Bernard to clean the mud from the heels of her shoes.

As the evening drew on, the voice of God was bothersome and shrill. His nagging repetition brought on a headache and a constant trickle of sweat running down Bernard's neck and back. During prayers, she fixed her eyes on the glitter of the crucifix and pressed her hands flat against the cold floor as she knelt, so that she was thrown forwards on all fours, her head thrust upwards, ungainly, and everything but the gilt cross blurred and swirling. Her breathing came fast and noisy. When the nuns around her stood to leave, she found she could not move and someone had to put an arm across her chest and pull her to her feet. Later, in the bitter dark of her cell, with God still hammering His complaints in an incomprehensible cacophony of spite, she could not sleep. She worried that Mother Catherine's interference would put the soldier off; she wished more than anything that she had not mentioned it to him.

She had to make amends, she knew that. She had to find a way to keep him. It was all that mattered. She went over and over the things he had said; she heard his warning fresh each time, she knew that he might leave her. And then she remembered Sister Jean, darting out of the pantry, wary. Something in the recollected movement was a shock. The dip of Sister Jean's head, the quick panic of her hands, was a revelation. She recalled other things she had heard, the gossip of snatched conversation. She remembered the way the other nuns talked of Sister Jean, with pity, as a transgressor. In Sister Jean's secrets there was an opportunity, she saw that. If she could only grasp it, she could make things right. She understood, all at once, what he had said about the war, the way it was upon them, distilling their desires. And through the confusion of God's chatter an idea came to her, a plan almost. Bernard realized that she could be indispensable to the soldier, if she were given one more chance.

# Four

Before the certainty of dawn was quite established, Thérèse pulled down the shelves. She stacked them neatly in one corner of her cell and kicked the objects that had fallen onto the floor into heaps. She laid her prized possessions respectfully on the bed – an origami swan folded for her over thirty years previously by a travelling salesman, a vase without a manufacturer's mark which she held to be Sèvres, a tiny wooden apple carved from a piece of walnut which she had won at a charity raffle and a large brass Buddha, its provenance unknown. Then she dismantled the system of empty orange boxes and cardboard tubes that ran around her small cell. She placed all the remaining objects on the heaps, stacking them high, and cleaned out the alcoves in the corridor to either side of her door. Finally she took the things from the bed, one by one, looking at each of them slowly, with love, and she pushed them all together, systematically smashing everything with a heavy-headed hammer she had found in the cellar. She worked methodically, trying to make the broken pieces as small as she possibly could. Chippings and splinters flew up and around, a momentary display of something magical, and then there was just the dust, and the debris, a mishmash of spoilt things, old and pointless.

She left the Buddha. The brass, she knew, was solid. She had dropped it once by mistake when she had been cleaning and it had not dented. She sat it upright on the bed and looked at it, fingering a cut on her cheek where she had been caught by a piece of flying glass. It looked back, unblinking, unfazed by the destruction around it. It still wore its serene smile.

The noise brought Bernard scuttling from her cell. She could think only that it was workmen, sent by the diocese, come already to strip, or even demolish, the convent. Then she saw that the debris in the corridor was only outside Thérèse's door, and as she came closer some of the shards of broken ceramic and coloured glass, odd, tortured remnants of moulded plastic and splinters of wooden shelving, seemed to her familiar. Wearing only her slippers, she trod carefully, sliding past the worst of the rubbish to push open the shutter in Thérèse's cell as she did every morning.

'Good morning, Sister,' said Thérèse from behind the bed, peering around the Buddha. 'I will tidy up after prayers.'

Bernard clipped the shutter against the wall, looked up briefly at the heavy sky, and turned back to Thérèse.

'There's a piece of broken pot under the bed,' she said, nodding towards a lump half-hidden by the trailing end of bedcover.

Thérèse did not look. Bernard bent and picked it up and put it slowly down on the end of the bed. It was nothing any more, a broken leftover, and Bernard shrugged, apologetic, feeling that the fault was hers. Thérèse smiled back. The brightness of her eyes was unnerving. Nothing about her seemed quite steady. She clasped her fingers across the Buddha's sleek head and rubbed her palms back and forth, the brush of them quiet on the brass.

'I'm sorry,' said Bernard. 'About your things.'

'I told you.' Thérèse held her voice flat. 'It's a new start.'

'Yes.'

Thérèse's attachment to the things of this life had always marked her out. It had been little more than a handful of cheap souvenirs at first. But then it had become a pleasure, a passion, everyone could see that, and the growing collection of bits and pieces, old tools and bottles, decorated boxes and plates stuck with shells, models of the Eiffel Tower and the grotto at Lourdes, coloured sands layered in gourd-shaped jars, ribbons and wrappers, had attracted attention. On more than one occasion items had been stolen. Some of them were found after searches of the other cells; several pieces were never seen again.

In the early days, before the Buddha and the Sèvres vase, the Mother Superior had gone into Thérèse's cell one afternoon while she was teaching and had emptied all the clutter into cardboard boxes which she had locked in the basement. When Thérèse had come back, her cell was as stripped and bare as the ascetic cubicles of the most righteous. Without a word she had lain out flat on her bed, where they had found her when she was missing from evening prayer. She did not move again and refused to eat until her collection was returned. After less than two days, the Mother Superior's resolve had been broken

51

by the stubbornness of Thérèse's spirit and the fear that she might be answerable to God for the reprobate's life. Thérèse was given permission to go for the boxes and she spent an entire day rearranging the objects on her shelves. Since then, no one but Thérèse had touched her things.

'It'll be better,' said Bernard. 'Without it all.'

Thérèse was wearing day clothes rather than her habit, a neat dark skirt, thick tights and a high-necked black jumper against which her cross sparkled. She wore no veil. Her thin hair was cut shorter than Bernard remembered. It had been dyed. As she rubbed her hands across the Buddha's head, she looked strange, unrecognizable.

Thérèse stopped. 'I can't work out what to do with it,' she said, nudging Bernard's glance towards the Buddha. 'It won't break. It won't burn, of course – whatever I do, it seems dangerous. It's indestructible – like the kingdom of heaven.'

She laughed slightly, closing her hands again across the statue's head. Bernard was watching her hair, glittering a burnished purple in the early morning light, draining the colour from Thérèse's skin, erasing her. It seemed wondrous that she had managed to dye it in the shared bathroom without leaving a single stain.

'What are they going to do with this place anyway?' asked Thérèse. 'Do you know? Are they going to sell it? It must be worth something.'

'I don't think it's decided,' Bernard said, knowing that the convent could not change, its sturdiness impregnable. When they left it would go on as it always had, that was all, its vacancy finally uncontested.

'I heard talk of a holiday village or something, for tourists,' said Thérèse. She glanced around her small cell, seeing something else. 'It would need a bit of work, but it's possible, I suppose.'

Bernard too thought about the solid grey building.

'Perhaps they'll knock it down,' she said, unconvinced. She was unable to conceive how this would end things.

'Whatever it is, they'll rip it out. Change it completely,' said Thérèse. 'They're bound to.'

Bernard did not understand. She nodded.

'Good then,' said Thérèse. 'That's fine.'

And she picked up the Buddha and hurled it with a long graceful action through the window. The narrow bars holding the small panes snapped instantly, the glass splintered and Bernard had a view of a chubby Buddha bottom disappearing towards the ash tip at the edge of the grounds. Thérèse stood with her arms outspread in the direction of the throw, statuesque, embracing the puff of morning air that came to them through the broken glass.

'I don't think you should have done that,' said Bernard.

Thérèse held her pose a moment longer, like a plea for something. Then it looked as though she would fall. She put out a hand and steadied herself on the bed, reaching too far across, suddenly ungainly.

'It won't make any difference,' she said sharply, her words too slight for her tone. 'If they're pulling it all down, it'll all go anyway. And if not, well – the windows will be the first thing they'll have to change. They're quite rotten.'

'But throwing a god out of the window – that's what I mean. It doesn't seem right.'

Thérèse frowned, unsettled by Bernard's unexpected confidence.

'I'd never thought of my Buddha as a god.'

'What else is he?' Bernard did not mean to sound accusing. She was puzzled by how they all fitted together, the obscure ecumenical arguments they had tried to teach her but that she could never quite grasp. She was curious about the Buddha; his round features seemed cosy and kind. She felt the unfairness of his ignominious fall and wanted to go after him.

'I just thought of it as a statue,' said Thérèse. 'It was an aesthetic thing.'

There was a long pause. Thérèse righted herself, and brushed down her skirt with quick hands. She did not look at Bernard. Bernard went to the window. Fingering a piece of the broken frame she peered across to the overgrown verge, trying to see the Buddha. But the autumn sun was full over the horizon now, dazzling, and everything below was misted and uncertain.

'I think they could say the same about the Sacred Heart, or the Crucifix, or even the Virgin Mary, if they wanted,' she said at last. 'I heard that once – that they were just statues.'

Thérèse sat heavily on the bed.

'Well, you know,' Bernard went on, less sure of herself. 'These days. They say things like that.'

The mutability of things was too evident. They did not look at each other. Thérèse buried her face in her hands, throwing her head forwards so that the dye of her hair changed colour. It was several seconds before she looked up.

'Why didn't they say something, about me having it in my cell? What must they have thought?'

Bernard turned her back to the window and drew a foot through the clutter, clearing a narrow path. She could not think of an answer.

'Didn't you think it was strange?' pressed Thérèse. 'If that's what it is – a god… didn't you think it was strange?'

Bernard wanted to escape. The disintegration around their feet was too much.

'I don't suppose it matters,' she said.

Finally Thérèse looked at her. 'I'll fetch it back. I'll brush it down, give it a wash. I think I'd better. Just in case.'

'Just in case?'

'Just in case it is a god, after all.'

'I don't suppose anyone will know,' said Bernard evenly.

'But doesn't God know everything, Sister?'

This, of course, was true.

'So then the Buddha, too, if he's God, would know,' Thérèse went on logically.

Bernard was confused. She felt the familiar un-controllable flap of ideas in her head, like wind-blown laundry.

'I said he was *a* god, not *our* God,' she said, thinking her words were too quiet now for Thérèse to hear. 'I don't suppose he knows everything like our God, the real God.'

He didn't look like he would know everything. He was too fat for a start. And too cheerful. There was good reason why God was never cheerful.

'Jesus never laughed, you know, Sister,' she said more distinctly.

Thérèse looked wistfully towards the broken window through which her Buddha had soared, and then full at

55

Bernard. Bernard did not know what to say. She smiled at Thérèse, conciliatory, but Thérèse looked away. They did not know each other. In the ruins of the small cell, with only the scraps of an old life between them, they could not begin. They were too old for that, and too alone.

Thérèse was sulky. 'I feel like I've profaned something.'

She gazed at the wreckage on the floor. It all seemed as though it were Bernard's fault, the loss of the convent, the cramped room at Les Cèdres, the destruction of her collection.

'I liked my things,' she said. Then suddenly she was prickly. 'They were… you know… I liked having them here, Sister.'

She looked hard at Bernard, driving the accusation home.

'I told you to take them with you,' said Bernard flatly.

'Yes, but I couldn't, could I? Not *there*. Going *there* – with you – I've got to start a new life. I've got to, I don't know, do as I'm told. It's the only way.'

Bernard could hear high faint sounds now from the end of the long corridor as Sister Marie greeted the day with a hymn.

'I didn't know, did I, when I agreed to it.'

Thérèse couldn't mention Corinne, but she already knew that she would mourn the loss of her collection for ever and this, too, seemed as though it were Bernard's fault. 'I didn't know it would be like this.'

For the final flourish, Marie's singing was clear as birdsong, her voice trilling on the high notes. Thérèse, hearing her now, looked to the open door.

'I should go,' said Bernard. 'Sister Marie is at the end of her hymn. I should get her up before she starts again. Or she'll not let me…'

She turned quickly, without finishing what she was saying, and she pushed her way through the worst of the debris. She moved briskly down the corridor, her relief making her steps light.

The singing stopped and Thérèse's world was silent again. She looked around. The plain ash-coloured counterpane, the same as all the others in the convent, sagged about her. She rubbed her ears. She had been awake the entire night, kneeling sometimes on the floor, sitting sometimes on the bed, restless, unable, in the end, to ignore the old routines of observance. Alone in her cell, as some kind of compromise, she had recited rosary after rosary for the trapped souls in purgatory, hoping that her solitary prayer would not be too scant to matter. And it had been a special night, holy. The thick autumn silence had seemed to have a softness about it. With the dawn she had begun ripping down her collection. She had felt elated, renewed. She had demolished her attachment to earthly things with the fervour of those who had lived and died glorified by God and honoured by the Church.

But then had come the Buddha, and Bernard's confused theology. And now her courage had left her and she just felt tired and old. The wet November day was upon her. She felt trapped between one life and the next, sure of neither and frightened by both. She had never felt so helpless.

*

Bernard knew she could leave the sodden sheets where they were, unlaundered. It would make no difference. But she wrapped Sister Marie in her dressing gown and sat her in the chair under the window while she stripped the bed, folded the linen as best she could – it was very heavy – and took everything downstairs to soak in the sink in the scullery. As soon as the sheets were submerged, she took a dry cloth from its hook by the door and retraced her steps, bending every few yards to wipe the drips from the floor and stairs, turning her head sharply to one side to catch the glint of urine against the tiles. She moved quickly past Thérèse's cell, keeping her eyes on the floor, and followed the trail to the end of the corridor. Marie was half-dozing where she had been left.

'Do you think,' asked Marie, as Bernard was attempting to slide her habit over her head, 'do you think God will still love me when I leave Him?' She sounded lucid. It was a trick she had.

'You're not leaving God, Sister, only the convent. God will be with you wherever you are,' said Bernard. She had told herself this many times, but she could not believe it was true.

Marie took Bernard's hand for a moment. It was not a comfort.

'You will soon settle,' said Bernard.

They walked slowly to the refectory. The dim light was spun from the past; it had little of the morning in it. It gave an unexpected solemnity to their passage, and Marie leant more heavily than usual on the older nun.

'You can sit here, Sister Marie,' Bernard said in the refectory, as though offering a choice.

She pulled back the bench and held it steady as Marie shuffled in.

'If God still loves me,' said Marie, 'why is He sending me away? Why is He banishing me? What have I done?'

Her voice was scratchy with tears. Bernard unfolded the napkin that they kept by Marie's place and tucked it carefully into her habit around her neck. Then she pulled the plate to the edge of the table, reachable, and turned away to put some water on to boil. The hiss of the burning gas filled the room, and soon after came Thérèse's footsteps, echoing down the corridor as she made her way to the refectory. It was a morning the same as all the others, indistinguishable. That was the way of things.

'I've cleared most of it, but I'll need to borrow a broom, Sister,' said Thérèse, making her way to the table and kissing Marie in greeting as she passed. 'There's a lot of pieces of glass which I should put somewhere safe. Do we have a box?'

'I can find one, after Sister Marie's gone. I think there's some in the storeroom,' said Bernard.

'Thank you, Sister, that would be kind.'

Bernard served the coffee. A frozen baguette was still warming in the oven. There was nothing left in the freezer now except for two small frosted bags right at the bottom, shoved into the far corners. Bernard could not see what they contained and could not reach them to find out. After taking out the bread that morning she had simply closed the freezer lid, taken the plug out of the socket, and wiped the top surface with a damp cloth. She already missed its familiar hum.

Bernard loitered by the stove until the baguette was warm, unready to begin the ordinary, everyday, unremarkable breakfast that would be their last together. Finally, though, it could not wait any longer without spoiling. She took the long loaf from the oven on its flat tray and broke it into pieces with burning fingers. She slid them onto a wide plate which she carried to the table, putting it carefully in the middle, where they could all reach their share. Steam rose into the cold air, and the smell of sweet dough and the years that had gone before. They waited for a moment, as Bernard made her way back to the bench, and then Thérèse said grace; she had not quite finished before Marie, grinning, made a grab for the largest piece of bread. Thérèse took another piece and dipped it in her coffee. She held it up to drain, the colour seeping through it like old blood. It dripped onto the table. Bernard made a note to scrub down properly when they had all finished. There was so much to remember, even now.

Thérèse began tentatively, still letting the bread drip.

'So... our lives are changing, starting afresh.'

She paused.

'There're a lot of memories here to be leaving behind – our whole lives are here.'

'You've been here fifty years, Sister,' said Bernard.

'Fifty-two. It's a big change for me.'

'Yes.' Bernard dipped her head low over her plate, breaking the bread into tiny pieces, and slipping them into her mouth from her open palm.

'And you, Sister?'

Bernard looked up from the ritual, her hand flat out to Thérèse as if in some sort of supplication, the crumbs on it sticky. She did not know what Thérèse wanted her to say.

'God tests us, Sister,' she tried.

Marie took the last piece of bread.

'You must have lived through many such tests, Sister Bernard.' Thérèse looked straight at her, pressing so much curiosity into the question that her mouth hung open slightly.

'No, Sister,' said Bernard. 'None like this one.'

And now it came to it, this seemed enough. Thérèse nodded, letting her eyes fall gently from Bernard's small, flat face; allowing the revelations to remain hidden there in its openness.

'We should thank God for all His gifts, Sister,' was all she could say.

Bernard rubbed her hands together and reached for the empty plate in the middle of the table. Marie belched. There was a clatter at the front door.

'That'll be the men.' Bernard let the plate drop back onto the table. 'For Sister Marie. They've come early.'

Thérèse had only heard the noise faintly. She was surprised. It was actually beginning. They looked at each other for a moment and Thérèse raised her eyebrows. It was the only sign either of them was ever to give that they might have wished this parting to be different. Then together they heaved Marie up from the bench, pulling the napkin bib from her as two young men appeared at the door to the refectory, pushing an empty wheelchair.

Bernard and Thérèse went to the porch and stood in its shelter, watching. Marie was carefully seated in the minibus and the wheelchair folded away. The rain, falling lightly, obscured the windows and made the driveway dark. They did not wave as the minibus pulled away but remained outside until it had turned out of sight and the sound of it was gone.

Bernard shook the damp from her veil. 'I'll fetch the box,' she said.

'Yes, Sister. Thank you. If you leave it by the door, I'll empty everything into it.'

'You should mark it, too. So that when they come to collect the rubbish, they'll know to be careful.'

'I'll do that,' said Thérèse.

But for a moment neither of them moved, surprised by the sound of their voices in the cavernous building and unwilling to step away alone.

'I'll bring it up,' said Bernard at last, drawing back.

She went down into the storeroom and picked out a box for Thérèse. She brushed it clean and took it through the hall, leaving it on a small table by the door. But even with her task finished, she was drawn back, and she returned again to the earthy damp, descending the narrow steps and spending a long time in the dim brick cellars, letting the dust cling to her habit, treasuring it, as though it was all she had left now.

Later, when Corinne found her, Thérèse was kneeling on the floor of the corridor writing in large red letters on the box of shards.

'There was no one around downstairs,' Corinne said loudly, making sure she was heard. 'So I came for a wander to see what I could find. I hadn't realized – it's big this place, isn't it?'

Thérèse sat back on her heels. 'Too big for the three of us,' she said, her voice hard.

Corinne nodded. She looked over her friend's head into the stripped cell, but said nothing. Thérèse bent forwards and finished writing her warning on the box. When she looked up, her smile was fixed.

'I've been cleaning out,' she said. 'I used to, you know, hoard things. Collect things. I thought, with everything – well it shows, doesn't it, that I'm making an effort. That I'm trying.'

Corinne held out a hand and pulled Thérèse up from the floor. Then she pushed the box to one side with her foot.

'Let's go outside,' she said. 'It's a nice morning. We could walk.'

Thérèse hesitated. 'I don't know. I should pack.'

'You look pale. You need some air,' said Corinne, matter-of-factly, setting back off down the corridor.

'It was All Souls,' said Thérèse.

It was drizzling still; they stood under the porch. The bread van sped across the end of the drive, hooting, sending a pair of deer leaping into the trees.

'Have you decided, then?' asked Corinne, when the quiet had resettled.

'I can't come. I can't.'

'Thérèse, think about it. You can come and live with me and continue your life of prayer and devotion exactly as before, but comfortably. I can give you a good home.'

'I'm not a stray dog.'

Corinne did not laugh. 'It will be a change, that's all. But I'd like the company; I need someone now, around. And for years, we've said... We always talked about how it would be, if we lived together – always.' She pressed her foot against the wall and Thérèse noticed for the first time that she was wearing red shoes. 'Besides, it's different now. The vocational life is different in the modern world. You don't have to – I don't know – you don't have to punish yourself.'

'It's my duty to stay with Sister Bernard,' said Thérèse.

'Until now, it's been your duty, yes. You've been keeping the convent, sustaining its presence here, the three of you. But now – now… it's not your fault. You didn't ask to change. You didn't ask to move. They made you.'

'I can't help feeling it would be wrong.'

Corinne stepped out onto the gravel and looked at the sky. 'Why?' Her frustration made the question sharp. 'Why on earth would it be wrong?'

She wiped the rain from her face and came back under the porch. She went to take her friend's hand again, but Thérèse pulled away.

'Look, I'm sorry,' said Corinne. 'I don't mean us to argue – it's just…'

'I think it has to be a question of duty. In the end,' said Thérèse. 'That's all I can think. When I pray about it, all I see is Sister Bernard, left alone, cared for by strangers.'

'But that's what's happening to Sister Marie.'

'Yes, yes, I know. But she'll hardly realize what's going on. And I can't be everywhere, can I? I can't do everything. And I should look at it as… as duty, as penance. As something I've given my life to. As a prayer.'

Corinne did not reply for a moment. She took a tissue from her pocket and blew her nose noisily, taking her time to fold it carefully afterwards.

'Couldn't life with me be a prayer of some kind?' she asked at last.

Thérèse smiled sadly. 'It would be too much a pleasure,' she said.

Corinne pushed back through the door without saying anything more, walking quickly across the entrance hall. Thérèse followed. They were stopped by Bernard, emerging into the corridor from the storeroom steps, an apparition, sepia from the dust.

'Oh,' she said.

'Corinne. I'm Corinne. You remember, Sister?' Corinne held out her hand stiffly.

'You met Corinne once at church,' added Thérèse unnecessarily.

Bernard shook Corinne's hand lightly. 'Yes,' she said.

'You've been… sweeping, Sister?' said Thérèse.

'Yes. Perhaps. A little.'

'Sister Bernard gave me the box, for my scraps,' said Thérèse, turning to her friend.

Corinne looked at them both blankly. Bernard moved on, without dusting herself down, her boots leaving soft prints on the tiled floor. She disappeared into the refectory.

'I don't see, I just don't see, how she can be worth it,' hissed Corinne.

But Thérèse did not hear her; looking after Bernard, she did not know her friend had spoken.

At the nursing home in town they unloaded Sister Marie from the minibus and left her sitting outside in the wheelchair, protected from the rain by the overhang above the entrance. She sat slouched to one side, her wimple slipped low onto her forehead. Her hands were crossed neatly on her lap, and though no one could have known this, she was praying.

She waited for nearly ten minutes before a woman in a blue uniform hurried out and grabbed the handles of the chair, pushing Marie quickly through the front door without a word. They bolted around a horseshoe-shaped corridor and then took the lift to an identical corridor higher up the building. The woman stopped to talk in a low voice to another woman in a blue uniform carrying an armful of underwear. Moving on, they nearly completed the length of the horseshoe before turning through an open bedroom door. Then the woman in the uniform left and Marie was alone. She continued to pray.

'Ah, Sister Marie! You've arrived!'

Marie either did not hear the chirp of the sharp voice, or took no notice of it. Nor did she move when a young girl with thin hair ducked round in front of the wheelchair and crouched down to straighten Marie's veil.

'Let's get you sorted, shall we? Are you comfortable there? Good. I'll just move you nearer the window, out of the way, and I'll get your things. Good.'

Marie looked neither at the girl, as she bustled about, nor at the view of the autumn shrubbery, but at her clasped hands still welded to her lap. She was pleading with God not to abandon her. This place did not smell like heaven; she did not want to be left here, waiting.

'Where are your things then, Sister?' asked the nurse, pulling out a light drawer in a small dresser and finding it empty.

There was nothing in the wardrobe, on the shelves beside the window, or on the back of the wheelchair.

'I'll ring down.'

The nurse sat on the bed as she dialled the number on the oversized red buttons.

'I'm with the nun,' she said to someone. 'Just came in today. Yes. Her bags aren't with her… Yes, could you? And let me know? All right then.'

She put down the receiver but continued to sit on the bed picking at the cuticles of her nails. After a few minutes the phone rang with a high-pitched buzz. At the end of her second conversation the nurse came back and crouched before Marie.

'We haven't got your things, Sister. We can't find them. They might be on the minibus, but it's left, gone back. Do you know where your things are?'

She spoke too loudly and slowly and looked too closely into Marie's face. Marie looked back at her and smiled, but there were tears in her eyes.

'Never mind,' said the nurse, getting up, her words softer. 'We'll find everything, I'm sure. We'll ring the place you came from. They might have your bag. Let's get you cleaned up first. And then it will be nearly time for lunch. You'd like some lunch wouldn't you, Sister?'

Already the room smelt of Marie's farts.

The noise of the phone hardly stirred the convent quiet. But Sister Bernard heard it and promptly hurried along the corridor to answer it, her gait stiff and swaying from the creak of her joints.

'We put her bag on the minibus,' she insisted. 'They must have lost it. Ask the drivers again.'

Bernard had packed most of Marie's things several days before. She had not found the photograph of Monte Carlo, only a large number of prayer cards, grateful letters from parishioners, souvenirs of Lourdes and Assisi, and a selection of rosaries. In the end, there had been so little in the bag that Bernard had added a dark green woolly cardigan, a clouded half-used bottle of eau-de-cologne and a bulky encyclopedia of saints from the leftovers of past lives stored in the huge cupboard in the cellars below the convent. She presumed that Marie had edited her life's scraps at the first signs of illness, of mixing up her words, forgetting her name and wetting the bed, reinforcing years of dazzlingly public piety. She hoped God had seen Sister Marie's underhandedness.

'We're moving ourselves in a few days. We're very busy. You should have everything. It was organized,' Bernard said to the woman on the telephone, not quite daring to be stern.

She remembered bringing the bag down from Marie's cell after she had seated her at the breakfast table. She remembered putting it by the front door and looking through the little side window to watch a thrush hammering a snail on the rubble from the broken-down wall.

'Well then, we'll search again. I'll ring back,' said the woman wearily.

Thérèse walked the perimeter of her empty cell. It looked neat now, and clearer than it had done for many years. The outlines of her objects remained printed on the walls by the years of light and dust, the silhouette of a particularly spectacular city skyline, but the clutter was gone. It was possible to walk in a straight line from the door to the window and from wall to wall; the untrodden boards shone in the corners. She stopped at the window to look out over the edge of the garden to the autumnal oaks and the ash tip where her Buddha lay half-buried by the force of his fall. Then she closed the door firmly and made her way quickly along the dormitory corridor with its imperishable smell of enclosure. When she emerged in the refectory several minutes later with her box neatly packed with paper and labelled in red for the dustbin men, she found Bernard crumpled on the floor shaking with sobs.

'Oh, Lord Jesus, whatever is the matter, Sister?' cried Thérèse, putting down her box.

She helped Bernard to her feet, but Bernard's tears refused to stop and all Thérèse could do was sit her at the table and watch.

Bernard cried for almost two hours. There was no work to do any more, no duties, no rules, nobody waiting for her in the quiet corridors. There was simply the sorrow, at last. She let it come, mourning the loss of the soldier. She knew that her memories of him, Technicolor bright, mottled like old film, could not be shifted from the gathered shadows of the convent. He would have to be left behind. The abandonment overwhelmed her. For a while Thérèse hovered around her, making faint reassuring noises, sometimes taking the seat next to her and reaching out a hand. She brought a glass of water. She thought of beginning a prayer. But as the tears continued and Bernard seemed completely unaware that anyone was with her, Thérèse simply sat alongside her without speaking.

She completed two word puzzles and picked at the soft splinters at the edge of the table. There seemed no need for lunch. Some time after midday Thérèse offered Bernard a mint, but Bernard shook her head dolefully and Thérèse sucked her own sweet as quietly as she could.

When they heard the village clock strike two, Bernard stirred herself, lifting her head and pushing back the bench. She found her knees had stiffened and it was painful to flex them. She stopped crying as abruptly as she had started.

'I should carry on packing my things,' she said.

'Good idea, Sister.'

'You've done yours?'

'I have,' said Thérèse.

'Good,' said Bernard, but still she remained seated.

Her head drooped forwards again so that she seemed to be gazing at a spot on her knees. Her elbows rested on the table in front of her and her hands were pinned to the middle of her forehead. She could have been praying; Thérèse thought she was. She tried to recognize in the shapes made by Bernard's half-hidden mouth the words of familiar prayers.

'It's difficult for me to hear today,' said Thérèse apologetically. There was the slightest of pauses. 'If you would like to pray, we could pray together, Sister. We've been so busy, it might be rewarding to take some time in prayer.'

'I should pack my bags,' Bernard said.

'But if we prayed together, Sister… praying together is like…' Thérèse could not think exactly. 'It's a blessing, isn't it, to pray with people we love?'

The word made Bernard start. 'Love?'

Thérèse looked away as she corrected herself. 'To share God's love, Sister.'

Bernard only really prayed alone. There were orders, so she had heard, where this was encouraged, where each nun lived a solitary, silent, hermit's life in communion with God. This might have suited her. But her order believed strongly in the value of community and firmly advocated the merit of shared prayer. So Bernard had recited the words with hundreds, perhaps even thousands, of people. She had knelt with them, and bowed, and occasionally held hands. She had stood with them for long hours in the cold of the church. But it was only when she was on her own that she attempted to speak to God, privately and very quietly, even though she knew He would not understand.

'Shall we then? Shall we pray together, Sister?' Thérèse was looking at her expectantly.

'One prayer,' sighed Bernard. 'And then I must get on. You begin.'

Thérèse sat up straighter and folded her hands on her lap where she could feel the ridges of her rosary beads through the thick material of her skirt pocket. She waited for Bernard who, after a pause, bowed her head without otherwise moving. Then Thérèse closed her eyes. There was a moment's silence in which Bernard could hear the rainwater pouring out of the broken gutter by the outside door to the kitchen.

'Hail Holy Queen, Mother of Mercy. Hail our Life, our Sweetness and our Hope,' began Thérèse, emphasizing the capital letters as she had learnt as a child.

'To thee do we cry, poor banished children of Eve. To thee do we send up our sighs mourning and weeping in

71

this vale of tears,' continued Bernard quickly.

Their voices blended as they joined together.

'Turn then, most gracious advocate, thine eyes of mercy towards us, and after this our exile show unto us the blessed fruit of thy womb, Jesus. Oh clement, oh loving, oh sweet Virgin Mary.'

'Pray for us, Oh Holy Mother of God,' continued Thérèse alone.

'That we may be made worthy of the promises of Christ,' finished off Bernard flatly.

'Thank you, Sister,' said Thérèse. It was a moment she would remember.

'I'll go upstairs now,' said Bernard, rising.

# Five

They were leaning side by side on the stone edge of a farm well, its circular walls raised several feet above the long grass. It was tucked away in a small secluded wood up the hill from the convent, behind a collection of barns and low buildings. There was no one left now to run the farm. The young men were all away fighting somewhere, or dead; the old woman who had lived there alone had disappeared in the cold of the previous winter, leaving the cattle to tread dark paths in the snow. Weeds had grown and the pastures had become unkempt. The well was never used and already the metal bar that hung across the deep shaft was stiff and rusting. In response to Mother Catherine's warning, Bernard and the soldier met now in the haze of half-light dawn or dusk and came here sometimes, when they could; it was a safe place. Bernard liked the way the trees encircled them, seeming ancient.

He had been sent a small parcel from home: a cigar, two newspaper cuttings reporting on the successes of the much-depleted local football team, a robust pair of knitted socks and a small brass crucifix. He had brought the crucifix to show Bernard.

'It used to hang above my bed. My mother has sent it.'

The crucifix had meant nothing to him until now. Bernard took it from him and held it. It was warm from his hand. She tried to imagine many things – his room at home, his bed, his mother, the industrial town parish to which he belonged – but what came to her instead was the thought of her own bed in the corner of her cell, its sheets ruffled, and the soldier lying sprawled and hot within it.

'One day,' Bernard said, 'you could come and be with me at home, in the warm.'

The dew lay silver on the trefoiled leaves around her feet and she scuffed at them, making the green beneath brilliant.

He looked puzzled and Bernard repeated herself more slowly. But it was not the language that was confusing him.

'At home?' he said.

He took the crucifix back from her and put it away in his pocket.

'At home – you know, where we live.'

'*Ja, ja*, I know what it means – I know at home. But…' He paused. 'But where?'

He did not want her at his lodgings. He did not want anyone finding them together.

'In my cell,' Bernard said. 'At the convent.'

She felt no thrill in saying it. It was the picture of him, skinny and languid, still in her mind, which excited her. But he immediately felt the adventure of it.

'The convent? Your home?' He turned to face her. 'You want that?'

74

The questions were quick and sharp. He leant towards her. Bernard could not decide what he thought of her.

'Yes,' she said. 'Perhaps.'

'And you think…' He could not make the right words come.

'If we're patient… if it's what you'd like.' She wanted to promise him something. 'We'd have to be secret, that's all. We couldn't tell anyone. We couldn't let Mother Catherine find out. Or anyone.'

He swirled away, twisting his heel in the ground and spanning his arms wide, throwing his head up so that he was looking at the circle of sky through the trees. He let himself stand there like that, and Bernard waited. When he finally let his arms drop, and looked back at her, there was something bright and lively about his face, his expression would not hold.

But when it came to it, it was not easy to work out the practicalities of such an intimate visit. Bernard could see, even now, that there were difficulties.

'I could give you a key. Or I could come down and let you in,' she said, as they picked their way slowly back through the trees.

Both of these ideas frightened her. They walked further. She wanted to take his arm.

'Or you could hide somewhere, inside, until everyone has gone to bed. I could show you where,' she said. She did not know how she could have come up with such a plan. 'And you could creep up to me, to my cell. And stay all night.' She stopped and turned to him, grinning. 'You'd like that.'

He had no way of picturing a cell at the convent. Instead he thought, inevitably, of his own home, the bed jammed in under the eaves and his brothers sitting close on the floor, playing dice.

'Yes,' he said.

They both meant it. It was something like a prayer, or perhaps more of a wish. The boundaries were blurred: Bernard thought of the moment as sacred. She put her hand gently on his arm. He did not pull away. And she knew then how he could belong to her purely, to the different self she would become if he spent just one night holding her.

'There's something I want to tell you,' she said.

They were almost at the edge of the woods. The growth of trees was thinner here, though each of the trunks was sturdier. Bernard paused in the dappled shadows, the vault of branches framing her.

'It's about Sister Jean.'

There wasn't a great deal to tell. Bernard did not know much. Whisperings merely, half-heard conversations, references she did not understand. Not many of the nuns spoke to her, and when they did they reached her through the litany of God's complaints. But she had gleaned enough, and with the soldier impatient beside her, picking at the bark of one of the trunks, hidden by the fall of her veil, she found ways to embellish. She made things up.

'It's Sister Jean who runs the Resistance,' she assured him. 'She has meetings all the time – secret meetings. And they come to her, at the convent. She's in charge of it all. And they've got plans to do something… something terrible – to the German soldiers. To you.'

'You are sure?' he said at the end, wondering.

'Oh yes. Everyone knows.' She made it sound certain. 'You should tell someone, before it's too late. They'll be pleased with you then, won't they? They might reward you.'

'If it is true…' He sucked air through his teeth, whistling softly. 'I'll see, if it's true. Thank you,' he said, 'my little nun.' And he put a hand on her shoulder, like a blessing.

A few days later, before the sun sank completely, they skirted a field where the hay was high and followed a track until they came to a junction marked by a worked metal cross on a stone plinth, seasoned and fragile, the hanging Christ worn and misshapen. Where the metal pierced the stone there was bindweed and tall shoots with brilliant blue flowers. Bernard paused for a moment, picked several stems and laid them at the foot of the cross. Then they took a path that dipped away into the shade of the oaks, finally rounding the corner by a broken barn.

They had not planned anything. But they walked further than they had meant to, and first the rain came. It was not heavy but the drops were hard and hot, as though God was spitting at them. They kept closer to the edge of the path, to gain as much protection as they could from the trees. But the grass was long there, and the low mess of brambles made walking difficult, and when the wind came, it was so fierce and loud, and so many leaves and twigs were thrown to the ground, that there was no shelter at all.

'There must be a hut somewhere. Something,' he cried, but the wind was pitiless now and the rain pelting like stones and his voice was whipped away. Bernard heard nothing. He was several yards ahead of her, being blown along with the wind at his back, walking so fast that she could not keep up.

The storm howled. It was not normal. All around them trees dipped wildly, stretched and contorted. The sky was upon them, too close. Acorns spat at them from the trees, wrenched too soon from their cups, and the rain stung Bernard where it struck her on the head and shoulders. Her veil pulled at her hair, heavy and soaked.

'Here!' He seemed to disappear into the wet hedge. Catching up, Bernard could see nothing beyond the dense bushes and the dark wet stone of a wall. She stood on the path. The storm was like the rage of God; there was so much noise she couldn't work out what to do. She heard the crack of a tree splitting.

The soldier reached out a hand to grab her arm and for a second she saw his blond hair between the tangle of brambles. As he pulled her in, she realized he had found a *cazelle*, a small domed shepherd's shelter, carefully layered out of stone, the open entrance protected by the thick growth. It swelled from the length of wall, almost circular, a large, thick slab propped upright to make a doorway.

Inside, the earth floor was completely dry. Bernard could stand upright in the middle of the hut, but the soldier had to bend; he soon sat down on the ledge built into the circumference of the shelter. He wiped his face with a damp handkerchief. Outside, the tempest seemed to be getting stronger and louder. More trees and branches cracked and fell. The unrelenting howl of the wind scared them. Bernard was trembling so much that she did not see his hand shake as he wiped his face.

'It is good here,' he said. 'Safe.'

Bernard thought of a great oak branch tearing from its trunk and falling on the hut to crush them, but she nodded.

He puffed and closed his eyes. 'Is it always like this?'

Bernard was used to storms. Thunder and lightning never bothered her. But this absolute fury was new.

'Never.'

For a while they listened to the roar outside. It would have been natural for them to hold each other, but they didn't, although neither of them would have liked to be alone.

'We will stay. We cannot walk. It is dangerous,' the soldier said.

For a moment he pushed his head and shoulders out of the entrance to see what was going on. When he turned to Bernard his hair was wild, his face wet again and his eyes wide.

It did not last long. The storm blew itself out in little more than half an hour. But when the wind had died down and the rain was easing, it was dark and Bernard and the soldier were both breathless. The hut seemed safe and snug and hidden.

'We could stay,' Bernard said, not daring to look at him.

'Until the rain stops?'

'Just stay.' She kicked over some old ashes piled against a curve of the wall. 'I could make a fire.'

She did not think about how wet the sticks would be outside, and how difficult it would be to set anything alight.

She thought about the impossible romance of a private fire.

The soldier went to the entrance and looked out again.

'Is it raining?' asked Bernard.

'A little.' He turned to her as he spoke and caught the way she looked at him in the gathering gloom, her eyes blank and dull still, but her faith somehow in the folds of her skin and the way her mouth fell and in the uneasiness of her breath. There would be something special about staying there together, he knew that. It was that sort of place.

'You'll be missed,' he said. And then, though she said nothing. 'I can't.'

He did not move. Outside it was becoming quiet.

'I can't,' he said again, as if it were a sudden realization. He went to step outside. Bernard pulled him back. It was not much of a pull, a slight tug on the sleeve of his uniform, but it stopped him.

'What?' He was almost fierce.

Her face was too dark in the close shadows of the hut. It was now only the tremble of her voice that he could judge by.

'You must stay here,' she said. 'We could stay all night. It would be better than being at the convent; it would be better than anything.'

He could not bear it. '*Nein*. I will go.'

It was too much; he felt threatened by her, by what might happen. And so he moved quickly, before she could stop him again, pushing back the wet brambles from the entrance, not feeling them claw at him, setting off at a trot down the sodden path, not looking back, hardly breathing.

Bernard was alone again. She touched the stone ledge on which he had perched and let her fingers lie there. God began drumming in her head. She knew that something had been lost.

She was afraid of the noises left by the storm, the creaks that punctured the night and the unfamiliar rushing of water. In the utter dark she stumbled, and once or twice mistook her way. Her habit caught in the wet hedges and she heard the tear of it as she pulled it free. But when she got back to the convent, she had not been missed. Roof tiles lay shattered in the drive and one chimney had fallen completely, splintering stone. The dislocated branch of an old tree had crashed through a first-floor window. The corrugated iron roof of the henhouse had been ripped off by the wind and thrown halfway across the lane; dismayed hens were scurrying round in the dark, their panic noisy. The nuns were all busy. Bernard shooed a loose chicken up the path in front of her and was thanked for her efforts. Because of the light rain that had begun to fall, gentle now and silent, no one could see her tears.

Bernard was digging over where the early salads had already been pulled. The soil was not quite loose, stiffening around the mattock, making her strain. There was a pain lodged across her shoulders. When she saw someone approaching, she was pleased to rest, leaning hard on the trunk of the cherry tree at the edge of the garden, her head in the shade.

'Sister Bernard.'

The Mother Superior's face was intently serene. God cried out. Bernard felt the sweat gather under her habit.

She knew she had done something wrong.

'I was finishing,' she said. 'The soil is dry; I was slow.'

'I will send Sister Benedict with the seeds.'

Mother Catherine looked slowly around, gauging things. Bernard wiped her face with her sleeve, smelling the earth there. She pressed closer to the shade.

'You might like to come inside, Sister,' said Mother Catherine slowly, not yet settling her eyes on her nun. 'Your father has died this morning. He was very ill, I understand. We are praying right now for the repose of his soul.'

Bernard blinked. The tricks of sunlight and shade disorientated her. She was silent.

'You might like to come and pray with us, Sister.'

Mother Catherine spoke carefully, as if to a child, looking hard at Sister Bernard in an attempt to thrust the words home.

'I haven't finished,' said Bernard.

Mother Catherine sighed. 'You have permission to leave your work, Sister. This once. It can be finished later.'

Bernard glanced up at the clear sky through the threaded cherry branches.

'It'll be hot,' she said. 'The soil will dry even more. I won't get it dug.'

'Sister—' Mother Catherine looked across at the neat patch of turned earth. Her lips were tight now. 'Very well,' she said at last. 'As you like. I will leave you to finish.'

Bernard did not watch her go. She turned immediately from the fruit trees and picked up her mattock to dig again. With relief, she felt the crunch of it in the soil and she worked her way through the unbroken earth, bending to pick out weeds, the sun hot through her veil. Her hands stung, the skin already blistered, but God was languid in her head, hardly a bother, only pressing her sometimes to break up the larger clods.

When the angelus rang at midday, Bernard was still working. She did not stop for the bell, and no one came to fetch her in to pray. But the digging was nearly done now; only the slightest ridge of hard soil remained, and in the hot sun she paused, pushing her veil from her face.

Severine was standing a little beyond the convent wall, a wide hat shading her face and shoulders and two of her children sprawled on the grass alongside. Bernard did not know how long her friend had been there; her bovine gaze was unhurried and incurious as though she might have been watching for many hours. But when Bernard finally stopped, peeling her scorched hands from the wooden handle of the mattock and straightening in the sun, Severine cocked her head, a greeting. The bell finally came to an end, the last toll fading; everything was sudden silence.

Bernard pulled her habit flat at the belt and brushed her hands against each other, spreading the stains of dirt. She went slowly towards the wall, picking her way through the strawberry plants that were low to the ground there.

'I was with him,' said Severine. 'All night. I was there. We prayed together.'

Something about this annoyed Bernard.

'Right,' she said.

Severine did not seem to mind the sharpness of Bernard's tone.

'And we talked about you. He asked for you,' she went on steadily.

Bernard looked at the uneven stones on top of the wall and pressed her hands against the warmth of them. But her voice was hard still and her words curt. 'Everyone was there.'

It was not a question, but Severine nodded.

'It was a good death. We called the priest – and the other women were all looking after him – doing everything he needed. He just drifted away.'

Severine paused and looked down at the children, letting her arm fall towards one of them before she continued. She smiled at Bernard, some kind of apology.

'They're all still there now.'

Bernard wanted to imagine what this would be like, but she could not even see how the house would look with them crowded into the dark front room, her father flat on the table and the candles lit, making the old shadows shiver against the beams. She looked up at her friend, blank.

'Really – he asked for you,' said Severine again. 'He thought about you.'

Bernard did not move, and her gaze seemed fixed. Severine flicked her head so that her hat fell backwards and her face was plain.

'Sister?'

Bernard heard the plea and knew there was something she should be making of the moment. But she could think only of the soldier, everything about him coming clear and close; the pain of her longing was so new to her then, and so keen, that she staggered, reaching out for the wall to steady herself, the sunlight lurching around her.

Severine put out a hand and Bernard grabbed at it. And they stood together, with the wall between them, the meadow stretching away towards the village and Severine's children nudging at their mother's legs, impatient in the heat.

'They will let you come to the burial,' said Severine at last.

Bernard shook her head. 'I don't think it's permitted,' she said.

She looked down at their clasped hands, as though surprised to find herself held there. She heard God, cheerless.

'I'm late,' she said. 'I've been too long.'

And she pulled away, dragging the mattock over the ground behind her, on her way to wash her hands at the butt. Severine stood and watched for as long as she could, seeing Bernard store her tools in the shed and leave her clogs at the back door before disappearing into the convent, its windows milky in the high sun. Then there was the sound of a vehicle strident in the lane below, distracting her, and Severine stood back to watch a small German truck as it rattled along by the wash house, turning out of the village, fumes puttering from its exhaust and hanging in the quiet air. She frowned at it, and scratched hard at something on the bare flesh of her arm. Then she pushed at the children, starting them down the hill, sniffing viciously at the caustic smell of diesel, out of place there.

# Six

Bernard's cell bore very few traces of her. There were unfilled holes along one wall, inexplicable now, and sinister. Here and there were the blots that sticky tack had left on the paint when she had taken down faded church rotas and diocesan calendars. And around the ceiling line were one or two stains where she had reached up to crush mosquitoes with her shoe. Otherwise there was only the luminous Christ and the dints in the wooden floor made over time by the wheels of her bed rocking backwards and forwards during the night.

She did not look around. She concentrated on her task, shaking out her sparse collection of clothes, sliding them from the two drawers in the boxwood chest under the window, and refolding everything into a saggy kitbag which someone had provided for the move. She ran a clean tissue over her one spare pair of shoes, her best, which were kept in a clear plastic bag. These she also transferred to the bottom of the kitbag. The personal wash things which she was permitted to take to Les Cèdres fitted into another plastic freezer bag which slipped into a side pocket without filling it.

Finally, Bernard sorted through the square tin biscuit box. She had used it mostly as a step for reaching the top of the door and window frames when she needed to clean. Its lid had buckled slightly under her weight, the pink and gold Alpine landscape distorted and worn away in places by the rub of her shoes, the dull gleam of the tin pushing through. She had to lever it off at the corners with a key. Inside was a small uneven stack of papers. She lifted them out gently and put them on top of the chest. The cell filled for a moment with the smell of damp ink, like incense. Underneath, at the bottom of the tin, was her mother's wedding ring; four obsolete coins; a single pearl earring; a button from a German military uniform; a plastic pencil sharpener souvenir from Lourdes; a tiny wooden crucifix, split across the grain; six paper clips and a glass marble, the captured twists of its undimmed colours marvellous. There was nothing of any value, and nothing that matched the list of Les Cèdres permissibles. It could all be left behind. The only thing that Bernard took from the tin, to keep, was the dark brown knot of old umbilical cord, so desiccated and small now, so archaeological, that its past seemed long beyond her. She could hardly recall it or how it had come to her, the memory stuttering and fearful. But she prized it, nonetheless, instinctively, and she held it tightly for a moment as though it might still connect her to something. She put it into the kitbag with care.

The village clock sounded ten. Bernard counted the chimes and almost immediately afterwards heard the clatter of the doorbell. She could not imagine who it could be; the unexpectedness of it alarmed her. She pushed the tin box away across the bed and tried to hurry, looking around in the dormitory corridor as though the sound of the bell might have disturbed something there. When she was halfway down the long stairs, she saw a green beret below in the hall, bobbing, and then Sister Thérèse coming forwards in her best black coat. The beret slipped backwards and Bernard saw Corinne's upturned face, smiling.

'There's no hurry, Sister Bernard. We have plenty of time.'

Bernard stopped on the stairs and peered at the visitor.

'It's only five minutes in the car, after all.'

Thérèse was fastening her buttons. She did not look at Bernard. And in the end, because they seemed to be waiting for her, Bernard made her way to the end of the staircase, but slowly now, as if the descent pained her. In the hall she stretched.

'I haven't had a chance to tell Sister Bernard of your plan,' said Thérèse, smiling lightly at Bernard. 'You see, Corinne rang just after breakfast to suggest she drive us to the Armistice service in the village,' she went on. 'For a change. To save us walking.'

'I didn't hear the telephone,' said Bernard. 'How did you hear the telephone, Sister?'

'You were upstairs. You were packing. I was right there. It was chance,' explained Thérèse, still seeming somehow uneasy about the way her buttons were fastened.

Corinne grinned. 'I just thought of it,' she said. 'It was just an idea.'

Bernard noticed a tiny tear in the green beret, and threads hanging loose around it.

'I think your beret—' she began.

Corinne put her hand to her head. 'I know. Isn't it lovely? I love it.'

Bernard nodded. 'Yes,' she said.

'Even for Armistice,' added Corinne. 'No one'll mind.'

'Corinne said it was a shame that you'd never been, because we had to walk usually, and stand around in the cold.' Thérèse was suddenly loud. 'She thought it would be better with the car, Sister Bernard. She was thinking of you.'

'It's true. I never go to the village for Armistice,' said Bernard.

'You're shouting, Sister,' said Corinne, laughing and taking Thérèse by the arm. She turned then to Bernard. 'But you'll come today, won't you? I've told everyone we're coming.'

She looked hard at Bernard, and Bernard guessed it was a test of some kind. But she could not quite understand it. Her thoughts were still fractured by the moments of unmeaning memory in her tin box. She stared at the tear in the beret.

'You'll need your coat, Sister,' said Thérèse.

The day was bright and clear; the early winter sky a wide flat blue. A donkey bellowed somewhere, far away. Waiting for Corinne to turn the car, Bernard could feel a breeze that reminded her of an old summer.

Corinne had music playing on the radio.

'Music is so good for the health, don't you think, Sister? It's so relaxing,' she said, as she pulled down the drive. But Thérèse did not hear the question, and Bernard, sitting in the back, did not think it could have been for her.

'We should start a choir. At church. It's a shame there's no choir,' Corinne went on, raising her voice this time. 'If a few of us began I'm sure there'd soon be others. A small choir to begin with, doing simple things. Hymns. You would join us, wouldn't you, Sister?'

Again, the question went unclaimed.

'You're not in our parish,' said Bernard instead.

'No. But at La Collegiale we already have a choir. A good choir. I sing every week.'

'She sings very well. I've heard her,' said Thérèse, although really she had seen the way the choir lined itself up around the altar, regimented, and had caught bursts of the music, undefined and slippery.

'Well, I'm not musical,' said Bernard.

Corinne looked at Bernard in the rear-view mirror. 'But of course you can sing?' she said, and she hummed a few bars of a bright tune as encouragement.

'No,' said Bernard. 'I don't think I can.'

Corinne tutted, as though this was ridiculous, and narrowed her eyes at Bernard in the mirror. On the radio, a boy band replaced a girl band, and an upbeat tune turned to a ballad. Bernard squeezed her hands and legs together. Her fear was suddenly unshakeable.

There were other elderly drivers parking their cars where the streets narrowed and beginning the slow climb up the hill towards the square. The skeletal plane trees, knobbled and bulky, made the village seem bare. Only the photocopied yellow posters were bright, advertising a dance to celebrate the end of the chestnut season. There were few other distractions. And Bernard could not help seeing the people gathering around her, recognizing the faces without meaning to. Everything was enduring and familiar. She recognized the turn of the common nose and the usual earthy hair colour. The roll of gravelly voices had been always known. And yet she did not belong here, with these people. Her memories had never been the same as theirs.

Preparations for the event were still under way. As they emerged into the square, Corinne walking steadily between the nuns, someone was trying to reattach a decorative bow to the mound of flowers which would act as a wreath. A young woman was connecting a portable cassette player to a long extension lead which snaked out of sight down an alley, and broken glass was being swept from between two bare flowerbeds. A ribbon of onlookers was gradually thickening behind the small raised wall which fronted the church.

The limestone memorial glistened in the sun. The names were stacked on it, each one cramped above the next. Bernard looked for her old name, a relic of the family she had given up. The tug of it was warm, a belonging; she read it over and over. But she could not be sure now whether she had ever known the brothers whose deaths were carved into the stone, and she turned aside in the end, letting the name fall away. It was too long past.

'You see,' said Corinne brightly. 'It was worth the effort, wasn't it, Sister?'

She seemed to bear down on Bernard, who stepped back.

'We could have walked,' said Thérèse. 'It's an extravagance really, taking the car.'

Corinne winked at her, Bernard was sure. 'It might have rained,' she said.

And all three of them glanced up at the divine blue of the sky.

'Anyway,' Corinne added quietly, after a moment, 'I wanted to come with you.'

Thérèse bent close to try to hear. 'It's true,' she said. 'It seems special. When we're at Les Cèdres we might not be able to do this kind of thing any more. We won't even come to this church any more. To this village.'

'You can come to La Collegiale with me, and sing,' said Corinne.

'Not from Les Cèdres – it's too far.'

'From my apartment,' said Corinne.

Thérèse's sudden anger was loud and out of place. People nearby turned to look at the thin nun.

'Enough, Corinne. I have already said. I'm not coming to you, to your apartment. I can't come. Sister Bernard and I are going to Les Cèdres.'

Corinne flapped her hands at Thérèse. 'All right. All right. It was nothing. We'll talk about it.'

'We will not talk about it, not again,' said Thérèse.

Something with the taste of clay swelled in Bernard's stomach. She found it difficult to breathe. She began to recite the well-known rhythms of the rosary in her head, repeating them meaninglessly, but they did not soothe her and could not distract her from what was going on. She edged away from the squabble. She could see how Thérèse avoided looking at her. She knew she was not wanted, and she was drawn to the shadow down the side of the church where no one was standing. She understood that Corinne and Thérèse were hurling accusations at her, silent, camouflaging them with the noise of their argument; she could not bear their anger.

The small crowd continued to gather. One or two people noticed Bernard as she stood apart. No one spoke to her. Corinne watched where she was going and threw her a little wave. A heavy red four-by-four was parked in front of the village memorial. All the other cars had been moved for the ceremony, but no one could find the owner of the jeep. Straddling the stone plinth, it made the memorial all but invisible from one side of the square. There was a last effort to find the owner; doors were knocked on for a second time, questions asked, but no one knew where it had come from. It had an unfamiliar number plate. There was nothing to be done but to work around it. The young woman lifted the cassette player onto the bonnet and, after finding her place on the tape, stepped to one side. A crocodile of children, holding hands in twos and threes, arrived at a trot from the school, but was not late. The children seemed baffled by the solemnity of the occasion and were quiet.

Just before eleven, the mayor emerged from the crowd and made his way to the four-by-four. He stood with his back to the driver's door and thanked everyone for coming. There was a short pause and then church bells rang the hour. The young woman stepped forwards and pressed the button to start the tape. 'The Last Post' wailed out into the late autumn air followed by a jolly but scratchy rendition of 'The Marseillaise'. The crowd stood solemnly, arms crossed or tucked behind their backs, looking sadly at the four-by-four as a young boy took the flowers, edged around the back of the vehicle, and laid the tribute out of sight.

The opening bars of 'The Marseillaise' struck up again as the tape automatically rewound. The mayor reached over the bonnet to stop it. There was, for a moment, unsmudged silence. Then he spoke briefly about the futility of war and the debt owed to those who had given their lives for freedom. He invited all those present to join him in a glass of wine and a slice of sweet cake to honour the fallen. He encouraged them to attend a concert the following Saturday at which dinner would be served. There would be dancing, he promised, and the view of the stage would not be obscured by mystery off-road vehicles. There was a trickle of laughter. The war was nearly forgotten. Only the ceremonies remained, faint and unreal, and occasional stirrings of emotion, bubbling briefly to the surface of contaminated lives.

Bernard knew, when she heard the bells, that the past was upon her. Fleeting, for the slightest of moments, the soldier was there, in the square, his uniformed figure uncertain, his blue eyes unsettled. Then there was just the priest, coming towards her, smiling at her. She knew she should not have come.

'Come and have a drink, Sister. Don't be shy,' said the young priest. He was new to the parish and his cheeks were pinched pink with embarrassment and enthusiasm. 'You must know everyone. And there's fruit juice if you would prefer.'

He stepped away to make room for the schoolchildren filing in turn to the memorial behind the jeep, each laying a paper flower there. A teenage boy began to squeeze out a sorrowful melody on the accordion. Bernard slowly followed the priest to the drinks table, where he left her.

Two women skirted round the edge of the table, sticking down the white paper cover with tape to stop it blowing up in the breeze. The drinks were served by a dark-haired woman of imprecise old age, in a tight blue coat and a fitted hat. She filled the cups evenly and mopped up spills without fuss.

'We heard you might be coming, Sister Bernard,' she said, too loudly. Her face was drawn, the wrinkles in it cut deep.

Bernard took her cup of orange juice and moved away. She could not, for a moment, think who it was who had spoken to her. She could not place the other woman, the odd contortions of age making the features inexact. But then she remembered. Faces came back to her, crowding; the odd creased eyes of the boy who was shot with the ambushed Resistance unit, and this, his younger sister, who many years ago had been pretty. She looked again, to make sure; the memory was faint, unused.

The villagers knotted around the table. Corinne was talking to a small group of women, her green beret easily visible, and Thérèse was at the edge of the gathering, bending to pat a dog on a long lead. Bernard tried to slip through the crush but in the end had to push, suddenly anxious to reach open ground. She felt the crowd of people too near. She looked for Thérèse again, but could not pick her out in the mass of dark winter coats, and so she began to make her way down the hill towards the cars, knowing she could not stay.

The woman at the drinks table watched her go, overfilling one of the cups until it spilt. Unapologetic, she surprised the young man she was serving with her hostility.

'How can she show her face here?'

The man shrugged and smiled. He did not touch the brimming cup; he had no idea what was going on. But when he moved away from the table, a woman in a green beret took his place; heads bent towards each other then, repeating an old war story, infected by time, discoloured and brittle.

Bernard saw them coming, a group of five or six old women, at first, marching down the hill to the car park, the blue of the winter sky brilliant behind them. She felt their anger from a distance. She looked for someone she knew, but Thérèse was out of sight and only Corinne's beret was visible, at the back of the crowd. Panicking, she tripped as she hurried to find Corinne's car, confusing it with other small white cars, and only finding it in the end by chance. But when she tried the door, it was locked, and she could do nothing but turn to face them as they came towards her. She tried to think of something to say, but everything was confused and out of place and there were no words for it. When one of them slapped her, the open hand cold against Bernard's face, her plastic cup slipped from her hand to the ground and she felt splashes of juice through her tights. The women pushed closer. Bernard flung out a prayer, calling for help. She heard laughter, and hoped it wasn't God's.

The voices all around were shrill, too quick and harsh. The accusations fell too densely, like the confusion of sudden hail. Bernard could not make out what was being said. But then the dead boy's sister spoke again, low and quiet, uncertain of her tone after sixty years of fury.

'You should never have been allowed to stay,' she said, and Bernard understood this.

If she could have chosen, this was not how the old woman would have had it. She had not imagined a confrontation so ragged and public. She turned away, pushing through the crowd, shaken by tears. The rest of the small mob rearranged itself, men sidling to the front for a better view, and one or two of the schoolchildren, having broken ranks, squeezing between adult legs. The sight of Bernard, small and dark in her worn habit, disappointed them all.

The rest of the women kept coming closer. Bernard took several steps back and was pinned against the side of Corinne's car. Someone stretched out a hand, as though wanting to touch her. A globule of spit flew past the side of her veil and landed with a wet splat behind her on the car window. It might have been aimed at her. Bernard could not think now why this was happening; she couldn't remember anything. There was only this moment, too luminous, enduring for ever.

There was damp around her feet, spilt juice or a shameful trickle of urine. She tried shutting her eyes, but the din around her, the laughter and spiteful talk, echoed in her head and the women pressed in on her even more, closer, their breath a flavour now in the air. Someone reached forwards and pulled the veil from Bernard's head. She felt a rush of cold on her scalp and had to open her eyes. One of the children gasped at her baldness.

There was still no sign of Thérèse or Corinne. They had been pushed away, perhaps, by the crowd, or had not seen what was happening. All Bernard knew was that she

97

was alone. And it was the young priest, finally, who stepped in to restore a measure of calm. The sight of Bernard's dry pate in the sun shocked him.

'That's enough. Enough. This is a day for peace, not for violence. And a sister of Christ…'

'She's not a sister of Christ. She's a Nazi whore.' It seemed old-fashioned, even as it was said.

Someone spat again; the spittle landed like bird droppings on the front of Bernard's habit. She thought she felt it sting.

'No, no. *Mesdames*. Really. She's an old woman.' From the back of the small crowd, the priest had tried to piece together what was going on, but it seemed confused to him and ridiculous, an odd leftover of some old quarrel, pointless. 'Perhaps you should get in the car, Sister. Perhaps it would be better if you were to leave now.'

'I can't… I don't…' Bernard tried to explain.

'Here, Sister, I have the key.'

And Corinne was suddenly there. Bernard heard the click of the automatic locks opening. But she still could not move.

'Sister, it's open. You can get in,' she heard Corinne say.

'Don't come back here. Don't show your face again,' she heard another voice.

But still she could not move.

'I'll help you, Sister. It's been a shock,' said the priest, putting his arm across hers and trying to turn her so he could open the car door with his other hand. She was unwieldy; he had to tug at her. It took some minutes to manoeuvre her into the back seat. Then the priest passed in her veil. Bernard noticed that it was damp, stained down one side. She clung to it, trying hard not to look at any faces. The crowd waited, as if to make sure that she really was leaving, and Bernard, her eyes fixed ahead through the windscreen, knew they were still there behind her.

The car did not move. Neither Thérèse nor Corinne got in. Bernard made herself as small as she could on the back seat and tried to pray. But she found only a memory of the soldier, propped above her on his elbow, chuckling with delight, bending to unbutton the tight tunic of her habit, looking at her with something she thought was tenderness, leaning down, his hair falling softly against her skin. It did not seem long ago. It was a comfort.

Outside, Thérèse was standing apart. She saw the villagers loitering, no longer concerned with Bernard, finishing new conversations before they started for home. She saw how Corinne smiled at the women around her, and shook hands with the priest. She saw Bernard's bald head, framed by the back window of Corinne's car, and in the distance beyond she saw the smeared grey walls of the convent, unnecessarily solid, a fortress against the petty evils of a country parish. She waited. The children filed back to school; someone shouted something from the square. It all seemed significant but she could not think quite why.

'Well then,' was all Corinne said when she finally came. She looked towards the car, but Sister Bernard was hardly visible.

'I didn't know,' said Thérèse.

'No.'

'I mean, I knew things happened, during the war. I'd heard one or two… stories. But not that. Not that she'd, you know…'

'Informed.'

'Betrayed them,' said Thérèse, letting the strange words come slowly.

'The Resistance was strong around here, in all these villages,' said Corinne. 'There was a lot of support for them; they made good progress. But afterwards, after the ambush... and the information the Germans got. Especially from that poor boy – the things they did to him.' She looked away for a moment, her face creased. 'It gave the Germans the upper hand for a while.'

'But it's terrible.'

'It made a mess of things, certainly. There was chaos after that – all sorts – recrimination and murder and executions... No one knew what was going on or who to trust. You know what it's like in a small place, everyone watching everyone else, little things getting out of hand. People still remember it.'

Thérèse felt her hands tremble. 'But how did you know... about Sister Bernard?'

Corinne clicked the car keys against her hand. 'Lots of people know, or knew, at least. But it was mostly glossed over. The convent hushed things up. They've always been good at that.' She smiled. 'Anyway, it's a long time ago now, I suppose.'

Thérèse knew it was not, and she did not move towards the car.

'I always assumed... I always thought... I always thought she must be good,' said Thérèse. 'She always seemed so good. So simple.'

Corinne shrugged and gestured towards the car. 'We should take her back,' she said.

'Yes, yes, I suppose. I'm sorry. It's a shock, that's all.'

Corinne nodded. 'Does it alter your plans, Sister?' she asked.

Thérèse did not understand the question. And then, in an instant, she grasped it all, and how the past had freed her. She sucked in a sharp loud breath, as though surprised by a sudden pain.

'Oh,' she said.

Corinne saw such doubts in her friend's face that she wanted to say many things, but Thérèse put her hand up, silencing her. She looked away to the convent.

'I'll walk,' she said. 'I'll walk back.'

'Don't be silly. You might as well have a lift. It's uphill.'

'Just take her. I'll walk. I don't know what to… I don't know anything. I need time, to think. I need someone to help me – I need to pray.' And before anything more could be said, Thérèse had turned away from the cars, cutting down towards the wash house to the path that would take her up the hill.

Corinne watched her go and then was brisk.

'Good, Sister Bernard. Let's take you home,' she said, pulling the car door open sharply and starting the engine.

Bernard did not thank Corinne, nor turn to wave as she went in through the convent porch. She did not stop to wipe her boots on the mat. She thought she heard the car pulling away behind her, but she could not be sure, and she did not look. She went straight up to her cell, letting the village and its memories fall away.

The following day, the minibus was coming to take them to Les Cèdres. She had very little time. That was all she could think of now, the rush of it making her head spin, and only this mattering, nothing else. She put her packed bag at the threshold, and moved the tin box into a corner. Then, from the top of the chest of drawers, she picked up the pile of papers and shook the dust from the top sheets. It fell like glitter in the clear light.

She hurried from her cell, anxious, unable to make an ending. On the stairs she stumbled, the air fluttering around her too fast, everything passing. Some of the papers slipped away. She did not stop to collect them. The doorbell rang and she thought it must be Corinne again. She saw a shape through the stained-glass panels of the door, indistinguishable, but she turned away from it and carried on across the hall. Thérèse, coming in the back way, through the refectory, saw Bernard hurry along the corridor, a little old woman carefully holding high a stack of papers as though to protect them from an encroaching sea.

Even through her deafness, Thérèse heard the clatter of the doorbell and, after a very short pause, it sounded again. In her mind, there was still nothing except the anger of the Armistice service, the villagers pushing forwards and bitterness pricking everywhere at the close seams of things. The bell seemed a part of it, a summons. She thought they might have been followed up to the convent, so that it would all continue, and if she could, she would have resisted that. But the bell was too insistent. By the third ring, she was in the wide, marble-floored hallway, her heart loud, even to her spoilt ears.

'I didn't know if you would still be here. I didn't know when you were going. I couldn't remember,' said Thérèse's nephew, Claude, breathlessly, as he kissed her. 'And I've got the day off, for the Armistice holiday, so I thought I'd come and…'

'Soon. We're going soon,' said Thérèse, bewildered by the sudden change. 'Tomorrow.'

She wiped her sleeve hard across her face, in case the tears still showed. But Claude was looking past her, into the wide hall.

'Then I'm glad I came.' He remembered to shout. He always did.

From the corner of the porch he lifted up a huge potted plant, rampant with luminous pink flowers.

'I brought you this, for your new home,' he said, waving it in front of him as he entered.

'It's beautiful,' said Thérèse.

'I thought so.'

They were awkward together. Thérèse reached to take the plant as he thrust it towards her; it caught her in the face. They both had to step back.

'I was going to write. I promised I would,' said Thérèse. 'I'm sorry.'

It was by the slenderest of chances that they had kept in touch since the death of Thérèse's sister fifteen years before. But Thérèse prayed for Claude and his family every day and loved him better than anyone else on earth.

'I'm glad you came,' she said. 'God is good.'

Claude grinned at her from behind the pink plant, waiting.

'Would you like some coffee?' Thérèse asked.

'I'd love a coffee.'

'Right. Good.'

Bernard had stacked her papers on the small table in the snug. She saw the plant approaching and was surprised that behind it was the fat nephew with big ears.

'You must both come and be comfortable,' she said. 'You should come and join me.'

'I had thought we would go to the refectory… to let you…' Thérèse sighed the slightest of sighs.

'As you like, Sister,' said Bernard.

And Thérèse could not refuse her then. 'I'll bring the coffee through, when it's ready,' she said.

Bernard praised the plant as Claude set it carefully on the floor. Three flower heads, loosened by their journey, dropped gracefully onto the tiles where they lay like cartoon butterflies.

'It's quite rare, I'm told,' said Claude. 'I thought she'd like it. To brighten things up.'

'I'm sure she will.'

Claude coughed a breathless cough. 'You must be sad to leave, Sister,' he said.

'I am, very sad.'

'You have been here…?'

'Seventeen days short of seventy-six years.'

Claude could not imagine the monotony of this. 'A long time,' he said.

They heard Thérèse drop something in the kitchen; the thin metallic echo was like bells.

'It must have been a very different place when you were first here, Sister Bernard.'

Bernard thought about it, recalling with absolute clarity the day the convent had finally accepted her father's meagre dowry offer and she had waited by the front steps for someone to find her there, too afraid to knock. She recalled the smell of bread and blood and soap. She had thought, at first, that it was the smell of sanctity, but had soon realized that it was merely the stench of communal living.

'No,' she said. 'It was much the same, I think. I can hardly remember – I feel the same.'

'Life's like that,' said Claude, wanting his coffee.

Thérèse brought in the small glasses on a round tray. They trembled slightly, clinking.

'Isn't it a beautiful plant, Sister?'

'Beautiful,' said Bernard.

'It's nothing,' said Claude. 'Just a little gift.'

'It's very kind,' said Thérèse. She set the glasses on the table. 'We're not disturbing you, Sister,' she said as she sat down. 'Sister Bernard is going through her papers,' she added to Claude.

'I haven't started,' said Bernard. 'Would you like the television?'

'We're fine,' said Claude.

The smell of the coffee was somehow out of place. They held their glasses away from them and a light steam rose into the cold air. They talked for a while about the weather and Claude's work. Bernard predicted that rain would come in a day or two, and high winds from the coast. Claude entertained them with tales of his new computer.

'There's a change, anyway,' said Thérèse suddenly.

They thought she hadn't heard their conversation. Claude leant forwards, closer to her.

'I'm not going,' said Thérèse, not looking at him. 'To Les Cèdres. I'm not going there after all.'

For a moment, Bernard thought something had happened to save them.

'You have heard from the diocese, Sister?'

'But you said you were going tomorrow,' said Claude.

Thérèse shook her head at them both. 'No, no,' she said, but neither was quite sure if the answer was for them. 'You see – look, I'm sorry… I'm going to live in town, with Corinne.'

Bernard said nothing. She was not even sure, not yet, what Thérèse might mean. She watched as Thérèse smiled at her nephew and explained, her cheeks flushing. She heard her tell him about Corinne's apartment and how much nicer it was than the room assigned to her at the rest home.

'I couldn't do it. Not finally. Not when I thought about it – I couldn't end up in that place,' she said.

Claude threw back his head and laughed.

Bernard hated him.

'I thought it would be all right. I thought I could make a new start. But in the end… well, you have to live, don't you?'

It did not seem an odd question. Claude beamed at his aunt.

'Of course you do. You've been shut up here long enough, I'd say. Take a break for a while – see a bit of the world.'

'It'll just be… it'll just be a change, that's all. Not to be in an institution.' Thérèse knew she could not explain. 'I'm looking forward to it.'

Bernard moaned.

'We should leave Sister Bernard to her papers,' said Thérèse, as lightly as she could. 'We shouldn't disturb her. We'll go next door for a moment. We'll be better talking there.'

And Claude followed his aunt into the refectory, taking the tray of glasses. Bernard heard the rattle disappearing.

When Claude left the convent half an hour later he was still laughing a little, his mouth wide and his words springy. He took Thérèse by the shoulders and kissed her, holding her afterwards for longer than he needed. As she watched him walk down the long drive, she knew that what she was doing was right.

'Sister Marie's bag is by the front door,' she said brightly when she came back into the snug. 'Claude found it; he nearly tripped over it.'

'If you go into town with that woman—' Bernard began.

'I'm leaving the convent, Sister, one way or another. They're making me leave. It's not my choice. What difference does it make where I go? Everything's changing, breaking up – I can't help that.'

'I didn't imagine going on my own,' said Bernard.

Thérèse pretended she had not heard. 'Yes,' she said. 'The bag. Sister Marie's bag. It's by the front door.'

Bernard rocked back on her heels, unsteady. 'The hospital rang about it,' she said.

'Nursing home, Sister. It's not a hospital.'

'They rang to say she didn't have it. I told them we'd put it on the minibus.'

'No, Sister, it's by the front door,' said Thérèse, narrowing her eyes.

Bernard could not believe this. She presumed Claude had made a mistake.

'You think it is still here?'

'Yes. Here. I saw it just now.' Then, as if making a concession, she continued. 'I went to wave Claude off, and as he was leaving, that Dutchman came to pick up the cultivator from the yard.'

Bernard started at the thought of the Dutchman.

'But I have the instructions. I wanted to give him the instructions,' she said.

She had mended the cultivator herself for the last twelve years since the mechanic's workshop in the village had closed. She knew now, after much trial and error, exactly how the engine worked. She knew what to do when it threatened to stall and with what care it needed oiling after each use. Only she knew all this. So when a small ad had been placed in the free local paper, and a sale agreed, she had written instructions and scratched out a few diagrams, working on them with great care over several weeks. Thérèse had watched her compile them.

'Claude helped me start it up and we ran it round and then the Dutchman put it on his trailer,' said Thérèse. 'And when he'd gone, we stood in the porch for a moment, to say goodbye, and that's when Claude saw Sister Marie's bag. He joked about it being a bomb.'

'Did he give you the money?' asked Bernard.

Thérèse frowned. 'The Dutchman? I thought you'd already done that.'

'No, Sister. We agreed the sale, that's all. He was to pay us when he came to collect it.'

'Well then – no,' Thérèse huffed. 'He didn't. I didn't know.' She thought Bernard was about to cry. 'Don't worry, Sister. I'm sure he'll bring it. I'm sure he simply forgot.'

She wanted to put an arm round Bernard's sloping shoulders, but she did not dare, and then Bernard stepped away.

'I wouldn't have known how much you'd agreed, anyway,' said Thérèse.

'You should have fetched me. I could have done it.'

It seemed an enormous treachery suddenly, and Thérèse was ashamed.

'I'm so sorry,' she said.

'It was for the parish fund,' said Bernard stiffly.

Thérèse nodded. 'What shall we do about Marie's bag?'

'I told them we had put it on the minibus.' Bernard could not bear the thought of another mistake. She imagined God's spluttering dismay. 'I told them.'

'I thought it might be Claude's. But he had the plant. He couldn't have carried anything else.'

'I'll have to ring them.' Bernard started for the telephone, but a sudden thought stopped her. 'Did you give him the spare spark plug?'

'For the cultivator? No.'

'He'll need it.'

Thérèse waved away the thought of this. 'He looked a capable man.'

'He's Dutch,' said Bernard. It sounded like an indictment but neither of them was sure exactly what it might mean for the future operation of the convent's only piece of agricultural machinery.

\*

The girl at the nursing home knew nothing of the search for Sister Marie's bag, but she went away for a long while and came back to the telephone with cheerful confidence.

'Will you be there later this afternoon?'

'At what hour? We haven't got much time. We're moving soon. Tomorrow,' said Bernard.

The girl went away again.

'Our deputy director has an errand near you. We can call her and she can stop at your house for the bag on her way back to town,' she explained carefully when she returned to the telephone. 'Where do you live?'

Bernard gave the address.

'That's a convent!'

'Yes.'

There was a pause.

'Please ask her not to be late. We're very busy, with everything,' said Bernard.

Thérèse was in the snug cleaning the mud from her shoes onto a piece of newspaper.

'They're coming later for the bag,' Bernard said.

'All right. Good.' Thérèse poked hard at the treads of the soles with the blade of a kitchen knife.

'I said we couldn't wait, because of the minibus.'

'We can always leave it out under the porch.'

Bernard hadn't thought of this. 'I'd rather not,' she said.

She picked up a sheet from her pile of papers.

Thérèse looked at her. 'Sister…' But she could not think how to explain. 'I didn't mean you to be alone,' she said at last.

Bernard unfolded a letter and laid it flat against her hand.

'We always have God, Sister,' she said.

Thérèse knew this was true, but something about it did not satisfy her.

Bernard glanced at the handwritten address. It was nothing, a brief note from the daughter of a Spanish woman she had met through the church cleaning circle. For several years they had been on the same rota. Bernard had mopped and swept, while the other woman had dusted and refreshed the flowers. Afterwards, although this had never been agreed between them, they would share a biscuit and some coffee from a flask that the Spaniard would bring, sitting in the annex at the back of the church, tidying the piles of hymn books and missals while they talked. Mostly they would discuss next week's dirt. They had in common a devotion to vinegar as a cleaning fluid. When her husband had retired, the Spaniard had moved south to be closer to her family. She had died a little over a year later. That was why the daughter had written. Bernard had forgotten to reply and had not attended the funeral, but she had included the woman specifically, by name, in her prayers for the dead. She put the letter on the floor to one side of her chair.

Thérèse was watching .

'You're doing well, Sister. With your papers,' she said, as she rolled the newspaper deftly around the mud from her shoes, careful not to spill any onto the floor.

'I have very little time. I should have started earlier.'

'Everything seems like that, at the end. A rush. When

we've known for months that we'd have to go,' said Thérèse.

Bernard took the next sheet from the pile. 'Yes.'

Thérèse could not believe there was nothing more to be said. 'It didn't seem – when they told us – it didn't seem that it would be like this.'

Bernard did not look up. 'We must obey what is meant for us, Sister.'

'Meant by God or by the diocese?' returned Thérèse, sharp.

But Bernard could not answer this. And when Thérèse came back from throwing away the muddy newspaper, she was stiffly bright again.

'What have you decided to keep, Sister?' she asked, bending towards Bernard.

'Very little. There's no need. But I would like to keep that photograph of Rome. I would have liked to go to Rome.'

'You should ask Sister Marie. You know she went twice? To the Audience? I'm sure she would tell you about it.'

Bernard knew Marie would have no memory of it.

'I will, Sister,' she said.

She picked up the next sheet, a scrap of newspaper, clearly torn out in haste.

'And that next one. The newspaper. Are you keeping that?' asked Thérèse, eager, envious for a moment of the chance to sort and classify and choose, to arrange things.

The scrap was dated April 1986. The rest of the date, giving the day itself, had been torn off. It was part of an obituaries column, two or three complete entries, each bordered in thick ink. One of the entries included a picture of a man in late middle age, unsmiling under a magnificent moustache.

Bernard handed the clipping over to Thérèse.

'Madame Sandrine Romero, née Marty, of St Grat,' she read from the top, 'died at home aged eighty-seven. Widow of Jimenez Romero of Madrid and much-loved mother of the late Paul Romero and of Melanie Oustal and Micheline Henry, grandmother of Stefan, Lucy, Philippe, Paul and Odile, and great-grandmother of Simone.'

Bernard did not stop her. Thérèse went on to read the short prayer-poem at the bottom of the obituary.

'Was she a friend?' Thérèse asked at last.

'No. It's the one below,' said Bernard.

'Philippe Pourcel? Died 4 April, after a long illness bravely borne. That one?'

Bernard nodded.

Thérèse looked more closely at the grainy photograph.

'I don't know him,' she said, holding the clipping at arm's length to see if a new perspective didn't somehow trigger a memory. 'Was he special? Why is there a photograph?'

Bernard knew he was not special. He had been the ugliest of rebukes, the hardest of penances.

'He was director of finance at the town hall,' she said.

'But a religious man?'

'I don't know. Does he look it?'

The doorbell sounded again and Thérèse jumped, susceptible now to noises that burst upon her silence.

'I'll answer it,' she said, standing up and resting the piece of newspaper on the arm of her chair.

'Perhaps it's the Dutchman come for his instructions,' said Bernard.

Thérèse did not hear her. She was almost across the hall, realizing already from the slim dark shape through the glass that it was not the Dutchman, nor Claude.

'It is too late anyway, for any of that,' said Bernard.


'This is Sister Bernard,' said Thérèse. 'She has lived here over seventy years. Won't you sit down?'

Veronique nodded slightly towards Bernard and then chose the chair opposite to her, sitting uncomfortably on the edge of it.

'I really can't stay long. I must be back at the home before the shifts change. If you could just let me have the bag.'

'Sister Bernard is going to Les Cèdres,' said Thérèse, adding to Bernard, 'This is the deputy director from the nursing home. She's come to collect Sister Marie's bag.'

Bernard and the woman looked at each other.

'It's nice,' said Veronique. 'At Les Cèdres. I know some people there. Working there,' she corrected herself quickly.

She looked tired. Her face was pallid and meagre, uninteresting.

'You have come promptly,' said Bernard.

'When they phoned they said it was urgent. To be done this afternoon. So I made an effort.'

'It's because we're moving,' Bernard felt obliged to explain. But Veronique was looking away, at the empty corridor and the inexplicable hardness of the convent light. She was not paying much attention.

'Sister Marie would be honoured, if she knew, to have

114

the deputy director come to pick up her bag,' suggested Thérèse.

'It was easy enough for me to pass by.'

'Good of you though,' pressed Thérèse. 'On a holiday too, on Armistice.'

'We work a shift rota. We have different holidays.'

Veronique shivered. The convent unnerved her. From the outside its blankness was disturbing, tainting the centre of the village. It was out of time, somehow, neither a part of the tumbled roofs and stone barns that had been there for ever, nor in keeping with the new-build bungalows tucked onto spare land, the pristine bar or the glass-fronted *salle des fêtes*. Inside it was simply sordid, the old nuns crawling around like slow spiders, their movements clogged with dust. She leant back in the armchair, dislodging the scrap of newspaper which Thérèse had laid on the arm. It floated down to the floor at her feet.

'You must be sad to be leaving,' she said.

'It's a chance to try something else,' said Thérèse.

'We are,' said Bernard.

Veronique reached down for the scrap of newspaper and put it on the table. She glanced for a moment at the grainy photo. Then, bending forwards, she looked at it more closely.

'Sister Bernard has been going through her papers,' explained Thérèse.

'But I've nearly finished, Sister,' said Bernard.

'Have you? Then that's excellent.'

Veronique picked up the obituary and turned it over at the edges with anxious fingers. Then she looked at the two nuns expectantly.

'Sister Thérèse is not coming to Les Cèdres,' said Bernard, as though in reply. It was intimately said, a secret. Thérèse could not hear it. 'I have to go on my own.'

Veronique held the scrap of newspaper towards them. 'This is my father,' she said quietly.

Again, Thérèse had not heard. She smiled and nodded. 'I'll fetch the bag,' she said, going back to the hall.

Bernard felt something flicker in her stomach. They sat across from each other, not moving. Veronique looked away from the nun, towards the bend in the corridor. She imagined the building stretching away beyond, the gloomy air still and unchanging. As soon as she heard Thérèse's footsteps coming close again she got up to leave. She placed the photograph of Philippe Pourcel back on the table without further comment. She picked something from her skirt. Her hands trembled.

'Good luck with the move, ladies. Sorry, Sisters. It's a long time since I was in a convent.' Veronique spoke too brightly. She took Marie's bag from Thérèse. 'I can let myself out if you're busy packing.'

'It's all right. I'll come with you,' said Thérèse.

Bernard watched them round the corner towards the entrance hall, and sat back. As Veronique's car pulled out of the long drive and along the track to the newly renovated wash house, she sat with her hands in her lap, her thoughts spun with shadows. Nothing came clear. Many minutes passed.

Thérèse came back to the snug and turned on the television. Someone had won a holiday to Florida and was hugging the presenter energetically, bouncing and squealing, jubilant. Bernard sank back further in her chair.

# Seven

Something about the soldier's tightness was new. His thin frame was too fragile; he seemed to be concentrating on holding it steady. He lay on the cold floor at the back of the church with his head in her lap, but she could hardly feel the weight of him.

They were away from the draughts but the door was slightly open so that they could see anyone who came up the steps. It was a fine dusk. The bats had begun their low swoop over the village square and the stone glowed golden. The air smelt already of summer dust, the promise of hot days. For a while they heard the low drone of a plane, somewhere distant, something to do with the war, perhaps. Two Germans crossed the square together, briskly, talking loudly. But then it was quiet; the birds were hushed, there were no voices.

He drank from a cloudy bottle, hardly lifting his head, letting the beer dribble down his chin and settle in pools in the creases of Bernard's habit.

'I can't miss evening prayer,' she said quietly.

'It is time?'

'Nearly.' She turned to judge the light outside but the high walls of the square held the day and she was confused. 'I don't know. They'll notice if I'm not there.'

'Go then.'

'A minute more.'

She wanted to close his head in her arms, sweep up the gold of it, but she did not risk it. Instead she took the slightest wisp of his hair in her fingers and held it. She did not twist or pull or caress it, but she pressed the hair tightly, as though it might float away from her. He might have felt the pull of it if he had fidgeted, but he was absolutely still and did not know she had secured a part of him.

When she let the hair fall, she said, 'I didn't think you would stay like this – with me – so long. Usually you go.'

He flipped sideways, sliding from her lap, his head on his elbow and the beer bottle suspended. 'I have permission.' He watched her as he said it; did not smile.

'To stay with me?'

'You have been useful.' He drank his beer and rolled back into her lap, gazing at the damp-pocked ceiling as though there were beauty there. 'The information you gave was very good.'

For a moment they let this hang between them. Then, with a start, Bernard wriggled her knees, bouncing his head.

'Wait. Look.'

With a grunt, he turned to see. Two children were emerging from the shadow at the side of the square and heading for the church, a girl of perhaps nine or ten, and a much younger boy who she was yanking along by the hand. The children trotted across the open ground to the bottom of the church steps where the girl turned to help her brother climb up. By the time they reached the top the soldier was standing just inside the open church door, his uniform tightly buttoned, his feet confidently planted, his pistol visible in his hand. Bernard had slipped further back out of sight, but she was able to see a sliver of what was going on through the crack where the heavy church doors hinged to the stone.

The girl noticed the soldier and stopped, not quite at the top of the steps. She pulled her brother to her side. She said nothing. The boy smiled and rubbed his nose.

'Go home,' said the soldier, his voice gravelly with borrowed age. 'You cannot come here.'

'I have to collect the altar cloths for washing.' The girl was matter-of-fact.

'You cannot come here.'

She gave the slightest of shrugs but did not otherwise move. She looked back hard at the soldier, daring him. He straightened the arm holding the pistol.

'What are you doing anyway? You shouldn't be in the church. Soldiers shouldn't go in the church. I know that. It's a safe place.'

Bernard shifted so that she had a better view of the child's face. She thought she might know her, but the light was unsteady and she could not be sure. The soldier swayed slowly backwards and forwards, his heels clicking softly on the worn stone. He looked over the heads of the girl and her brother, to the low blank buildings on the far side of the square and the dense dark gathering in the open ground beyond, the country trapping him there, a stranger.

'Go home. Now.' There was some panic in the way he

said it, an urge to scream at the children; the words spat
from him viciously.

The girl moved backwards down the steps, reluctant,
one at a time, as her brother made his way down sideways
like a crab. At the bottom of the steps Bernard saw the girl
let go of her brother's hand. The boy moved away from
her then and Bernard could no longer see him. The girl
turned back, emboldened now by the distance between her
and the soldier.

'I'm going to tell them that you were in the church,
with a gun. They'll come and get you for that,' she said.

His reply was low and soft and foreign, a whisper of
the village night. And for the first time he moved out of
the shelter of the porch.

'Stop!' he said in French, though the girl was still,
letting him speak. 'I'll give you the cloths. Wait there.'

He was visible now, to anyone that wanted to see, and
he straightened himself, his fragility absolute.

The girl smiled at him slyly as though she had won
something.

'They're folded up on the sacristy table.'

'What is that?' He turned to find Bernard. He did not
recognize the word. 'What did she say?'

Bernard nodded. 'I'll get them.'

The soldier stood at the back of the nave, in the dark,
while Bernard went to the sacristy where the cloths were
neatly piled on the corner of the table as the girl had said.
There was the faded smell of old stone and worn wood,
and the faint sounds of the village behind him, the squawk
of a blackbird sounding an alarm above the square and the
hum of evening. When he closed his eyes, it was familiar

for a moment, a place he knew already; everything was as it had been when he was a child. But then there was the squat nun picking her way back down the aisle and the pull of his uniform, heavy on his thin limbs.

He still held the pistol in his right hand, so he took the cloths in his left. There was a stain of wine on the top fold. Bernard went in front of him and pushed the door further open for him to pass through, returning into the shelter of the porch. At the bottom of the steps the girl and her brother were waiting patiently. There was no one else to be seen.

'Here,' said the soldier. 'Come and take them.'

The girl was pleased with her success. She skipped up the steps between them and took the cloths in both hands. Through the long crack in the door frame, Bernard could see the way she smiled at the soldier. Then, as the girl turned to go down, Bernard saw him catch hold of her light skirt with his free hand, and tug her back towards him, whipping her round as he did so until she was facing him. She watched as he pulled the girl's skirt up slightly and, in the same movement, deftly moved the hand with the pistol underneath. She watched him jerk his right arm, his pistol arm, upwards, saw the cloth of his uniform shift as the muscles tightened beneath it, saw the colour drain from the girl's face and her mouth and eyes open wide, saw the soldier and the girl sway together, almost dancing for a minute or two, the altar cloths bright in the gloom. She saw him twist his arm sharply, three, perhaps four times and a patch of dark sweat in the small of his back.

A bat passed close to the girl's head and made the soldier, for the first time, take his eyes from her face.

Bernard watched as, with a sharp tug, he pulled his arm and the pistol from under the girl's skirt. The girl let out a noise, a huff, as though she had been winded. He gave her a push back down the steps. She stumbled, still holding the bundle of cloths. When she reached the bottom of the steps, Bernard saw her stumble again. Steadying the cloths with one arm, the girl reached down with her other hand, touching her skirt lightly at one side, as if she might feel something there. She started as if burned. Then both she and the boy moved out of Bernard's field of vision.

The soldier came back into the porch and wiped the barrel of his pistol on Bernard's habit before putting it in his pocket.

He spat something in German, dismissive, and picked up his bottle from the floor, swigging the remaining beer quickly and noisily. Then he put the bottle neatly onto the small table that was pushed back against the wall, took Bernard's face in his skinny hands and pinched her cheeks hard. He spoke to her, in French, but he spoke too fast, scrambling his vowels, and Bernard could not catch anything except the stale heat of his breath. She was frightened of him for the first time. His face did not look quite right.

'Kids,' he said, more clearly, stepping back. He shrugged at her, a plea, his eyes on hers as though what she might say would matter.

But she could not think of anything to say.

'I shall have boys only. Four sons,' he said.

'We must accept God's will in these things,' Bernard replied, her voice stiff and small.

For a moment he snorted a laugh. 'Is that what He says to you, Sister?'

He turned away and was leaving. She saw the unsteady grasp of his hand on the edge of the door.

'You'll be a good father,' Bernard said.

He did not turn back. '*Ja*.'

'Your sons will be strong.'

It was dark now. Bernard heard the click of his boots on the stone steps, and then silence. She had stayed too long. She picked up the bottle, meaning to tidy it away somewhere, but there was nowhere else for it to go and she put it back on the table. She brushed down her habit and her veil, trying not to touch the place where he had cleaned his gun. As she returned to the convent, rather than trying to come up with a convincing excuse for being late for prayers, she imagined the soldier's four sons. God grumbled.

Next time, when he saw her sitting on a stone that had fallen from the wall, only half-shaded, her face in the morning sun, he quickened his step, almost ran to her. She watched him come quickly up the side of the field where the hay was thinner, smiling, and as he came closer he put out a hand to pull at the stems which swelled towards him, presenting her in the end with a loose bouquet of floppy white daisies and tall clover and meadowsweet, ragged robin, seed heads and the light stalks of ripening grass.

'We've got them,' he said, his breath coming fast.

She took the flowers and felt the immediate fear that they would die before she could remember what it was to have this kind of gift. She held them upside down, to let the moisture run to the heads.

'Three of them. One or two got away. It was dark.'

The stone was not large enough for them both. She moved across onto the amber earth and he took her place. She reached out her arm stiffly so that the flowers would be in the shade.

'We followed that nun of yours all the way. It was easy.'

'I didn't know,' Bernard said.

'It was only last night. Late.'

'I haven't seen Sister Jean since evening prayer.'

He leant back. 'She will be all right. We did not touch her.' He closed his eyes for a moment against the bright sun. 'Silly old bitch.'

Bernard had heard a scream some time in the dark hours before dawn, but had thought nothing of it. The convent was not quiet at night. There was always the creak of pipes and floorboards, the scurry of animals and the wails and sobs of the nuns, noisy enough to interrupt the lamentations of Bernard's sleepless God.

'Why did you leave her alone?'

He opened his eyes, surprised. It seemed obvious. 'The Church. She belongs to the Church.'

'Oh.'

Bernard looked away into the thick tangle of the field. A butterfly skimmed past, flashing yellow. He had closed his eyes again; was perhaps asleep. What Bernard said next seemed like a departure.

'What does your name mean? Schwanz?' She took the bouquet back onto her lap and twisted at one of the petals, its colour crushing dark. 'I like it. I like your name.'

The soldier sat up. 'It is…' He shook his head. 'It is German.'

'Yes, but – doesn't it mean anything? Doesn't it have a translation?'

He did not seem to understand. 'It is German,' he said again. He reached towards her and pulled at the fabric of her habit. He was wide awake, suddenly restless.

As he unclasped his belt she kept talking. 'I don't know any German names,' she said. 'Only French names, and names from the Bible. My name's a man's name. Do you like it?'

He had never thought about it. 'Yes, I suppose.' And he pushed her back so that he could lie on top of her. She puffed at the sudden weight and the heat of him.

'I'm named for Bernard of Clairvaux,' she said. But he was anxious now, preoccupied, and she did not receive a response. 'I wanted to be Clare.' She shifted on the hard ground, trying to ease the rub of a pebble in her back. 'Like Saint Clare, who sewed the altar cloths.'

Still he said nothing. He had his face buried now in the thick clutch of habit around her breasts.

'But Mother Catherine preferred Saint Bernard. She had a picture of him, in a book.' Bernard still remembered his glowing Aryan splendour, tall and broad shouldered, fierce. She could not know how many hours Mother Catherine spent with the page open on her knee, the fervency of her prayer alarming her. 'She showed me some things about him, historical things, writings and sermons. I couldn't understand them,' she said.

He was breathing fast. She could not be sure if he could hear her. She spoke more loudly.

'My real name is Lucie,' she said, and the thrill of the confession split open inside her.

He pulled back, his face flushed. He rested on his knees, steadying himself. He seemed confused, discomfited.

He repeated the last word.

'Lucie.'

It sounded foreign and fragile the way he said it. It had nothing of her in it.

'No one calls me that now. I'm not Lucie any more,' she said.

He stood and started to brush himself down, rubbing hard around his knees and in the creases on his jacket. Then he stretched and turned to look over the wall. The field beyond was also full of hay, busy with insects, discordant. Bernard looked hard at his profile and felt so many things about him that she could not make sense of them.

'Bernard and Schwanz,' she said. 'It sounds nice.'

He spoke quietly. 'But it is not right.'

'Because it's two men's names? That doesn't matter. Not to us. We know the truth.'

He flapped his hand at something.

'Schwanz.'

She said his name again very softly, the sound of it intimate and artless, pastoral, belonging there between them like the breeze in the long grass and the insects and the gentle movement of the leaves.

He started. He did not want her going on.

'I think there's someone coming,' he said, straining his neck as though to look over the drift of hay.

'Up through the bottom gate?'

He nodded. When he turned to her his face was fixed.

'I will see you soon, Sister Bernard.' He set off briskly down the length of wall. Bernard slunk back low, hiding herself behind the long grass. She took the wilting bouquet of flowers and held it close. She trembled slightly, waiting for the danger to pass, but it remained quiet; no one came.

She wished she had told him how she had managed the problem of having a patron saint whose chivalric heroism and medieval theological disputes intimidated and confused her. She wanted to tell him about the saint she had created, an entirely imaginary Bernard who at first had been simply someone amiable with whom to share a name, but who had, in time, acquired a body and a face, gestures that had become familiar, personal idiosyncrasies, freckles and moles and winks and farts, an extremely old man, wiry and gnarled, with silver hair and inexplicably squeaky shoes. Bernard rested against the wall where the soldier had been, and prayed for a moment to this man, a man of very few words, undemonstrative learning, unworked miracles, unregarded piety and undefined theology. When the voice of God came back to her, brusque and demanding, she repeated the prayers again, screwing the bunch of flowers in her hand in her desire to be heard. The petals fell across her lap.

# Eight

The days were blue and airless, suspended in summer. The classrooms acquired warmth like glasshouses and everyone was restless. Sister Thérèse had tried being stern but mostly the girls had ignored her. They were loosening their clothing, lounging back in their seats, weary and hot. They looked and felt older than the young nun, in her first year of teaching, pacing up and down in front of them. Outside, the hay was high, and very soon they would all be out in the fields, the stems scraping at their skin, their arms and legs pricked and sore, working through the short nights in the glow of the moon, the freedom of it exhausting them. In anticipation, they dozed. Thérèse tried everything she could to rouse them. She scolded and blustered. She strutted, hurling questions, slapping her hand on her desk until her palm tingled. But they could not forget the heat. It curled around them. The girls hardly moved and Thérèse's desperate pacing slowed and finally stuttered. She stumbled, reaching out for her seat with one hand, her veil falling thickly about her head.

Closing her eyes, she saw a swarm of dancing coloured

dots. When she opened them, the dots were still there. She bent forwards, drooping her head over her knees, a flash of heat across her neck and face.

'Are you all right, Sister?' chimed several voices.

'Go back to work, girls.'

But Thérèse could not lift her head without the classroom sliding away from her and the silence she had won was brief. No more work was done. The girls began to giggle. She dared not raise her gaze from her knees.

'Are you having a baby, Sister?'

The shock of it, icy, was a restorative. Thérèse forced herself to look up. Marie-Hélène, sitting in the middle of the back bench of older girls, was watching her with a curious expression of defiance and concern, refusing to drop her eyes to her desk, waiting instead for an answer. Thérèse, still faint, could not think straight.

'Don't be stupid, Marie-Hélène. You're being childish.'

'I was just asking, Sister.' The girl was calm. 'I thought if you were having a baby, you might not be feeling well.' She smiled, first at the young teacher she liked so much and then around at the rest of the class, her grin stretching.

'Nuns do not have babies,' Thérèse pointed out.

'Some do.'

It was the animal smell of high summer, the heat, the sense of days that would never end. It made them go on, as if the rules were simply melting away. When the bell rang for the end of the class, Thérèse sat with her head in her hands as the girls filed past, not understanding how it had come about. It had been unwise, she knew that already. It had started something that could not be contained in the hanging heat of these uncommon days.

The ache of Thérèse's curiosity would not pass. School ended. Anvil clouds began to build in distant valleys, threatening rain, and the girls hurried home to change into their work clothes, coming out again quickly to dot the fields with smudges of colour, none of them ever quite alone. Thérèse tried to pray, but even long after dark the heat remained, suffocating her thoughts. She did not sleep.

Confused, she went to Mother Catherine the following morning, knocking on the study door shortly after dawn. Mother Catherine was old now, bent over with some kind of pain, unsmiling. Since the end of the war she had been almost silent, except in prayer or, like now, when one of the nuns came to her and forced her to speak. She did not eat in the refectory with everyone else; she did not go down to the church for Mass. She spent most of her time at the window of her study, her colourless eyes gazing out, looking for something. She did not turn from the familiar view now as she spoke to Thérèse.

'You should not have let them talk about it, Sister. It's idle curiosity. Gossip. Wicked.' Sweat trickled from under her wimple where it was pulled tight to her hairline.

'I'm sorry, Mother, truly. But what shall I say if it happens again?'

'You will not let them speak in this way again, Sister.' The reedy frailty of Mother Catherine's voice was somehow cutting. 'You need more discipline in your classes. If you cannot keep control of them some other job will have to be found for you. Perhaps you are too young.'

Mother Catherine turned finally from the window and peered at Thérèse, her eyes narrowed, looking for evidence of failure. She laced her fingers tightly together across her body and Thérèse noticed, for the first time, how skeletal her hands were. Their papery blueness made her recoil; she stepped back.

'There is no problem with my classes, Mother.' To be forced to spend her days closeted inside the convent was unthinkable. 'But this thing, this idea, has taken hold of them. The best way for me to deal with it would be to refute what they are saying absolutely. When they come back from haymaking I could admonish them; I could send them to seek penance. That would be an end of it.'

Mother Catherine looked back at her and showed no sign of wanting to speak.

'But can I do that? Can I say it's all lies, stupid, childish lies? Can I? I have to know, I have to know whether or not I can say that. And if I can't say it, I have to know what I can say, or it will come up again and again, with this class and with others.'

Rumours that Thérèse had hardly heard, whispered things half-known, became suddenly important. In the heavy heat, with the clasp of Mother Catherine's hands sharp before her, it all seemed to matter. It became something personal for a moment. In the few years that she had been at the convent, Thérèse had rarely spoken to Bernard, had barely noticed her in the bustle of shared life and the daily demands of her teaching. Even now, she could not clearly picture Bernard's face. But the stab of her curiosity was a physical pain, sickening, and it threatened to overwhelm her.

Mother Catherine bit her bottom lip.

'Prayer, Sister,' she said. She inclined her head slowly towards the door. 'I think you need to ask for guidance in how to deal with this gossip.'

'It is gossip then, Mother?'

'It was a long time ago, Sister. These things happened a long time ago. Long before you came to us.'

'But if the children remember it—'

'They don't remember anything, Sister. It's their mothers, their neighbours and aunts and… it's nothing but gossip. They have nothing better to do. They are peasants.'

Mother Catherine walked slowly to the door and placed her hand flat against it for a moment, perhaps steadying herself. Once it was open, Thérèse knew, the convent's unflinching routine would knot around her.

'I must know, Mother. Does Sister Bernard have a child?'

Mother Catherine looked away. Her thin voice was bitter.

'Ask yourself, Sister, why you are so anxious to know these things,' she said. 'God will reveal to you all you need to know. Trust in Him only.'

The unfamiliar desire prickled still under Thérèse's skin, but there was nothing she could do. Mother Catherine said no more, but stood by the open door watching as Thérèse made her way along the corridor to the chapel. There she spent the whole day praying for guidance, pinned to her knees, unable to shake the thought that Mother Catherine was making her pay for something. She offered up as penance the missed meals which Bernard had prepared.

Nearly two weeks later, the hay safely stacked in the barns and the rain falling hard on the dry earth, Marie-Hélène told her teacher the story of a nun found one day on the floor of the open wash house, giving birth to a son.

It had happened quickly. The nun had collapsed with a screech, folding on the cold floor with her arms tight across her. For a while her sisters had ignored her, going on with the washing, thinking it might be nothing, until one of them had noticed the filmy puddle seeping from under her habit and the swell of her stomach, clear now in the way she was lying. She had run for Marie-Hélène's mother, knocking furiously on the door of their small house, but there was no one at home and the noise had only brought several of the German soldiers onto the street. The messenger had ducked away through the narrow alleys and finally, desperate, run round to the shared rows of vines that cut up the hill behind, finding the makeshift midwife there, clipping shoots, her hat pulled low across her face. Then the two of them had started back, a flap of habit and wide skirt in the pinched streets, other women calling out, laying down their work, knowing what it must be. The soldiers, too, had followed, unstoppable, their dark uniforms silhouetting them against the cream stone.

By the time they arrived at the wash house, there was a little crowd, chattering and pushing, all the women trying to see who it was that was giving birth so publicly, ducking in under the low tiles to have a better look, and the soldiers hanging back, watching, the tedium of occupation shifted for a moment. When the women saw that it was Sister Bernard, many of them moved away. The chatter faded. There was an odd quiet, crammed with complaint, and one or two were heard to say that Marie-Hélène's mother should step away, too, from the contamination of the collaborator, leaving Bernard where she was, to die there, if that was God's will, in the filth of her wickedness.

The bed sheets, piled on the floor of the wash house waiting their turn to be scrubbed, were put under and over the whimpering nun. Billowing in the breeze, threads catching against the bare stone, they created a kind of tent to protect the ruins of Sister Bernard's modesty from the onlooking village, and to mop up the blood. She writhed and panted and screeched, adopting an ungainly squat and calling on her God several times during the birth, none around her recognizing the form of prayer.

But the delivery of the baby was quick and the boy was healthy, sliding onto the stone floor without injury. Immediately Bernard bent to pick him up, holding him out far in front of her, his head wobbling and his face creased in a scream, his dark hair plastered to his scalp still with the wetness of birth. To everyone's surprise she ran her hand hard through his hair, easing it from his red skin and then pulling at it, somehow unbelieving. Over and over she pulled at it, as if she would pluck every strand from his head. The boy yelled but the nun kept on. She was so obviously distressed – so terrifyingly disappointed – that the women around tried to explain that things might change in a matter of days. No baby was quite beautiful after birth, they said. But when she could not make the hair come loose, she put the baby down on one of the flared scrubbing stones, disgusted by the dark features that seemed somehow to damn him. She untwined clumps of wet hair from her fingers and flung them into the pool at the centre of the wash house. Someone else wrapped the baby in an unlaundered cloth until he was almost invisible.

Bernard, unsteady, was helped back up the hill by three of her sisters who supported her under the arms so that she could walk. The soldiers slipped away, as though they had not been there. The rest of the village stayed for a while, talking quietly, and finally made their way home unwillingly, indignant, slowed by the rankling feeling that justice had been cheated. A little later, two nuns appeared back at the deserted wash house to collect the ruined sheets and to clear up the mess. They were still there at dusk scrubbing blood from the stone; stubborn dark stains remained for some years, blotchy and brown. Marie-Hélène's mother was never thanked for her intervention, nor was the incident ever mentioned to her again by anyone from the convent, but two days later the family found a large ham on their doorstep when they woke.

Marie-Hélène's story was detailed and convincing; when she was finished she looked away from her teacher for a moment, out through the long windows to the clustered village squatting in the rain beyond.

'Thank you,' said Thérèse, the sound of the water falling from the roof making her words musical.

Marie-Hélène nodded. 'I'm sorry now that I said about it, the first time. I shouldn't have. It was just... Anyway – I'm sorry.'

'Well, it's all cleared up now, for good.' Thérèse was brisk. 'It needn't be mentioned again. We've got to the bottom of it and it's forgotten.'

Marie-Hélène still would not turn back fully into the classroom. 'Yes, Sister,' she said meekly.

'These things are for God,' said Thérèse.

But when her pupil had gone, pulling the door softly behind her, Thérèse sat for a long time, drawing dense spirals on her wooden desk with the chalk. There was the sound of young children playing close by, and a tractor at a distance, whirring. The rain continued to be loud, resolute. The thrill of the story had already faded. But the sadness of it, the melancholy of satiation, was a surprise and she could not shift it.

Thérèse could not calm herself. At the end of the evening, her prayers would not hold steady, and she did not go to bed. She tried rearranging her small collection of things, as yet little more than a shelf of souvenirs along one wall of her cell. But somehow this unsettled her the more and with the summer light fading, and no permission to have her lamp on, she took instead to walking the short length from window to door, marking out a straight line by following a fracture in the floorboards. It was a long dusk but Thérèse was still pacing when dark finally came.

She opened her door gently and slipped down the corridor. The damp of the day lingered there, making the air thick. She walked slowly, so as not to make a noise, passing in turn each of the identical grey doors pressed into the long wall, brushing past the prayers, sobs and night terrors that punctured the silence. At Bernard's door it was quiet. She dared not knock, knowing even the tiniest rap would be heard as it echoed into corners far away, so she pushed lightly until there was enough of a gap for her to stand half in and half out of Bernard's cell, the door frame rigid against her shoulder. She was unsure of exactly what she was going to say.

The room was not dark. Two candles were lit on the small table to the side of Bernard's bed. One of them was burning low and would soon be out. Both stuttered, casting unsteady shadows. Bernard was kneeling on the bed, her nightgown unbuttoned and rolled carefully down to her waist. Her heavy daytime chain hung around her neck, its crucifix nestling in the cleavage between her breasts. She was still, her head bent forwards, as though exhausted or asleep, or perhaps praying. But even by the light of the candles Thérèse could see the great red weals on her arms, shoulders and back, shining with new blood, the skin torn over old wounds. The cuts criss-crossed her flesh, making it seem unnaturally white and fragile, the webbing of the scars meshed more darkly around her, holding her together. On the bed beside her lay the whip, carefully knotted and tied from lengths of leather, the handle worn.

Thérèse stood in the gap in the door, watching. But nothing happened. Bernard remained perfectly still and quiet. All Thérèse could hear was the sound of her own regular breathing. At last a noise from somewhere above her – the cracking of a beam or a floorboard – made her start back from the door. It was impossible to look again, knowing this time what she would see. She stood very still for a moment, watching the moon rise red through the small barred window at the end of the corridor, and then she pulled Bernard's door shut, went quietly back to her own cell and prayed.

The following morning, Thérèse asked Sister Assumpta to stay behind in the chapel for a moment.

'I need help, Sister,' she said.

Sister Assumpta nodded gently, as though this were to be expected, and waved a hand towards the bench beside her. Thérèse did not sit down.

'I... I have something to tell you,' Thérèse went on, knowing it sounded like a confession. She smiled. Sister Assumpta turned the page of her prayer book and bent towards the altar, benign and quiet, a middle-aged servant of God. Thérèse began her story.

'Of course,' Sister Assumpta said at the end of it, without looking up from the pictures of her prayer book. 'I know.'

'You know that Sister Bernard...'

Thérèse could not finish.

Sister Assumpta sighed. 'Sister Bernard has much to ask God's pardon for,' she said.

'But flagellation?' Thérèse whispered the word.

'Sister, it is not for us to judge another's relationship with God,' Sister Assumpta said, more sternly than Thérèse expected. Sister Assumpta looked up from her prayer book now and Thérèse could not understand whatever it was that showed in her face. It looked something like envy.

'But what should I do, Sister?'

'Do?' The idea was cut down by the disdain of Sister Assumpta's tone, but she flattened her voice again carefully as she went on. 'Sister Thérèse, we are a close family here. We are not all as young as you are. We have lived through many things. We are aware of Sister Bernard's imperfections. We are, God forgive us, none of us perfect.' She closed her prayer book, and stood up to leave, looking especially hard at Thérèse now. 'There is nothing you could tell us about Sister Bernard that we do not know. There is nothing to be done.'

Thérèse could not quite believe this. But she bowed to Sister Assumpta, letting her pass out of the chapel ahead of her, and she never again ventured out after her own cell door had been closed. Yet sometimes, even with others around, preparing for late prayers on a winter night or taking her turn to lock the outbuildings, there was something, a smell in the air or a tone in the unsteady darkness, which reminded her of Bernard slumped on her knees. At these times Thérèse wished she had gone on and disturbed Bernard from her reverie, touched her perhaps, held her even in the places where the flesh was intact. All kinds of things, she thought, might have been different then. But she found that after each time her memory came back to her in this way she spoke less often to Bernard, who seemed in any case always entirely absorbed in her chores.

It was not until several years later that Bernard was finally called into the Mother Superior's study.

'A letter has arrived for you, Sister. It is marked personal,' said Mother Catherine, so curled with age that she could hardly be seen behind the desk. The letter lay in front of her, unopened, the envelope crisp.

'Take a seat, Sister Bernard, if you would like.'

Bernard hesitated. The convent was smaller now than when she had arrived. The order was aging and in decline; many of the old routines had changed or even been forgotten. Discipline had slackened. Mother Catherine, wheezing noisy breaths, seemed no longer to care about what her nuns might be doing. She spent the entire day and most of the night in intense contemplation of bitter mysteries; the nuns spoke of her now in whispers, knowing she would soon be called to her rightful reward. But still her study reeked of the power of the Church. Its calm, warm silence disturbed Bernard, the watchful gaze of the Sacred Heart testing her in ways she did not understand.

'Could I take my letter to my cell, Mother?' she asked, not sitting down.

'I think it better that you read it here.'

So Bernard read the letter standing in silence and slowly, because the writing was confused in places and because the thump of her heart was making her vision swim.

Philippe introduced himself without flourish as her son. He had tracked her down, he said, with difficulty. Although his adoptive mother – his 'real' mother, he had called her – had been happy to tell him all she knew about his personal history, this had amounted to very little. As no formal adoption had taken place, with no agency involvement and no paperwork, she had only been able to tell him the story of a baby made available by the diocese and a kindly parish priest suggesting that it might prove a consolation to young parishioners lately bereaved of their second child and without natural hope of another. Philippe's 'real' mother had not asked too much at the time, for fear of finding out something that might put the promise of the baby at risk, and in the intervening years the priest had died, and the diocese had become determinedly silent.

He explained how he had found her, visiting every parish in and around the town, talking after Mass to the priests and the older parishioners, making himself amiable, slightly forlorn. He had kept notes, recording in a small black notebook all the possible clues that might help him track down his mother. He had been thorough. And eventually he had found rumours he could cling to, half-memories, stunted stories. He had found her out, his mother but not his 'real' mother, the nun who had given birth one bloody morning in spring, on the floor of the village wash house. He had hesitated, he said, before writing to her, on account of her vocation. She might not, he appreciated, want to rekindle her shame. She might want to forget him. He would understand. He was in any case, he assured her, in all respects other than biological heredity, already a son to someone else. He hoped soon to be a father. This had made him anxious about his own paternity and conception, that was all. It had taken hold of him, the need to know himself. He wasn't sure why. He hoped she didn't mind.

'Is it bad news, Sister?' asked Mother Catherine, as Bernard crumpled the letter in her fist.

He must have visited Bernard's parish without her ever knowing, sitting perhaps a pew or two behind her habitual place in the second row, listening to the old priest intone the Mass, watching with her the host lifted above the solid stone altar in trembling hands and joining her in the ragged chorus of hosannas.

'I don't know,' she said.

One Sunday, to Bernard a Sunday like any other, she had shared communion with her son, and God, grumbling in her ear, had never let on.

'I would like to see the letter. If I may.'

Bernard handed it over. Mother Catherine uncreased it carefully, her bony fingers clawing at the paper, and she read it through with her face close to the page, peering. It took some time.

'Indeed,' she said. 'Unexpected.'

There was a pause.

'You would not want to respond, Sister,' she asked, though not as a question.

Bernard, who could hardly make out anything above the roar of God, shook her head.

'Our sins find us out – always, in the end. We cannot hide our true nature from God.' Mother Catherine looked hard at Bernard with something like satisfaction. 'I'll keep the letter, shall I?'

'If you would, Mother,' said Bernard.

Bernard thought about her son as she went about her chores. She turned over every word of what he had written, finding nothing but stony ground beneath. Then one day, a long time later, from the phone booth by the fountain in the village, during office hours, she rang the finance division at the local town hall where Philippe, in his letter, said he had worked.

'I have an enquiry about… pensions,' Bernard said.

'Yes, *madame*. And how old are you?'

'Fifty-seven.'

'And do you work?'

'Not exactly.'

'Have you ever worked?'

Bernard did not think about the long hours of painful labour she had submitted to the glory of God. 'Not really,' she said.

'Very good. Please hold the line while I connect you,' said the voice.

In time Bernard was put through to a young man who knew about pensions. It was not Philippe, and he was unable to help her with her financial planning once she told him that she was a nun. But he was polite and she had imagined him sitting behind a neat desk in the well-lit offices of the town hall, perhaps only a room or two away from her son.

Over the next few years, irregularly, Bernard made calls to the finance office. Each time she rang she changed the nature of her enquiry so that she was put through to a variety of departments, none of which could ever help her with her imaginary query but all of which were unfailingly polite and cheerful. To her relief she was never able to speak to Philippe himself. But over time she discovered that he was a team leader within the accounts department. This was already a responsible position and from there his career continued to flourish. Bernard's son became a successful man. Sometimes, when she thought about this, she felt the swell of too much breath, but mostly she hated him the more. She imagined him having everything he could wish for – a big house with vines and fruit trees, a car with space for the children, holidays each summer at the coast. She thought of him always in the sunshine.

Hurrying across the kitchen early one morning to reach a pan of foaming milk, rising, almost boiling, Bernard knocked a jar of pickles from the crowded shelves. Disgusted by her clumsiness, God yelled at her, pestering her to go into the storeroom to find some old newspapers in which to wrap the sticky shards of glass. She cleaned the pan and wiped up the worst of the mess before going down the narrow steps into the dark storeroom, the smell of drying onions and hung garlic thrown up in the dust as she pushed the wooden door. She took two papers from the top of the pile, long stored and fading, and hurried back, flaying them sheet by sheet to wrap the broken jar. She had almost calmed God's wrath, was almost finished and was adding a final layer of paper for extra safety, when she glanced down to see the obituary of Philippe Pourcel, town hall director of finance and victim of lung cancer.

It was the name in bold type that caught Bernard's attention. Pourcel was a local name, common on shop fronts and garage signs, but even so it was enough to suspend Bernard's hand, shaking, over the wrapped pickle jar as she read down the short entry. She read slowly and awkwardly, tripping over words, but nonetheless there was enough to convince her that the dead man was indeed her son. The obituary made much of his long service to the town's finance department. It listed, briefly, some of his professional achievements. She looked hard at the unappealing photograph of the man she had never seen. She was able to come to few conclusions.

Bernard tore off a strip of newspaper including the obituary and used the remainder of the page for the final layer of wrapping. It was almost time for morning prayer and she was hurried. When the bell rang to summon her, she wedged the torn piece of paper deep into her pocket and set the wrapped jar carefully on the refectory table until she could find time to take it to the bins outside. She bustled along the corridors to the chapel and was not late, although all the rest of her sisters were already assembled and on their knees. Kneeling herself, choosing a worn corner of the chilly floor away from the rest of the pews,

Bernard took her rosary into her fingers as usual and was about to begin the morning office with the others when she realized that God was silent. Not pausing, not waiting, inhaling, pondering, choosing a phrase, licking His lips or considering her pleas. Just silent.

This took Bernard's breath away. She fainted.

It was the first time she had ever been to the doctor. In the dark waiting room at the front of the house she sat next to a farmer who advised her pleasantly on the best way to birth a calf. Opposite, perched on a low cane stool, was a boy with a bulging goitre which pushed his head up at a strange cocked angle. He winked at her. But the silence filling her head was so pristine that she was hardly aware of any of this; she did not know where she was.

When her turn came to go through into the surgery at the back, she sucked in so much air so suddenly that she exploded into a coughing fit that she thought was going to kill her. The doctor, less alarmed, sat back in his chair and waited. He found something on his cuff to interest him. When the coughing subsided, he asked her to unbutton the front of her habit so that he could listen to her chest. He came round to her and bent towards her, pressing the side of his face against her bare flesh. The skin of his ear was warm, unexpectedly soft, like summer butter. Bernard wondered if most ears were like his. Her own, as far as she could tell, were more sinewy, like spinach stalks. He asked her to breathe, long and slow.

He pressed her tongue with a stick and examined her throat. He looked closely at her eyes, pulling at the thin skin below them. Finally he shone a light into each of her ears.

'There's no infection, Sister. Nothing I can see.'

'No,' said Bernard, unsurprised.

'Do you have soreness, or discharge, something on your pillow?'

'No, Doctor.'

'And ringing? Like bells, all the time?'

'No.'

The doctor leant back. 'What is it then? What exactly is your concern?'

'I used to be able to hear God,' Bernard said. 'And now I can't.'

The doctor grinned. 'I'm sure He can still hear you,' he said, breathing a soft laugh through his teeth. But her face was tight and he saw that she was serious. He pushed back his chair with a quick squeak and turned away to the sink in alarm.

There was a difficult pause.

'Have you spoken to the priest about this perhaps?' he said at last.

'I thought it best to seek a medical opinion,' said Bernard.

'But I'm not sure it's a medical matter.'

Bernard nodded quickly, pressing him. 'Oh yes, I'm sure it is,' she said. 'I'm sure He's still talking – I just can't hear Him. It'll be a blockage somewhere, I should think, like a drain.'

The doctor steepled his fingers stiffly. 'No,' he said. 'There's nothing. I've done a thorough examination.'

'Perhaps I need an X-ray,' said Bernard, having no idea what such a thing was.

The doctor seemed to be thinking about this.

'When did this happen? When did you notice it?' he asked.

'Yesterday,' said Bernard, remembering the moment.

'You came straight away, then?'

'As soon as I could.'

'And it happened suddenly?'

'Very. Yesterday morning, during morning prayers, I stopped hearing God. I haven't had a word from Him since.'

'Perhaps you should give Him time,' suggested the doctor.

'There is no time with God,' Bernard reminded him.

The doctor looked unhappy and baffled. Bernard felt she should explain to him, the way God had been with her, scolding sometimes with terrible fury, but mostly grumbling, His commentary foolish and dull. But she could not think how to begin.

'It was yesterday,' she said again. 'There was suddenly nothing.'

'And you can't remember doing anything unusual,' asked the doctor. 'Bumping your head, falling, even eating something different?'

Bernard did not want to tell him about fainting at prayers. She thought it might distract him.

'It was an ordinary morning,' she said.

The doctor twisted in his seat and tapped the dark bound book on his desk.

'I don't know what to suggest,' he said. 'It's most unusual. It's not something I've come across before. Not exactly. I normally deal with things that are more... practical.'

Bernard's disappointment creased across her face.

147

'I'm sorry,' the doctor said kindly. 'I wish I could be of more help. You were right to come to me, Sister. Perhaps we could make you another appointment, for a week or so, to see if there's any progress, to see if you can hear Him again.'

He was reaching for his pen, putting an end to the consultation. But the sudden alarm in Bernard's voice made him hesitate; his hand hung in the air.

'You think He might come back, Doctor?'

The doctor seemed unsure what kind of answer to give.

'Who can tell in a case of this kind?' he said.

'But please. Tell me. In your opinion, do you think He might come back?'

'I don't know.'

Walking from the surgery, Bernard crossed under the dark arcades that surrounded the square. The ground sloped. At the top end, stone steps led up to a row of medieval buildings, their rooflines uneven and their top storeys open, a remnant of old trades. Here and there balconies had been added, mostly rusting now and unused. And planted at the foot of the steps, reaching up almost to the top of the houses, was a massive iron cross, elaborately worked, its Christ figure lean. Bernard went to the foot of the cross and stood there. She was full of the sweating fear that this might only be a temporary lull, a kind of holiday, a balm for her tired hearing, before it all began again, the endless, inane, bad-tempered chatter that was God; she pressed her hands tight against her ears, trapping the sound of her own breathing. She looked up at the suffering Christ, splattered here and there across the shoulders with white streaks of pigeon droppings. A man came to the balustrade above her, leaning over and watching her for a moment. A slight bird swept across the sky above the cross, disappearing over the maze of streets. She wept.

When she arrived back at the convent she kept noise simmering around her. She put herself in the busiest places, she scraped furniture and clanked dishes and slammed doors. When there was nothing else, she whistled. She could not allow the quiet to settle in case it let Him back in. But when the night came, there were only the faintest of sounds, lingering, and nothing more Bernard could do. She knelt by her bed and waited. She noticed how soft the air of the convent was, coming quietly to her in this way, what comfort there was in the barely perceptible breath of it. And as the night passed, tender and undemanding, blank, bereft of God, Bernard offered praise. The relief was glorious.

Somewhere towards dawn, as the dark lifted very slightly, Bernard felt in her skirt pocket for the torn piece of newspaper. She stared at it hard in the still dense grey, trying to make out something. She wondered what it was about the distorted man in the photo that could silence God. She was newly afraid of him. She threw the cutting away, hard, but heard it flutter to the floor too near to the bed. She felt for it, feeling panicky, but she could not find it and it was not until the first light edged round the hinges of the shutters that she managed to pick out the tone of the newspaper from the flat colour of the floor. With shaking hands she picked up the ragged obituary and put it with her pile of papers on the top of the dresser, tucking it purposely away from the top so that it might not catch her eye.

The balm of divine silence soothed Bernard for a while, making the days light and easy, new sounds filling her head with surprise: the birds cackling in the trees by her window and the buzz of insects like music. But before long she found the noise too loose; she could not make it mean anything. When she fumbled a glass one evening, sending it toppling and the water spilling out across the table, the hum of the world continued unabated, unraging. The horror of this magnificent indifference astounded and then terrified her. She wiped the water from the wood with her cloth over and over, pushing at the dark stain, not sure what else to do. In the end, one of the other nuns touched her on the arm, pulling her back from the table. Bernard's face was slack and empty, as though something had been taken from it.

She realized that the absence of God was a loss. She was afraid. For several days she considered what she could do that might make things better, but finally all she could think of was to go to the priest. When Father Raymond came to the convent to lead the nuns in confession, she arrived late so that she would be last to take her turn and she waited until the end of the routine ritual before whispering her concern.

They were tucked into a corner of the chapel, a plain board screen set up to make the recess seem private and a curtain of dark velvet slung between them. Bernard saw the folds of thick material shift.

'Is this a spiritual crisis, Sister?' Father Raymond asked, drawing back from the absolution he was about to offer her. He was bent with age and his voice came muffled. Things wearied him now; he did not want this.

Bernard did not know.

'I just wondered if there was something I was doing wrong, Father,' she said. 'If there is something at fault in me – something that has made God quiet.'

Father Raymond let out a long breath. That Bernard might have been singled out by the Almighty to be a vessel of His utterance, that she might be in any way holy, seemed to him impossible.

'Sister, I am sure this is not a case of wrongdoing, of specific wrongdoing. I have heard your confession these many years and...' He stopped himself, remembering something that stripped the sheen of cautious sympathy from his usual tone. His next words came bare. 'You do not hear God, Sister,' he said.

He heard the quick catch of a sob, deadened by the close acoustics of the makeshift box; he could feel the grip of Bernard's distress even through the curtain that hung between them.

'Calm yourself, Sister. Calm down.' The old priest already felt at fault; he began to understand his sin for the first time. His voice was stern. 'It's not necessarily a question of wrongdoing, Sister. We all of us do wrong. We are none of us... iniquity is everywhere. Do you think I don't know that? But... but – we cannot hear God, not any of us, not directly. That is our poor human state.'

'But I *could* hear Him, Father – directly.'

Bernard looked hard at the slice of light that cut

151

towards her feet from one edge of the curtain. She shuffled on the wooden kneeler and felt her bones shift.

'But now that I can't, I don't know what to think,' she admitted. 'It's not… it's not the same. I don't know where I am. I think I'd like Him back.'

Father Raymond hooked his thumbs under his chin, his hands drawn up together towards his nose. He did not say anything. He knew that the casual comfort he was used to bestowing would not do. And while he wanted to dismiss the nun's peculiar belief that she could hear God, he found he could not. His usual ways of judging seemed suddenly unreliable. He blew soft quiet puffs through the steeple of his hands.

'Can't you help me, Father?'

He nodded quickly to bring himself round and opened his hands in a priestly gesture of authority.

'Yes, yes, Sister. Of course. It is… it is my duty. But you should have come to me sooner. We could have prayed together.'

'It seemed so small a thing, I didn't like to mention it.'

'Having God speak to you is no small thing, Sister.'

'Doesn't He speak to you, Father?'

The unthinking astonishment of her question confused him.

'I… it's not… I'm not sure that…' He settled his tone. 'Sister Bernard, when He stopped talking to you, that's when you should have come to me.'

Bernard could not tell him what a relief it had been at first. So she said nothing at all.

'Nothing is too small to share, Sister,' prompted the priest again.

'No, Father.'

There was another pause. Bernard thought she could sense Father Raymond peering through the curtain at her. His breath, as always, smelt of cigarette smoke, the thing she liked best about him.

'Tell me, Sister,' he said at last. 'Tell me what it is that you hear – what it's like, this voice.'

'I don't hear it, Father, not any more.'

He sighed. 'No, Sister. But before.'

Bernard brushed her face with her fingers while she thought how to describe it.

'It was the voice of God, Father,' she said, tasting the tobacco.

'And you can't tell me – exactly – what it was like… how you knew it to be the voice of God.'

'No.'

The priest sighed again. He could not bear to believe her. He could not allow the conviction that she was consecrated; it would damn him. And yet he was disappointed.

'And now that I can't hear it,' began Bernard again, animated now, 'I don't know… I can't tell if God is… how do I know He's still there, Father?'

The stool squeaked as Father Raymond sat back. He was aware suddenly of the damp cold in the chapel and pulled his cardigan more closely across his chest. He felt compelled to produce some theology.

'Your question,' he began, 'as I understand it, is how, when we cannot hear or see God, when He cannot communicate with us directly, how then can we be sure that He embraces us with His all-embracing love. Is that right?'

Bernard nodded, uncertain. He could not see this, but he took her silence as an affirmation.

'It is a question of faith, Sister. We can be sure because we believe.'

There was another pause.

'It's the same for all believers,' he went on. 'We are all of us forced to wander in the wilderness sustained only by our belief.'

'No, but when I could hear Him—'

'No, Sister.' The priest's voice was sharp. 'No. That is not so. We do not hear God, not directly. He is alive around us, in our prayers, in the communities in which we live, but He does not speak to us directly, Sister, like an announcer on the wireless.'

He was firm now, sure. He had a picture of Bernard in his mind, of the squat, flat-faced nun, ordinary, unpreferred.

Bernard was trembling at his ferocity. She did not speak. But he could not bear the accusation of her silence.

'Well, Sister – does that help?'

'Oh yes, of course, Father. Yes. Thank you.'

Bernard was given her absolution. The penance imposed upon her was the usual one. She passed out into the body of the chapel, pushing the screen to one side, and she knelt in front of the altar to begin her prayers. She wished she had not brought her trouble here.

When she raised herself stiffly from her cold knees she dropped two small coins into the unmarked box by the side of the Virgin statue and lit a candle from one which was spluttering to an end in a pool of wax. She set it in the brass holder, and then she left.

154

For a long while Father Raymond leant back on his stool, pressing his shoulders against the cold wall and looking into the dark corner of the chapel above him. He did not pull back the curtain.

# Nine

When they came to execute the three Resistance fighters who had been taken in the ambush, Bernard was summoned to see Mother Catherine. The message was brought to her as she was scrubbing the stone steps which led up to the convent entrance, and it took her some time to rinse down the soap, pour away the grubby water and dry herself. Her hands were numb with cold and God was rattling in her head with an odd complaint about the blueness of the suds that were collecting in puddles in the worn ridges of the stone.

'You must stop seeing the German, Sister,' said Mother Catherine. She chose to make her reasoning simple. 'It is wrong.'

Bernard felt the gaze of the Sacred Heart in the niche behind the Mother Superior's desk. Its bright heart was carved in relief over the sculpted folds of the statue's long gown, expertly butchered, inviting admiration. She looked away from it. She was sleepy. Her eyes itched. The thought of the soldier had disturbed her sleep. She felt the bulge of a yawn in her throat.

'The German?'

'Sister Bernard, sit down.'

Bernard sat, uncomfortably. Her hands tingled as the feeling came back to them in the warmth of the study.

'I don't know how we have allowed it to go this far,' said Mother Catherine. 'I don't know. I think we were confused. But now it must stop. People will talk. This war – it is a thing of gossip, of gossip and noise. If we are not careful, people will involve the convent. That I cannot have.' She glared at Bernard. 'There are things beyond you, Sister. That you don't understand – that you could never understand. You must respect that. You must be obedient. You have vowed to be obedient.'

Bernard could not suppress the yawn.

'Sister Bernard, perhaps I can tell you a story?'

Bernard still said nothing.

'It may be one you know.'

It was not. It was the story of Saint Agnes, who preferred having her throat slit to surrendering the virginity she had consecrated to Christ. It was the story of a miracle. For while the rest of Agnes' body was bruised, burnt, broken and slashed, her vagina remained immaculate, untouched. It was not a story Bernard had heard before, although she had heard many similar.

She felt her ankles tremble. She realized how little Mother Catherine knew.

'You, too, have consecrated your body to the service of God,' said Mother Catherine.

'Yes, Mother.'

'And I know that, when we are young, the devil tempts us in many ways. I know the flesh can be weak. I know

157

wickedness can put on many disguises. But you would not want to burn for eternity in Hell, would you, Sister?'

The question made Bernard jump. Mother Catherine's tone had not changed, but she was looking directly at her now.

There was no proper response. 'The German – the soldier?' Bernard said weakly.

Mother Catherine sighed. She would never shake off the idea that Bernard was miraculously stupid.

'We spoke about this, Sister. We spoke about you being circumspect. I thought we had agreed. But since then you have been seen in the village, in the convent even, with a young man. The same young man. A soldier. When I had already asked for your discretion.'

Mother Catherine knew what Bernard had done, but it was not time for accusation. She did not mention the executions.

'We are doing the work of God, Sister,' she concluded, smiling unexpectedly.

Bernard's God was urging the counsel of her superior in her ear. But her heart was thumping.

'What if I love him?' she said at last, after a pause, never knowing where the words came from.

Mother Catherine made a sound like a wail. 'Mercy upon us.' She was fierce. 'You cannot. You cannot love him, Sister. It's not possible; it's not… it's not permitted.'

Bernard stepped back, thinking that the Mother Superior might hit her or shake her. It was already as though they were clinched in a fight, but she was unable to see how that could be. She simply shook her head, knowing she could not explain.

'Sister Bernard, you belong to God, to the convent. You love God. Him only. You are nothing. A simple foot soldier in the battle for righteousness – a... a... you do not even understand what is going on here. You are just... stupid.' Mother Catherine pulled herself tall, forcing her breath to come steadily. 'There is God's love, Sister, set aside for you. There is no other love – not for you.'

Bernard knew this was not true. 'But if there *were* someone else...'

There was the slightest of pauses. 'Then you would have to leave the convent, Sister.'

The Sacred Heart continued to beam down on the two women, barely three yards apart, not looking at each other. Bernard gazed at the floor. Mother Catherine laid her hands flat on the desk and examined her nails. It was so quiet that God needed only to whisper and Bernard wondered if the convent had been emptied somehow.

'Think about it, Sister,' Mother Catherine said at last. 'There are some things we cannot change. Think about sin. Think about Sister Jean, who has already trespassed in her folly – her disobedience. She already knows the pain of sin. We must be good, Sister.'

'So I have to stop seeing him?'

'Yes. Entirely. You cannot be trusted.'

At the time, Bernard did not understand what this would be like.

'And then I can stay at the convent?'

'There is more rejoicing in heaven over one sinner who repents than over ninety-nine who have no need of repentance,' said Mother Catherine, more easily now, not quite believing it. 'Pray with me, Sister.'

159

Bernard bent her head and clasped her hands on her lap. The words of the prayer came over her, beating the air softly like mayfly wings. She thought of the buzz of the early summer fields, and the patch of earth that the soldier had flattened under her, dusty and unforgiving, fragrant with the crush of wild mint.

Sister Jean would not come out of her cell for five days. She constructed some kind of barricade behind the door which prevented all their most strenuous efforts, and the other nuns could only pause as they passed by on their way to bed, praying for her, perhaps. No sound came from within, and when she finally emerged she was gaunt and silent. She said nothing about the ambush. When a man with a limp, a young mother and a boy of sixteen were pushed up against a wall in the square and shot, the boy's screams seemed everywhere, shattering the thick air of the village, but it was not clear whether Sister Jean heard them.

Bernard, peeling a pile of onions in the kitchen, caught the panicked screech through the open window that looked down the long drive, but she thought for a moment that it was the squabble of cats. She paused, leaning forwards to look past the drooping willows at the well and pushing the point of her knife into the wooden worktop, but God was instantly upon her, scolding her for her neglectfulness and she resumed her work, slicing steadily through the onions, her eyes washed clear. She did not look up again, and the noise ended abruptly. The long slow ring of bells that followed, hanging in the valley, swelling, caught its stately rhythm in Bernard's head, but she hardly noticed it.

It was only when Father Raymond came later, joining

them in the refectory for supper, that she realized what it was she had heard. The priest sat at the furthest end of the long table from her, alongside Mother Catherine, his head low over his wide bowl of soup. For most of the meal Bernard paid no attention to him, finishing her own food quickly and rubbing at the dry skin that peeled from her fingers. He spoke solemnly and with hardly a pause – she could tell that from the constant burr of his voice, in duet with God's, and from the way the nuns at that end of the table leant towards him, not eating. But she could not catch his words and she did not, for a long while, associate his visit with anything out of the ordinary. She gathered the plates as she always did and took them through to stack them by the sink. Beyond the kitchen window the dark was falling quickly.

'Is that not so, Sister Bernard?' the priest asked her as she came back through.

She paused by the table and blinked at him. Mother Catherine, more used to Bernard's apparent idiocy, took it upon herself to explain, speaking slowly.

'The girl from the village. Madame Roux – Severine. She was a good woman. Kind. That is what Father is asking you, Sister.'

Bernard did not understand. There was something in the quiet of the room that was new, she sensed that, and the faces around her were tearful.

'She came to see you, Sister. Regularly, I think. She was very persistent.'

Mother Catherine did not expect a response from Bernard. She turned and smiled at Father Raymond, shaking her head slightly.

'You wouldn't have thought it of her – getting involved,' she said to him, marvelling. 'A girl like that. You wouldn't have thought she was capable.'

The priest smiled back. He spoke to Bernard.

'It is a shock, Sister, for us all,' he said. 'We are not accustomed to this kind of thing. The war has upset us… upset our way of doing things. People have done foolish things. Your friend – she did a foolish thing.' He looked along the table. 'But I, too, have found it hard, most hard. I have prayed.'

Bernard went back to her place. There was bread to be passed around, and a plate of sunken cheese, the smell of it sour. Bernard poured water into her glass but the clink of the jug was too loud and she let her veil slip forwards, hiding her face. When the priest stood to leave she was surprised by the bustle.

'Shall we pray together, Sisters, for those poor souls who were lost today, here amongst us?'

The priest stood at the end of the table and looked along the lines of them, fierce almost, as if there was some blame there. Most of the nuns bowed their heads, but Bernard had her head high now and she stared at the priest, her eyes wide and her mouth open, the realization of what had been said suddenly coming upon her in a way she could not resist.

'For the people of this parish…' the priest began.

'Severine!'

The name burst from Bernard in a despairing wail, and as Father Raymond paused, all the nuns turned to look at her. She saw the mourning repeated over and over in each of their framed faces and she understood what she had done.

Mother Catherine nodded towards Bernard. 'Comfort her, Sister,' she said briskly, and one of the nuns alongside Bernard reached towards her and pulled her from the table. The priest began his prayer over again, his voice steady, and Bernard felt an arm through hers, leading her from the refectory.

They passed the long corridor windows. The flat dark had already closed around the convent but Bernard stopped nonetheless, pressing close to the glass, peering out, as if she might see something of her friend's body, torn and contorted, punctured by bullets. But there was only her own reflection, docile and unsurprising, and the other nun tugged on her arm again, leading her away.

Bernard was alone in the kitchen, skinning rabbits. One by one she slit the brownish fur across the stomach and pulled it back, easing out the legs and finally peeling the skin away from the head and the glassy eyes. It came off over the ears in a single piece, and each time she could not help stroking it, newly amazed at its softness. She stacked the skins to one side and butchered the meat, cleaving through the joints and separating the hearts and livers into a tin dish. Finally she put the heads and feet to stew. Then she washed her hands carefully in a bowl and took off her shoes, tucking them under the flap of fabric that was pinned under the sink to hide the slop buckets. Her habit came almost to the floor, and with her feet still covered in thick dark stockings, it was not obvious that she was not wearing shoes. But it made her footsteps soundless and sent the thrill of trespass sparking through her.

163

She moved more quickly and stealthily than she had ever done before, padding up the wide steps to the dormitory corridor and sliding along towards her cell. She was not allowed here during the day and she kept to the shadows where she could, though the grip of them discomforted her. God was so shocked by her boldness that He spluttered incoherently; she was surprised by the feebleness of His objections.

In a small worn sack she had stolen several days before, Bernard packed some underwear. She had no outdoor clothes that did not belong to the convent, but she had a cardigan of her own and some old skirts that she wore under her habit on cold days. She packed these, too. There was the fleeting half-thought that when she went away with the soldier, she might have new things, but this was too strange an idea, and she put it aside. She did not think of anything.

She moved around her small cell gathering things and when she had finished she wedged the sack under her habit, securing it as best she could with the belt. In the kitchen she put her shoes back on and picked up a trug, rolling her sleeves to the elbow. She went outside and knelt in the patch of lettuce. She picked the leaves carefully, pulling off small slugs and filling the trug. On her way back, it was with only the slightest of odd movements that she cut away from the open ground and down towards the convent gate, putting the lettuce in the shade as she tugged the sack from its hiding place and shoved it hard into the summer hedge. She did not look behind or around. And as she made her way back towards the kitchen she blessed herself, offering vague thanks. But the words were slack in her head, splayed by the overwhelming exhilaration of having broken the rules.

Bernard volunteered to go into the village to collect some young plants, late leeks that would soon need planting for an autumn harvest. But there was no sign of the soldier, nor of any of the Germans. She walked as slowly as she could; she stopped now and again to resettle the basket on her arm or to flick an imaginary fly from her habit. She rejected the shortcut through the cemetery in favour of the wider, longer path along the stream. She stood and watched the languid pull of the water against the weeds. God grumbled at her for dawdling. But still there was no one. The village was closed down, the shops dark and the house shutters pulled tight, the paths deserted. The shock of the executions seemed to be echoing still, the sound of gunshot ricocheting against the stone.

Bernard went slowly past houses she knew. Her own house, the place where she had been born, was small and obviously deserted now, its roof rotten and sinking. Ivy had begun to grow up over the front wall, its roots already pulling wide the joints in the stone, and Bernard pulled a piece of it away, dislodging dust. A plum tree was just visible behind the house, laden with fruit. It occurred to her that the harvest was hers, and all of a sudden she longed for the feel of the warm plums in her hand. But she could not find her way through. The press of her footsteps in the long grass seemed like a trespass; God was alarmed. She turned quickly back to the street.

She was at the bend behind the church when she heard a quiet whistle. It came again, moments afterwards, odd and squeaky, distinctive, but it took her a while to see where he was, pressed tight in the entrance to one of the grain stores. She stumbled. And before she had steadied herself he had started on ahead, cutting quickly through the maze of paths that twisted between the close-packed houses and gardens. She could not keep up with him. But he whistled more loudly now, taking up a tune she did not know, and she followed the music, sometimes taking paths parallel to where he must be, sometimes turning back on herself, befuddled rather than purposely devious.

They ended up together at the house on the edge of the village where the soldier was billeted, a blank-faced building with blistered shutters. He pushed the door and went in first. She stepped in behind him and the door closed, cutting out the stream of light. She stood very still. He pulled the broad chair closer to the fireplace and took off his shoes, placing them together under the table. There was no fire, only the unswept ashes piled high, but nonetheless when he sat down, the soldier stretched his legs towards the grate. Bernard was surprised by how dainty his feet looked, even in their shapeless socks. He turned to her and smiled, patting his knee in invitation.

She began to be aware of things in the dim room, another, smaller chair in a far corner, utensils pinned to the wall, a besom propped upright. She put her basket on the edge of the table without moving her feet.

'Come on.'

She had to go to him. He spread his arms to draw her in.

'Come on, Sister Bernard,' he said.

She perched on his lap, trying to hold up her weight, wrapping her arm around the back of the chair to support herself. His bony knees were not comfortable.

He fingered the cross round Bernard's neck and muttered something to himself in German. Bernard shifted. She waited for him to begin. Normally he was ready for her, eager. But this morning there was just the reticent press of his penis against her thigh and the idle twist of his fingers on the buttons of her habit. She believed, for many years afterwards, that this languid slowness was evidence of his growing affection.

She was going to tell him about the conversation with Mother Catherine, about the packed bag and the way she had been feeling. But she did not have the chance.

'May I?' he asked before she could speak. He looked at her with a flick of the head but she did not know what he intended. Then he slipped the wimple back from her forehead and let her veil drop to the floor. Bernard yelped. She pulled up both her arms to try to cover her head, placing her right palm flat against the top of her skull and letting her weight fall for the first time full upon his knees so that he gave a small puff. The nakedness of her head, and the indecency of him knowing the full bodily weight of her, made Bernard's cheeks flame.

He laughed.

'I wanted to see,' he said, trying to peel her hands from her scalp.

He seemed to like her thin brown hair. He ran it through his fingers quickly, tangling it. Bernard thought about the smell of her hair on his hands. She heard the clock strike outside and then, a few moments later, a tinny echo from the back room of the house.

'We should be quick. They'll ask me why I've been so long.'

'Tell them you have been collaborating,' he said, still smiling.

The word was new to her, and strange, because of his quaint accent and the playful way he looked at her as he spoke. It was the longest word she had ever heard him speak in French.

His smile had gone and his fingers were slower now in her hair. She waited, thinking he was trying to organize his words but he did not immediately speak again.

'We had to shoot them,' he said at last, his accent murky. 'We had to take them and line them up – even the boy, even after… everything, after promising him it would be all right. We had to shoot them. They danced, you know – when the bullets went into them they danced.'

He pushed her from his knee and stood.

'I wish you hadn't told me,' he said.

The flap of his trousers was partly unbuttoned. His shirt hung loose at one side and Bernard noticed a streak of ash along one of his dark socks.

There was a sudden forlorn solemnity about it. Bernard wanted him to draw her down onto his knee again but he was stiff, still waiting for something from her. He could not be still. He paced along the length of the wide fireplace, looking sometimes at her and sometimes at the floor, his face drawn tight. When he stopped and turned to her, he tried to smile again.

'Will you pray with me, Sister?' he said.

She could not imagine it. He took her hand. She thrust the other deep into her pocket, clasping it around the string of umbilical cord that lay there.

168

The door clicked, a stream of light flashed across the floor and some kind of celebratory greeting was thrown in German from the threshold. The soldier let go of Bernard's hand. The light dulled again. Then Bernard saw the commandant striding towards them, his arm raised, his boots kicking up the dry sawdust from the floor.

The soldier was stepping away from the fireplace as the commandant's hand slapped across his shoulders. He lurched forwards, his feet insecurely planted. He was suddenly sharp and angular. He steadied himself with a hand against the wall but then he remembered his unbuttoned flies and hurriedly bent to fasten them. The commandant laughed. The soldier laughed back, his teeth showing. They exchanged a series of short phrases in German, but they did not look at each other as they spoke. They looked at Bernard.

Bernard tried to find her veil, but it was hard to pick out on the dark floor in the half-light. She bent low, almost kneeling, trying to feel for it with her hands. Then she heard the commandant laugh and when she looked up he was holding her veil aloft like a flag.

He tried it on. He could not fit the wimple fully around his face and head but it held long enough for him to toss his head one way and the other, trying out the feeling of the long thick material, heavy like hair across his shoulders and down his back. It was then, with the veil still on his head though sliding backwards, that he moved towards Bernard. She backed away, sure of what he wanted, knowing the look. The commandant laughed again, sucking in air between his teeth.

Bernard was often afraid of everyday things, the rickety walkway around the roof of the convent or the snakes that they chased from the henhouse with sticks. But this certain anticipation of pain and humiliation was different, like the astonishing displays of divine wrath, awful and disorienting. Her cheeks reddened. She had no breath. There was a murmur in her head that might have been God, but with the dark and the laughter and the confusion she could not make anything of the noise. She only had a clear sense of her soldier, creased at an odd angle, stiffened, his blond hair haloing his face against the soot of the wall.

The commandant stopped close to Bernard. She could back up no further without pressing herself completely against the rough side wall of the house. He rubbed his feet into the sawdust as though steadying himself on sand.

'I hear,' he said in good French, 'that you look favourably on the attentions of the righteous, Sister.'

Bernard tried to find a prayer, a way of saving herself from the brutality she saw in the officer's face. If she could only escape this she would offer penance until the heavens fell. But the commandant encroached on her still. He was all uniform. Bernard put her hands across her bare head, but she could not cover it entirely no matter how widely she spread her fingers.

'Look at me, a sinner!' he said, throwing both his arms open to display to her the full extent of himself. The veil slid finally to the floor. 'Have mercy!'

She screamed. A sound came from her soldier like a moan.

He came quickly at his commandant, pulling him back hard so that the officer fell awkwardly across the chair by

170

the fireplace, letting out a thick grunt, hanging there for a while, one arm and one leg dangling sideways, his head thrown back, panting. The soldier pulled at Bernard, too, trying to make her move, pushing her towards the door. He said something quick and fierce under his breath. It sounded like 'Make sure the apples are with you', but this made no sense. Either his French was garbled or Bernard had misheard him. In the end it did not matter. Except that, since she was to remember the words for ever, Bernard would have liked them to be more impressive.

With a renewed energy, his warning only a whooshing intake of breath through his nose, the commandant sprang from the chair and hurled himself at the soldier. He was a heavy man. Bernard saw them collide and heard the metallic ring of something – a uniform button, a coin? – fall to the ground as she reached the door. It was only then that she realized she was in the sunlight again, the air around her misted with the scuff of dust. The door was open already and above the crush of men blocking her exit she could see the implacable blue of the summer sky.

The Germans had waited outside in the shade of the house while the commandant went in. They had smoked. One or two of them had played with a kitten that had come to wind itself around their legs. But they had heard Bernard's scream and now they pushed across the threshold, blinking in the dim interior, shoving her aside in their efforts to reach the fighting men. It seemed to Bernard as though there was an army of them. It was mostly the energy of their movements and their thick uniforms and their shouts that made the room seem full, but it was enough to overwhelm her and she did not move.

She stood with her feet in the patch of sunlight, as around her everything shattered.

Her soldier was having the worst of it. He was too scrawny and slight, and it looked as though he would rather not have been fighting at all. He fended off the blows, his arms across his head, and only once or twice did he fling out in retaliation, his palm flat, a push. He was already cowering and unsteady. The blood from his nose was dripping fast onto the floor and his jacket was torn. When the commandant began to kick at his legs and knees, the sound of his boots cracking loud through the commotion, he would have soon fallen.

But the other Germans put a stop to them. They separated them, prying them apart, and holding them both. They scuffed at the splashes of blood on the floor and righted the furniture. There was an abrupt dusty calm, and then the commandant gave an order, and the soldier was dragged past Bernard in a flurry of uniforms, hardly visible. The commandant rested hard on the table, panting, his features swollen. The clock could be heard striking again from the back room. The last of the Germans brushed his hands against each other with a dry rasp. As he came past Bernard, still there, unmoving, he winked. But she did not make any response and so he pushed her aside, the murk closing around her again as he kicked the door closed behind him.

There was just the commandant, sitting now in the fireside chair twirling the veil between his hands, and Bernard still standing by the closed door. He looked at her again, his eye already swelling; blood was smeared across one of his cheeks. She wanted him to close his eyes, for a moment, so that she could leave. She could not bear the look of him. She tried to edge away, but with the fear and the darkness she had no real sense of where she was, and she stumbled over something solid bolted to the floor. The commandant laughed. As Bernard looked at him, he joined his hands in mock supplication and raised his eyes to the God in the beamed ceiling. Then he fixed his stare back on her again and she saw his distaste leaking from his face.

The sudden weight of him took her breath away. There was pain everywhere, all at once, and the smell of sweat. He was tearing at her habit, snarling, biting blood from her breasts, scratching his broken nails against her thighs. She felt the rush of it all, the hurt, only just real, so intense and such a sudden surprise that it might have been imagined, the clawing and clutching insatiable and frantic, and far away the sound of the commandant breathing hard with the sharp wheeze of an asthmatic. In the midst of it, a steady thought, untrammelled, Bernard wondered if what was happening now would make it all right for her soldier, and she lay as still as she could on the gritty flags. She said nothing. She hardly breathed. The commandant, when he was finished, wondered if she was dead.

When he slapped her around the face, she blinked.

'God be praised, Sister,' he said, standing shakily and smartening his uniform.

Bernard lay on the dirt floor and still did not move.

'You can go,' he said. 'In peace.'

He hardly had the energy to laugh.

He kicked at her, the mark of his boot dark on the bare flesh of her leg. But still she lay there, something on the grimy ceiling transfixing her, and the commandant brushed himself down and left.

Bernard lay for a long time where he had left her. Pain swelled and stabbed at her; tears came after a while, flooding from her wide eyes and soaking away in the dust. She was terrified of moving, in case that would bring it all down upon her again, so she suppressed the shivers that ran through her and stilled the tight tremble of her jaw. Her body felt heavy, exhausted, splintered.

She became aware of something uncomfortable beneath her thigh, and she shifted warily to pull out a tin beaker on which she had been lying. Still she did not rise. She would have liked to pray. But not a single line of prayer would come to her, not a verse from a childhood hymn, nothing from the Bible. In her loneliness she closed her eyes, and she heard God weeping. Inconsolable, His tears of anger and frustration and shame broke the quiet with piteous sobs. This, finally, she could not bear.

She hauled herself to her feet, her legs buckling and all kinds of terrors converging upon her, and she stumbled out of the house, making her way up the hill to the convent, seeing nothing of the women gathering fruit in the orchard or the children at the well or the soldiers clustered together, conspiratorial. All she knew was the soreness deep inside her, and the howl of God in her head. She tried to run, to make the blood pound in her veins and thump in her heart, drowning out the misery of His lament for her disgrace. But she could not.

When the owner of the house returned later there were few signs of disturbance. He put a pan of water on the stove to warm and shook off his boots. Unthinking, he swept a cobweb from the corner of the fireplace with his hand. It was only when he noticed the rounded worn-handled basket on the table that he was puzzled. And when he went out into the village in the nightingale twilight after his supper, he heard a story which astounded him.

# Ten

Veronique's car spluttered through the village. She did not quite notice where she was. All she could see, reflected back at her from the windscreen, was Bernard's still face, framed by the fall of her veil and gripped with questions. She tried to shake it away. She opened the window wide and let the cold rush in. She drove too quickly. At the edge of town, the traffic confused her. She failed to notice a junction and someone hooted as she sped across. She forgot to stop for bread, as she had intended. The nun was there still, too close.

When she pulled into her parking space at the nursing home and turned off the engine, she hauled Sister Marie's bag towards her across the seats, unzipped it and rummaged inside. She had no idea what she was looking for. When she uncovered the encyclopedia of saints, its paper cover rubbed and tatty, she turned to the entry for her namesake, Saint Veronica, and found a rose-toned picture of a young woman wiping the bleeding face of Christ with what appeared to be a bath towel. Veronique stared at it. She did not know that since the publication of the encyclopedia almost forty years earlier, the Church had agreed, with some embarrassment, that Saint Veronica had never existed. She was moved by this image of sympathy and love, of female humanity. She felt tears and a tightness in her stomach. She sat back against her seat and looked at the concrete wall in front of her and the door to the kitchens, propped ajar. She watched the steam seep out and swirl over the parked cars. Gingerly, she thought of Bernard.

She had to wait at the door of the nursing home while two elderly residents were wheeled out by nurses. She greeted everyone cheerfully. Then she placed Sister Marie's bag on the reception desk.

'I have the bag.'

The receptionist smiled conspiratorially.

'I'm sorry. Was it a nuisance?'

'It was fine,' said Veronique. 'I'll take it up. Where is she?'

The girl was anxious to save her further trouble.

'Don't worry. It can go later. I can put it on the trolley.'

'Thanks.' It was a relief. Veronique did not want to see Sister Marie. 'That's a good idea,' she said. 'I think I'll go home early. I'm tired out.'

The girl smiled at her again.

'Good idea,' she echoed.

Veronique locked her office and went back to the car park. She stood for a moment with her hand on the cold metal of her car roof, making her mind come clear. Then she drove the short familiar route to her apartment with determined care, as though it was important. She collected her post and cleaned the damp soles of her shoes thoroughly on the mat at the entrance to the block. She picked up a littered wrapper from the stairs. She made and ate a chicken salad; spoke to her mother briefly on the telephone; watched the television news and weather forecast and ironed two blouses for work. Her panic subsided; everything about the day was ordinary. But still she found she took too much notice of things, scrutinizing herself, debating the simplest of thoughts, waiting.

Exasperated, Veronique went through to the bedroom. The curtains and shutters were still closed and she turned on the light. She took off her shoes and stood on the bed to take down a photograph of her father that was pushed back on a high shelf. Dust was sticky on the glass. She ran her finger round the frame several times, then she looked hard at the photo. The man in front of the camera was seated on a bright blue towel somewhere sandy, the light behind him dazzling with the promise of the sea, but he was fully dressed and unsmiling. It was as she remembered him, unspecifically stern, irritated by her when she was young, vexed by her demands for inexplicable games, exhausted. She imagined the way he would have fretted as the photograph was taken, shaking sand from his hands, brushing down his clothes, unsettled and somehow bewildered. She made herself look again, examining the face that she did not quite know, every suggestion that might be poised there. It was nothing like the round-eyed nun's that she had seen earlier that day. Her father was thin, his features angled and brittle. There was no family resemblance. Veronique let the frame drop onto the bed and leant back, relieved. This meant things could be left alone. She began to feel that she had got away with something.

The minibus beeped in the drive at ten to four.

'Did you hear that? It's the minibus,' said Bernard.

Thérèse had been napping. She was startled. 'Already? What time is it? Are we ready?'

'Not quite. Perhaps they'll wait.'

'What have you been doing?' Thérèse was accusatory. 'You haven't finished your papers, Sister. You're not ready to go.'

'I have my bag. These things are not important.'

There were still two piles of papers, the one on the floor that was everything that Bernard meant to discard, and the other on the table still to be sorted. Alongside it was the newspaper obituary, lying where Veronique had left it the day before. Bernard picked up both piles and put the obituary on top. Then she moved across to the corner of the snug and stacked the papers at the feet of the Virgin, filling the niche.

'They're not important,' she said again.

Thérèse was busy with her own bag, trying to make the zip pull across, her fingers clumsy.

'You can't leave them there like that, Sister,' she said, hardly looking up.

Bernard ignored her. She went through to the refectory and reached above the fireplace for the matches. When she came back through to the snug, Thérèse had her bag fastened and was standing in the turn of the corridor, everything about her expectant.

'We should go. I think they beeped again, Sister. I think I might have heard it.'

The first match snapped and the head sizzled onto the tiles near Bernard's feet. The second burned slowly and Bernard angled it down to encourage the flame.

'Oh no,' said Thérèse, suddenly understanding. 'Oh no, Sister. You can't do that.' She let her bag drop and lurched towards Bernard. 'They'll – burn.'

'I want them to burn,' said Bernard.

She put the match up towards the papers, holding it against the edge of the newspaper clipping. For a moment there was the smell of charring. But the paper browned unevenly, resisting the flame, and soon the match went out with the slightest wreath of smoke.

Bernard began to strike another match.

'Sister, they're your things. The things you've kept.'

'You didn't keep your things, Sister,' Bernard pointed out.

'But I couldn't – they were… they took up so much space. And anyway—'

'Everything belongs here,' Bernard said, finishing Thérèse's sentence. She shook her head. 'I don't want it now. I don't want it – any of it.'

As she reached again to put a match to the papers, Thérèse pushed forwards, flapping her hands out to stop her. Bernard pulled the match away, trying to avoid Thérèse's arm; she raised her other hand to protect the flame, attempted to turn her back on Thérèse, her veil falling awkwardly across her face. It was confused and clumsy, their age making them slow. And somehow, between them, they crashed into the niche. The papers flapped up, the Virgin wobbled and then everything fell onto the floor between them.

Thérèse stepped back. 'Oh no – look at her! Look what you've done, Sister – to Our Lady.'

The Virgin had fallen on her side. The end of the nose was chipped, and one or two of the long white folds of veil were cracked and broken. The left arm was completely smashed to the shoulder; the robe down the left side was splintered into a series of jagged edges. The fall had revealed the back of the statue where the paint was unfaded and startlingly blue, a maker's paper label stuck near the feet. Smashed and deformed, there was something antique about it, a clothed Aphrodite, but from the back it was like something else, a toyshop mannequin.

The minibus horn sounded long and loud, and almost immediately afterwards the doorbell rang too.

'We'll have to leave it,' said Bernard.

She let the match drop, burnt out now, and she moved away to pick up her bag. Thérèse was still looking at the toppled Virgin.

'You couldn't have imagined it, could you,' she said, 'a few years ago? Even a few days ago.'

And she shook her head at the incredible mystery of it all.

Bernard allowed them to strap her into a seat near the back. She could see Thérèse's bare head several rows in front of her, bowed, the colour of her hair still unexpected. Their bags were on another seat, pushed together. Bernard kept her eyes fixed on the ridged plastic of the floor, pocked and worn by the rub of feet. She did not look out of the window. As the bus bumped down the gravelled driveway, she prayed to her silent God to release her from the world; she prayed without ceasing, without recourse to the learnt formulae, in her own meagre words. The bus paused at the entrance. A slice of sun lit the open gates and skewed back behind them, reaching up the convent walls. The plastic Christ nailed to the reconstituted wooden crucifix, atrophied now by the faint glimmer of afternoon light, hung still in Bernard's cell where she had left it.

Bernard prayed only for herself. She begged that the minibus journey might end, the rattling of the old seat ease and the draughts around the grimy windows be plugged. She prayed that she might be spared from whatever was coming. She pleaded with God to heal the old wound that seemed to be tearing within her, the irreligious urge to find Veronique and hold her. She implored Him to strike down Sister Thérèse there and then, as proof of His displeasure. But there was no sign that any of this was heard. The minibus continued to weave its way among the afternoon traffic, its engine noisy through the thin floor, as pain cramped weakly in Bernard's legs and feet.

'So then – Les Cèdres,' said one of the young men, leaning towards his passengers and lowering the volume of the radio.

Thérèse turned in her seat and looked at Bernard. The prayers in Bernard's head hammered on. She looked back blankly. Thérèse took it as an accusation.

'There's a mistake on your papers,' she said, turning back and summoning her teaching voice. 'We need to go to Les Cèdres, that's right. For Sister Bernard. But I have another address; I'm going somewhere else.' She gave the address to Corinne's apartment without hesitation. To her surprise the driver accepted her authority to make such a decision. He shrugged.

'OK. We'll go there first. It's nearer,' he said, raising the volume of the music again.

They drove on to where the roads became narrower and busier. Then they pulled into a quiet street of tall shuttered houses and narrow iron balconies. There was a *boulangerie* with a small window filled with large flat baskets of loaves: baguettes and round country breads and knotted lengths that Bernard had never before seen. Outside a café, several men sat drinking wine from tiny round glasses, their backs pressed against the wall and their hats pulled low against the wind. An alarm sounded as an automated garage door heaved upwards between two buildings. It was suddenly urban and unimaginable. Bernard bowed her head.

The minibus pulled up outside a neat apartment block. At a second-floor window a curtain moved. What seemed like only a moment later, Corinne appeared at the main door, waving. She was wearing a blue striped shirt neatly tucked into some kind of soft trousers, as though she had been sleeping, Bernard thought. Corinne came close to the minibus window and tapped at it, in front of Bernard's face. She mouthed something, a greeting of some kind, and turned to embrace Thérèse. The driver waited and handed Thérèse her bag. Bernard turned away.

At the threshold to the apartment block, Thérèse paused and looked along the street for a moment, as though there was something particular she expected to see there. Then, her face puzzled and drawn, she turned to Bernard and raised a hand, absolving the old nun of everything. But Bernard did not see it. Her anger had impaled her. She could not move. Staring at the grease-stained back of the headrest in front of her, she pleaded with God to make the world end. Thérèse went inside the building and the minibus moved off.

'Les Cèdres?' asked the boy.

'Yes,' said Bernard. 'Please.' She could not think of a different reply.

The cold seeped through the church, falling on the congregation with the weight of sin. Bernard's attention had drifted during the young priest's long sermon. She may even have slept. The heavy missal, which had come to her on the death of her father, dropped from her folded hands with a thud which shuddered through the church, startling and confusing her. When Sister Marie's name was read out among the notices at the end of Mass, Bernard was for a moment unsure of what she had heard. It was only when the priest went on to offer a brief summary of Marie's life, thanking God for the gift of her long vocation at the convent and leading the parish in a prayer for the dead, that Bernard was finally sure that the nun was gone. She looked up at the faint glow of the stained glass and the slender stone arches above her, blotched with damp and old dirt, and she rejoiced.

At the end of Mass, Bernard tapped the arm of the priest to ask him the details of Marie's funeral.

'Ah, Sister Bernard, how are you? How are you finding your new home?' he asked, distracted, his eyes not on her.

'It's fine, Father.'

'Good – that's good. Yes. I see someone is bringing you to church here, on the transport rota.'

'I've always come here,' Bernard said, unwilling to tell him how difficult a thing it had been to arrange with the staff at Les Cèdres.

'Yes, yes, of course. And sad news about Sister Marie. What a saintly woman! It was a blessed release, perhaps.'

'She was well looked after, Father.'

One of the altar boys skidded down the aisle to his parents. The priest glared at him over Bernard's shoulder.

'Is that right? Well, that's good,' he said.

Bernard traced the cross on the front cover of her missal with her finger, slowly following the indented gilt line right round before she spoke. The priest closed his hands, waiting.

'Father, could you tell me again the time of the funeral?' she asked in the end. 'I didn't quite catch it.'

'For Sister Marie?'

'Yes, Father.'

'Tuesday morning at ten. At Sainte Famille.'

This was a church to which Bernard had never been. The thought of it alarmed her.

'She would have liked to have it here. Couldn't it have been held here?' she said.

'Would she? Do you think?' The priest nodded, answering his own question. 'Ah well, it's Sainte Famille. It's the parish for the nursing home. Father Gabriel does a lot of work there.'

It was a new church. Its brick bell tower, punctured by an elaborate lattice of rectangular holes, dominated one end of the town, its colour odd among the dry ochres of the old stone. Inside it was hollow and bare, unwelcoming. Bernard sat firmly to one side, one of the smooth white walls almost within reach. The suited diocesan official who had picked her up from Les Cèdres sat in the pew in front of her, as though this might help to fill the space. There were only seven mourners. Three parishioners, who were there simply to attend Mass, sat together near the front. Sister Thérèse arrived a few minutes after Bernard, on her own. Bernard recognized the clipped rhythms of her step and glanced back to watch her come up the aisle. They smiled at each other, but Thérèse went to sit apart, on the far pews. Veronique and her colleague from the nursing home were alongside the looming coffin, directly in Bernard's vision.

Bernard knelt and dipped her head. Her veil fell around her, closing her in. When the priest entered, she did not raise her head. The sounds of the Mass went on, unequivocally solemn, and once or twice the bells rang. Bernard said the responses quietly but did not look up. She could not. She could not be sure it was not all some kind of shadow play, a manifestation of the terror of her first few days at Les Cèdres, an inevitable result of the disorientation and dismay that had made everything insubstantial and out of place, driving her into the corridors and the garden in the freezing hours of the night. She could not be sure that if she looked at Veronique, even once, her granddaughter might not disappear and leave her again, with only the unendurable ache of longing.

It was Thérèse who spoke to her.

'I didn't expect to see you again quite so soon, Sister. In such circumstances.'

Bernard raised her head, and her veil fell back to her shoulders. The Mass was over. The undertakers were fiddling with the latches that secured the coffin trolley and Thérèse had moved onto the pew alongside Bernard.

Bernard blinked, wondering at the solidity of things.

'May God grant her eternal rest,' she said.

Thérèse tutted quietly. 'It'll save the diocese some money, at least – with my moving in with Corinne and Sister Marie going to heaven. They must be relieved.'

Things were settling around Bernard, coming clear. Veronique was still there, bending in her pew to pick something from the floor, her bag, perhaps, or an umbrella.

'Maybe that was a comfort to her,' Bernard said.

'They found her in a heap, you know, on the floor,' said Thérèse. 'On the stinking linoleum. She'd been lying there for hours, her leg skewed from the hip at an unholy angle.' She shook her head. 'A torment, that's what it was. And unnecessary. If she'd only been taken care of properly...'

'She always had a special talent for sacrifice,' said Bernard.

The trolley rolled past them, one of the wheels creaking. Thérèse crossed herself and, for the slightest of moments, touched the coffin as it passed.

She was not wearing her habit, and Bernard noticed that the large metal crucifix which habitually hung between Thérèse's breasts had disappeared. A small cross and chain, perhaps gold, snuggled instead in the dint at the base of her neck.

'Is it working well, your... arrangement?' Bernard asked.

Thérèse turned from the coffin. Her voice was newly supple. 'Oh, it is, Sister, it really is. Corinne is such a marvellous cook, for a start. We have such meals! And I've signed up for a yoga class – for the spring and...'

She fingered the new chain round her neck.

'It was the right decision, Sister. That's the thing. I know that now. It must have been right. It must have been God's will. After all.' She let the cross fall lightly against her jumper and her face stiffened. 'And you, Sister? How is Les Cèdres?'

Even now, after several weeks, Bernard had only the faintest sense of the place, like a tremor in her stomach, the endless nausea of falling.

'It's fine,' she said.

'Yes. Yes.' Thérèse nodded hard. 'I thought it would be, in the end. I thought that.'

'I can't seem to find my way around,' said Bernard.

The church was empty now. The mourners had followed the coffin outside and the nuns' conversation, tuned for Thérèse's deafness, was too loud. It seemed like sacrilege. They were quiet. They slid along the pew and genuflected stiffly, side by side, as they came out into the aisle. Then Bernard and Thérèse made their way along the strip of bright carpet that split the rows of benches and stopped outside the wide door, on the top of the steps. The coffin was being manoeuvred into the back of the hearse and they stood to watch. The parishioners had left. The diocesan man in the suit took a cigarette from a crumpled packet of Gauloises in his inside pocket and smoked quietly, scenting the air. Bernard found herself standing next to her granddaughter.

Veronique did not turn. She looked far in front of her, at something on the building opposite or beyond, across the sloping roofs dotted with pigeons.

'I can't come to the burial, Sister. We must head back – to work.' She spoke wearily, as though she was continuing a conversation they had already exhausted. 'It's busy today – we've got a new arrival.'

'Yes,' said Bernard. And then, some moments later. 'It was good of you to come.'

'We always come to these things. It's part of the job.'

Veronique sniffed. The tip of her nose was red with cold.

'I thought of sending someone else, though. This time.' Her desire to avoid the nuns had been almost irresistible. 'I wasn't sure what to do, when I heard Sister Marie had died. I didn't want... I thought about it a lot. Even this morning, I wasn't sure.' She huffed a melancholy laugh. 'I was up and down in my office, trying to decide, pacing around. I knew you'd be here. And – well, I did my duty in the end, didn't I?'

Bernard did not think to reply. Thérèse was not sure of what was being said. She moved away, towards the smoking man. There was hardly a pause.

'The photo in the paper, of Philippe Pourcel. Of my father. The cutting I saw at the convent.' Veronique took short sharp breaths between the abrupt sentences. 'You had it... you'd kept it, because he was your son.'

It was not a question. Veronique drew the toe of her shoe along the bright yellow line painted on the top of the steps.

'I know all about it. It wasn't a secret. My father told us everything he knew. Not a lot really, but I knew he was the son of a nun.' It seemed nothing, when it was said out loud like that. 'And when I saw the cutting and saw you – well, I knew.'

She did not mention the bitter onion taste in her mouth the afternoon she had driven away from the convent. Nor that she still thought of the squat nun with disgust. Instead, finally, she glanced at Bernard, seeing nothing except the thick folds of habit and the round face and the glitter of something behind in the dark interior of the church.

Bernard was puzzled by the tone of what her granddaughter had said. She could not work out what was expected of her.

The hearse started its engine and for a moment its exhaust fumes were strong in the air. The diocesan man stubbed out the remains of his cigarette beneath his shiny shoes. Thérèse looked back to where Bernard was standing and swept an arm towards her, beckoning at her for something. Veronique shuffled.

'Well,' she said. 'I should go. I'm sorry if I've… you know, said something I shouldn't. I just thought it was best to be open about it. I mean, don't worry – I won't go telling anyone. I don't want people to know. I just wanted to tell you that I'd found you out. That I knew. That's all.'

Bernard thought there was something soft about Veronique's last words. It might have been an invitation.

'Is that why you came… to the funeral?' she asked. 'To see me?'

Veronique looked away. The hearse moved smoothly off and waited by the church gate for a break in the traffic.

'I don't want a fuss. Really. I wanted a clean break. I just thought I'd tell you, that I knew – that I'd worked it out.'

'Did you want to see me?' Bernard asked again simply.

Veronique frowned. 'I told you – it's my job. I needn't have come at all. I could have sent someone else. I was going to send someone else. I just thought…'

'No,' said Bernard.

Thérèse came and took Bernard by the arm to help her down the steps.

'He offered you a lift, the man from the diocese. He was going to take you back home, Sister. But Corinne's coming to take me to the burial and I thought you could come with us. That's all right, isn't it?'

Veronique stepped back.

'Wait,' said Bernard. 'Please. Just a moment.'

She tugged on Thérèse's arm and managed to move a few steps closer to her granddaughter.

'I'd like to speak to you again,' she said, her voice so low that, even bending towards them, Thérèse could make out nothing.

This was not how Bernard had thought it would be. She had known, already, the feel of the girl, the warmth, and she had thought, of course, of the soldier, the only person she had ever held. She had thought she would recognize everything about it, his musk a memory on Veronique's new skin.

Veronique looked hard at Bernard. Thérèse pulled on Bernard's arm.

'I don't know. I'll think about it,' said Veronique at last. 'You're at Les Cèdres, aren't you?'

Bernard nodded. Veronique smiled before turning away down the steps. Bernard was sure then that she would come.

Corinne joined them at the cemetery for the burial. Her pink trousers distracted Bernard's attention from the damp thud of the soil being piled back into Marie's grave and her bouquet of flowers seemed unnecessarily gaudy.

'I'm sorry I was late. I had an appointment, at the doctor's. I couldn't make the Mass.' She was bright. 'It's good to see you again, Sister Bernard. Poor Sister Marie.'

Thérèse was ahead of them, making her way through the long rows of clean stones. 'She had a long life. And happy – blessed,' she said, turning.

'She was a saintly one, they say,' said Corinne.

Bernard closed her eyes momentarily so that it might all pass.

'And you, too. You helped her with great patience, I know, Sister Bernard,' said Corinne. 'It's not easy looking after someone like that. It's a great strain.'

Nothing like this had ever been said before. Bernard stopped walking. The crisp light slanted shadows from the gravestones, cutting geometrics into the short grass. Corinne stepped across one of the sharp squares and laid her hand lightly on Bernard's arm.

She smiled. 'Have you got time to come back with us for a meal, Sister?' she asked. 'I could drop you back at Les Cèdres later.'

Bernard remembered the block of apartments she had seen from the minibus window, the drapes at the windows, neat and fresh, and the revelation of another way of living,

192

the unexpected craving. She shook her head.

'I have to go back,' she said. 'They wouldn't like me to stay out. They're quite strict.'

'But surely this once, Sister Bernard…'

It was Thérèse this time who shook her head.

'We shouldn't upset things,' she said briskly. And then, more gently, smiling. 'We wouldn't want to land her in trouble.'

Corinne took Bernard's hand. The offence of such sudden intimacy flushed Bernard's cheeks red; she went to pull away. But Corinne's skin next to her own was warm, a solace, and tentatively, Bernard pressed against it, the slightest of movements, as though everything might shatter.

Corinne felt the pressure and squeezed back. Then she let Bernard's hand fall.

'Well, I'm sorry, Sister,' she said, smiling. 'It would have been nice. We'll have to do it another time, that's all.'

'We'll drop you back,' said Thérèse. 'On the way.'

Bernard looked out across the graveyard. The studs of tall monuments drew her gaze away to where plastic bouquets of flowers were piled by the far wall, their anxious colours fading. Corinne and Thérèse started towards the car, but Bernard did not move; she was afraid to. Everything ahead of her was hateful, the sameness, the stupefying loneliness, the terror of waiting for Veronique and yearning for her.

Corinne turned. 'Are you all right, Sister? Can I help?'

Bernard pushed at her veil. 'You said… could I come… you invited…' she began, wanting to change things, but her voice was faint and Corinne, searching for her keys in her pocket and waving an arm towards Thérèse to direct her to the right parking place, heard nothing but breathy discomfort.

'You'll be fine,' she said brightly. 'You've been out in the cold too long, that's all. And it's upsetting, a funeral. It's always upsetting.'

She took a step or two back towards Bernard and stretched out a hand.

'Come on. We'll have you home very soon.'

Bernard did not take Corinne's hand this time. 'Yes,' she said.

Thérèse's fury was unstoppable.

'Why? Why did you invite her? She might have come.'

'Of course she might have come. That's what I wanted. That's why I asked her.'

Corinne laughed slightly. The soles of their shoes, squeaking on the soft plastic floor of the apartment block's underground car park, echoed the sound of her laugh, making it seem more than it was.

Thérèse stiffened. 'I don't see why,' she said. 'I still don't.'

'She looked sad. And cold. And lonely. I thought it might be nice.'

Corinne pulled open the heavy green door that led into the building, and they climbed up to the apartment without speaking. Thérèse had never felt so miserable. The unholiness of it shocked her.

'We can't abandon her,' said Corinne finally, unlocking the apartment door and holding it open for her friend to pass ahead.

They hung their coats neatly in the hallway. Walking through to the bright sitting room they brushed against Claude's pot plant and the pink flower heads danced.

'You wouldn't want that, would you?'

Corinne eased into a wide armchair with a puff and slipped her feet from her shoes. Thérèse did not sit down. She walked to the window, tugging back the curtain to look down onto the street.

'Really,' she said, trying to keep her voice steady. 'I don't understand. You suggest I come here, to live with you, because Sister Bernard is – I don't know – unworthy. Unworthy of my sacrifice, if that's what it is. I'd be better off here, with you, than making my life a misery for someone who, well, has sinned. So much; who has sinned so much. That's what you said, as good as. And now, now you—'

Corinne sighed. 'Sinned, Sister Thérèse. Exactly. Aren't we meant to forgive a sinner?'

'Forgive the sinner, of course, yes. Forgive the sinner.' It came out flat, without meaning. 'But this I don't understand.' Thérèse let the curtain fall. There was a pause. 'Oh, I don't know – what you say. That's right. I know that's right.' She fiddled with the chain round her neck, running it through her fingers. 'I don't understand why I feel that I can't... that I can't forgive her. That I hate her.'

She had never spoken such a word. It displaced her, threw her back many years to an indistinct past, with Mother Catherine prowling and the convent locked after dark and the intensity of their shared lives shut in with the dimming light.

'I shouldn't hate her,' she said, bewildered. 'I never

195

hated her before. I never hated anyone before – I'm sure I didn't. I don't understand.'

Corinne smiled. 'You don't hate her. It's just a hard day, a funeral. You've lost another of your sisters and now, well, there's not many of you left. Just the two of you. You must feel that.'

'I suppose so.'

'It's all been a lot, a big change. You'll be weary.'

Thérèse nodded. But the weariness had always been there, threatening. It was not that.

'I'll make us something to eat,' said Corinne. 'And we'll have an early night. That's all it needs – you'll see.'

Thérèse watched her go through to the small kitchen and a few minutes later she smelt the rich smokiness of slightly burnt butter. She followed through and stood for a while on the threshold, her hands twisted tightly together, watching, imagining the clinks and spits and shuffles of cooking in the small, closed space. She saw the bend of Corinne's back as she leant over the gas flame and the anger was inexplicably strong in her again, prickling and stinging, alive.

'You were pleased, though, weren't you, when I found out what Sister Bernard had done?' she asked sharply.

Corinne was concentrating on turning slices of fish in a pan and could not, for a moment, understand. She turned and flapped her spatula lightly in the air.

'What?'

'When I found out – at the Armistice memorial. When they told me about how she betrayed the Resistance, getting those people killed. Because – you know… because she was with the soldier.'

Corinne was busy with the pan. She did not look up. Only when she had slid the fillets onto plates and turned off the heat did she let herself speak.

'It was good that you knew. I thought that was important,' she said. She was puzzled at something in Thérèse's face. 'I don't know. I thought it was time for everything to come out, in the open. For everyone's sake.'

'Yes, I thought so,' said Thérèse.

Just before dark one of the staff knocked gently at Bernard's room. There was no answer. The nurse pushed the door open just enough to see inside. Bernard was kneeling by the side of her bed, her head dropped forwards to rest on the counterpane. Thinking that the old nun might have fallen asleep, and accustomed to the contorted positions of the elderly at prayer, the nurse left her quietly.

Bernard, listening hard, heard her come and go but did not move. She heard the door close. She heard the scrape of chairs being pulled towards the television in the room below and the sudden burst of sound as someone switched on the set. She heard shuffling zimmer-framed footsteps in the corridor and the heating system buzzing. She heard a metallic clank somewhere, and she thought she heard the brush of the breeze against her closed window and the fall of the night, like the breathy beat of moth wings. But no matter how hard she listened, she did not hear God. And she would have given her life then to catch a word, a whisper, a grunt; anything to suggest that she was not alone.

In her small, pink room, Thérèse was studying a guide to the Mediterranean coast. The apartment was quiet;

Corinne had gone to bed nearly an hour earlier. All the lights were out except the bedside light by which Thérèse was reading. She had not yet said her night prayers.

In the weeks since moving from the convent, she had already finished a short book about the Atlantic resorts around Bordeaux, a tourist board publication listing the most popular seaside excursions in Brittany and a first-hand account of a walking tour along Spain's Costa del Sol. She had reached no firm conclusions about the relative merits of any particular stretch of coast, but was beginning to understand that she had to go to the sea. She dreamt about it at night, the smell of it, indescribable. She tried to imagine the sound of it, the roar of great breakers thrashing up pebbles, pounding the cliffs on a stormy day, gurgling into rock pools, splintering into a million green and gold pieces. Sometimes, when she was sitting in the soft chair on Corinne's small balcony, she imagined what it would be like to look through the gap in the houses across the road and glimpse the water sparkling beyond. The sea was an expression of God, not quite graspable, an eternal prayer flooding the world. She thought that if she saw it once, the promise of it spilling over the horizon, she might begin to understand.

Her head dipped over the pictures of coastal spring flowers and she felt her eyes droop. She closed the book and sat up straight, her hands clasped, her usual prayers ready. She wanted to begin. She wanted to thank God for this wonderful new life, the opportunities and the pleasures it was bringing her, the joy of her soul. But something sank like a cold draught onto her prayer and all that would come to her was the familiar clutter of her cell at the convent, the origami swan and the unchanging Buddha, the scraping of the mice in the attic above her head, the soft unlit blackness of the rising land outside her window and the dim thought of Bernard, further along the corridor, silent and unheeded. Instead of praying, she wept. It was not at all the same thing.

The following morning, Thérèse made plans with Corinne.

'I thought we should have a holiday,' she said brightly. 'I thought I could treat us with some of my savings. If you drive and bring the car, I can book the hotel and pay for the petrol.'

Corinne dipped her slice of baguette into her wide bowl of coffee. She took a wet bite before she answered.

'Right,' she said. 'That'll be nice.'

'There's no use pining, is there? I might as well make the most of things – I might as well do the things I've always wanted and have a bit of freedom. I can…' Now that it came to it, Thérèse struggled to think what she might do. 'I can go shopping,' she said in the end, weakly.

Corinne smiled and took another bite. 'Good,' she said, still chewing. 'I knew you'd be all right. I knew it. All these years we've been friends – you're an intelligent woman, after all. I've always admired you. Ever since we were teaching together, I always knew you were – I don't know – clever. Proud and modern and clever.'

She dropped the unfinished baguette onto her plate and pushed back her chair, pleased with what she had said. It seemed to put an end to any lingering uneasiness. She looked at Thérèse's tired face and smiled again, clapping her hands together in a tiny, brief round of applause.

'Where shall we go then?'

'To the sea.'

'But which sea? Where?' asked Corinne. 'Like you said – we can go anywhere. Within reason.'

Thérèse was definite. 'The Atlantic,' she said. 'I've been thinking about it – the big beaches and the big waves. The power of God.'

She laughed uneasily.

Corinne smiled. 'Just the two of us?'

It seemed an odd question. Thérèse frowned, confused. 'I thought so. Is that no good?'

'Of course. It's fine. It's good.'

Neither of them mentioned Bernard's name, and she was only there with them, shadowy, for a moment, little more than a change in the light as the winter morning reflections shifted across the window. Then Corinne's certainty filled the room.

'It'll be wonderful, with the two of us. And easy for getting rooms. Rooms are always for two.'

Thérèse nodded. 'I know,' she said.

Later that morning they took down the road atlas from its shelf. Kneeling on the floor, to either side of the small round glass table in Corinne's sitting room, they traced a route across to the coast, choosing slow roads through the vineyards and along the wide rivers meandering west and then cutting across the open land on long straight roads that seemed pressed flat by the crisp light from the sea. They picked a small town, a fracture in the strip of yellow printed along the coast, and Thérèse promised to go to the library and find a hotel directory so that they could book somewhere to stay in advance.

'It's a voyage of discovery,' she said, her finger poised over the point on the map where their route would reach the sea. She wanted to use the word pilgrimage. 'It will be a new start.'

'It'll be cold,' said Corinne. 'At this time of year. And windy, too, probably. And more or less deserted.'

Thérèse sat back on her heels and sighed.

'Oh, it'll be fine, though,' said Corinne, not understanding. 'It's only a couple of days, after all.'

Thérèse closed the atlas.

'Perhaps we could invite Sister Bernard on a day trip with us somewhere,' she said. 'Before we go. That might be nice, mightn't it?'

Corinne tried not to look surprised.

'I think she'd like it,' Thérèse went on. 'It must be hard for her, having no one, being shut up with all those stuffy old priests at Les Cèdres. Like you said – she looked sad, and lonely. I saw that. It doesn't seem quite fair that I should have everything.' She ran her fingernail along the spiral binding of the map, not looking up. 'I can't help thinking about her, going off there so quietly, so obediently. And she has nothing, no family, no kind friends like I have.'

'Just that granddaughter,' said Corinne, with barely a pause.

Thérèse knew she should be curious. She had waited many years to hear such a scandal. There had been those days in the hot summer of the schoolhouse when such a revelation would have been wondrous, the answer to all kinds of questions. But that was too long ago now; she could no longer grasp the excitement of it.

'The woman at the funeral,' Corinne went on. 'The

woman from that home where Sister Marie was. Not the little blonde thing. The dark one in the suit. A funny-looking woman. She has an out-of-date face somehow. Anyway, that's her. That's the granddaughter. I can't remember the name but someone did tell me once.'

It seemed wicked now, such speculation. But Corinne was looking at her, expecting her to say something, and Thérèse could not help but smile.

'I didn't know,' she said.

'Really? I thought everyone knew. Everyone of a certain age, anyway. You do know about the baby, don't you? About Sister Bernard's baby?'

Thérèse nodded.

'Well, that's something. It might have been a shock otherwise.'

Corinne giggled and eased herself up from the floor, shaking out her stiff knees and feet and perching on the edge of the chair.

Thérèse wondered what there was to say.

'But how do you know, about the granddaughter? How would anyone know that?'

Corinne smiled. 'Oh, I'm a gossip. I keep my ear to the ground. I'm interested in what's going on,' she said lightly. But there was such bewilderment on Thérèse's face that she stopped herself. 'Really though,' she said, 'to be serious, it's been a bit of an issue, on and off. Not now so much. I haven't heard anyone mention it for years. But at one time her son was nosing around, making parishes uncomfortable, asking questions. I was a lay member on one of the diocese committees at the time, and it came up at the end of a meeting. No names, not officially, but we all knew.'

Thérèse had been to such committee meetings once or twice when something had involved the school. She pictured the brown rooms, somehow too dark, and tried to imagine someone recounting Bernard's story from a typed sheet, speaking quickly, keen to rush through a busy meeting.

'You discussed Sister Bernard officially?'

'Not Sister Bernard so much as her son. He was being a pain. Several of the parish priests had complained. One of the parish committees had sent us a strongly worded letter accusing him of harassment. It was bad for morale, you understand, having someone popping up every Sunday talking about pregnant nuns and illegitimate babies. It's the sort of thing that gets into the papers and then before you know it...'

Corinne threw up her hands and her eyebrows and sighed.

Thérèse began to see how little she knew. It was a shock. She had always thought herself different from the other nuns, unretiring, practical, with a grasp of secular affairs beyond the convent. She had presumed there was more to her life than her vocation. But Corinne's casual exposition of the unmargined immensity of the world made her tremble.

'I never thought anyone would care,' she said. 'I never thought anyone knew. It was never spoken about – not at the convent.'

'No one did care about Sister Bernard having had a baby as far as I knew. That had all blown over. As I say, it was just her son making waves. That's what bothered them. That's why we decided that someone would tell him where she was. To shut him up. It was nothing to do with me, of course. Not directly. It wasn't my parish. I just had to sign something, to say I agreed to it.'

Corinne stretched out her legs and arched her back, pulling herself tall.

'I can't remember how it was done exactly, but I know it did the trick. It all went quiet after that.'

'So all kinds of people would have known? All over the diocese?'

'And beyond, I suppose, in some kind of paperwork or other – reports and so on. You know how these things are.'

'I don't think I do,' said Thérèse.

But Corinne thought it was a joke. Laughing, she got up and went through to the hall to change her slippers for some bright pumps.

'I'm going for a stroll,' she said, calling through to where Thérèse was still wedged back on her heels. 'I'll call at the *alimentation*. Do you want to come?'

Thérèse did not answer. Corinne took her coat and scarf from the pegs and muffled herself carefully against the winter cold.

'It just proves one thing,' she said, as she left the apartment. 'We're none of us too small for God to take notice of. Like the birds of the air.'

Thérèse did not see how this made sense.


Veronique was sitting with friends under the wide awning of a bar alongside the main road. The waiter came with their order, wiping round the table quickly before placing the coffee cups in a circle. Veronique paid and he took a long while to dig out the correct change from the pouch at his waist, tearing the receipt on the table in some kind of temper, as if she had offended him. She was surprised that this bothered her. She lit a cigarette and fingered the raised crest on the wrapper of the chocolate square that poked from the edge of the saucer. Her friends talked around and across her.

'You're very quiet, Veron,' someone said.

Veronique had eaten lunch with her mother at a nearby restaurant, and had walked briefly with her afterwards by the river. They had sat for a while in the weak sun. Veronique had not said anything about the old nun she had met, and the difficulty she was having, despite everything, to forget her; her mother, too, had accused her of being withdrawn.

'I'm tired,' she said.

'You need a holiday,' one of her friends suggested kindly.

Veronique was sharp in return. 'Just an early night.'

They tried to bring her out of herself. They said she worked too hard. They made eyes, on her behalf, at a couple of young men sitting at another table. Then, because she still said nothing, they gave up. Not long after that, Veronique went home.

Crossing the road by the war memorial, the unexpected scent of flowers surprised her. The wreaths and bouquets from the Armistice Day service were still fresh there, their ribbons bright. She paused on the stone steps, and read, for the first time, the list of names carved into the stone, moving round from the panels of the First World War to the smaller ones of the Second, and wondering about the mysterious abbreviations that marked the ranks of the fallen. On the top of the memorial there was the figure of a French soldier in a round helmet, wielding a lance or a bayonet; he was looking ferociously over her head towards the encroach of foreign armies from the supermarket near the ring road. She had never noticed any of this before, not properly. And still it did not matter to her. She knew nothing about the war, nor how it was a part of her. It was a moment of undefined nostalgia, that was all. She was just unsettled. The unknown past was too powerful for a moment, pushing its way briefly into her attention. She brushed the inexplicable tears from her eyes with angry hands.

The following day, Veronique went into the church around the corner from her apartment. First she knocked on the door, but when no one answered she pushed it and found that it was open. The inside was bare and plain and warm. It smelt strongly of furniture polish. The pale wood shone, even in the dim light, and the carpet looked new. On a table near the door, a pile of blue books was neatly stacked, each copy aligned with the one below, and on the altar several gleaming pot plants were arranged in a close semicircle around the lectern. Everything was ordered and clean. She had not expected it to be so cared for. She had thought it would be rambling and cold, and not as small as it had turned out to be. She was disappointed at its domesticity.

Veronique sat on the end of a pew near the back. She did not fidget, or weep. She did not pray. She simply sat still, looking at the stone altar and the way the little red light hanging behind flickered and jumped. She remembered, again, a morning, a long time ago, when she had gone shopping with her father to the weekly market in the central square, the summer lingering and the stone walls sweating in the sun. It was the school holidays and the canopied stalls were colourful with summer vegetables and fruit, boxes of peaches and apricots, melons piled high and scenting the air. At the foot of the steps, two lines of old women sold eggs from baskets, carrier bags of green beans, rabbits and chickens trussed and panting. She had gone past all this and in under the stone arches, where the summer clothes and souvenir stalls were setting up in the arcaded shade, and hanging from one of the high rails she had seen the most beautiful soft yellow sundress, full and elegant, with the papery coolness of linen.

When she held it up against her, it had swirled and danced and people had smiled at her. Her father was smiling at her, too, as she twirled with it under the canvas shelter of the stall; she had assumed it was hers. So it had been a shock when he had said she could not have it. Sitting now in the cool silence of the church, she remembered exactly the way she had looked up at him in surprise, thinking he might be joking. But more than this, she remembered how, barely ten minutes later, they had jostled through the bottleneck of shoppers passing from one square to another under the huge stone canopy at the entrance to the parish church, and they had seen a cluster of nuns behind a small white-clothed table covered in unlabelled pots of jam and lopsided tarts, laid out for sale. And her father, without a moment's thought, had reached across for two swollen tomatoes and, in return, had given the nuns a donation almost three times the cost of Veronique's beautiful summer dress. The nuns had been only moderately thankful. She remembered the gentle dip of their heads as they took the money, and her father's heavy hands around the ripe tomatoes.

Veronique sighed out loud, and surprised herself. She felt the sudden grip of grief for her father and in a moment it came on her so suddenly that she could hardly breathe. She remembered everything about him, as though he were alongside her, the smell of tobacco in his hair and clothes, the freckles dark on one side of his nose, the way his hands would tremble sometimes when he tried to be still, the astonishing softness of his breathing, and she wanted to cry out, to cry for him, to make him turn to her, bright and smiling and alive. She wanted to make him buy the dress for her, so that she could twirl for him, as she would have done then, on that holiday morning that had been spoilt by the nuns.

For the first time, Veronique mourned her father. Everything was confused, her anger with him, her disappointment, her contempt for his clumsiness and foolishness, her absolute faith in him, unshaken, her longing. She shivered, feeling the coldness of the pew through her skirt. She leant forwards, resting her head on her arms, trying to make sense of things, but it was all barbed and tangled, and the more she struggled, the more the pain pulled at her.

'Please, God,' she whispered into the fold of her arms.

But nothing happened, despite her prayer, and she sat for a long time, bent over in the soft quiet of the church. Only when someone else came in, letting the door fall shut with a gentle bump, did Veronique move. She looked behind towards the noise. Seeing a man genuflecting a few yards behind her, his head bowed low and his hat held to his side, she blushed, suddenly embarrassed. She felt she was intruding. By the time he had straightened again, she was already past him, pushing the door open onto the street and breathing the cold air with relief.

Bernard's knees were so sore from a night bent on the floor that they buckled when she tried to stand and she had to edge herself around the room in a kind of ungainly squat using the furniture to support herself. In the course of the previous fourteen hours, she had thumbed her way through six rosaries, recited three full litanies of saints, and intoned the Lord's Prayer many times. She had, around four in the morning, cried out so forlornly for some kind of divine attention that the man in the room next door thought that her soul must at last have been freed by the Holy Spirit and he had offered a curt prayer for her peaceful repose.

But neither the pain nor the praying had done any good. Nor had the intercession of her neighbour. There was still no sign of God.

Bernard had been taught that everything testified to the presence of God, every flower that budded, every child's smile, every stranger's outstretched hand. Each of life's trials was a sign of His infinite desire to help her grow; each of life's triumphs a sign of His glorious benevolence. But this morning there were only her sore knees, the gathering clouds on the horizon and a dense ache in her stomach, and these seemed to belong to her alone, to mean nothing. She stretched, easing the pain through her body. She wondered how long she could go on like this, waiting, abandoned. The day gaped ahead of her, unremitting, and she wished she knew how to make herself sleep.

The refectory was already busy. Small fresh flowers were dotted about in vases on the tables and the window facing the elegant cedars was open. The birdsong was faint, depressed by the shuffling within. The peculiar smell of breakfast, of harsh coffee and death retreating with the daylight, drifted out into the corridors, greeting Bernard. She sniffed at it, unsurprised, and took her usual place at table. She ate diligently, hardly looking up from her plate except to take more bread. She could not be sure whether she was hungry.

Bernard waited, dozing, for something to happen. She waited for Veronique to arrive, expecting any moment to hear a car draw up outside on the gravel. She waited for someone to come and tell her that there was a telephone call. She waited for the post to be sorted and slipped into the pigeonholes near the front desk. She waited for the rain to begin. But none of these things happened and in time she was the only person left sitting in the refectory. Someone asked her if she was all right.

'I am,' she said.

She sat for many hours at the abandoned dining table with the sound of the first heavy drops of rain audible, at last, as they slapped onto the dry ground beneath the trees outside the window, waiting for her granddaughter to arrive to visit her, listening out for the whisper of God. She tried to remember how things had ended up like this. Something hung faintly for a moment at the back of her mind, as though it might be an answer, but it came to nothing. It was hard to be clear which memories were really hers, untrammelled, and which she had prayed and dreamt. When Veronique arrived, things would become clearer.

Veronique was sitting in her small, windowless office at the back of the nursing home. She could not concentrate on the pleasure of the neat new rota, hand drawn in five colours, ready to be pinned to the staff noticeboard. She was worrying about the nun. Going over and over in her head what had been said at Sister Marie's funeral, she understood that some kind of contract had been made. But she could not think about Bernard without horror. And she didn't know what to do.

She lit up and smoked determinedly. She answered a call from someone trying to sell her a new laundry contract. She swivelled in her chair and took a file to a rough edge of nail on the index finger of her right hand. She checked her emails. But none of this was satisfying. The day was ragged already, uncontained. Its rhythm was spoilt. Bernard was still there, nagging.

She knew it could not go on. She did not want the nun distracting and upsetting her. When she went to add up the monthly groceries bill, she stumbled over simple sums and had to recalculate the total several times before it tallied. When she closed her eyes, even for the slightest of moments, her father was imprinted on the darkness, tiny and distant, nothing more than a brittle stick figure, but somehow unhappy and accusatory. It was too much. Veronique wanted the matter properly finished, so that there could be no doubt. She had to settle her life again, confirming how it should be.

In the end, she chose to write a letter. Somehow she could not do this on her computer, as she normally would, so she took several minutes choosing a pen from her desk drawer and neatly folding a piece of blank paper in half, diminishing its emptiness.

*I'm not sure what to write to you about,* she began. *I don't want us to carry on with this. I'm not going to come and see you at Les Cèdres.*

Veronique thought about the little old nun opening the letter, reading these first few lines.

*That doesn't mean I'm not pleased to have found you. I have a grandmother, of course, though she's dead now, but still it's nice to know a little more about my family.*

She lit another cigarette without looking, reading back over what she had written in her looping hand. Could she stop there? Would the nun think it rude, worse perhaps than nothing at all? She fiddled with her pen, clicking the nib in and out.

*My father was sorry, I think, that you never replied to his letter, all that time ago. He really meant you to get in touch. But if you don't reply to this, I'll understand. I don't suppose there's much to say.*

She sat back and it was a long time before she began again.

*I heard him mention his letter a few times when I was small, though not so much after that. I suppose he forgot about you.* She crossed this out immediately and changed it. *I suppose he forgot about it.*

She began to wish she had used the computer so that she could make corrections. She would have to rely on the old nun's eyesight being too poor to trace the letters

212

of the words she had crossed out. Just to make sure she added a few more lines, zigzagging them into dense patterns.

*He even went once to the convent. He had been waiting for the reply. I don't know exactly how long, but a long time I would think. He was a patient man usually. Anyway, he told us how he went to the convent to try to see you. Did you know this? Did anyone ever tell you? They were quite helpful, I think. They even took him to the Mother Superior, so that he could tell her all about it. But after that, when he'd spoken to her, he didn't go through with it – in the end it was too much, I suppose. He got too nervous, perhaps. Anyway, he left without talking to you. I don't know whether he saw you or not, he never said, just that, right at the last moment, he thought it might not have been such a good idea, after all. I don't think he bothered much about it after that.*

Veronique tried to imagine her father at the convent, waiting as she had done on the wide porch as the clatter of the doorbell ebbed away. She thought of the tap of his shoes on the marble floor of the hallway, and the corridor closing around him. She understood that he might have been suddenly uncertain, intimidated even. But, try as she might, she could not imagine how it had ended. She pictured him there, poised, expectant, being led through the sticky brown shadows to tell his story, but she could not see him after that. Nothing would come. She could not think how he might have felt; he had never seemed to her a disappointed man.

She read back through the letter and wondered if this was the sort of thing the nun wanted. She had finished the second cigarette.

*If there's anything you want to know, you could write, I suppose, but as I said before, there's not much to say. I don't have much to tell. I don't mind you writing.*

She tried not to think of the need to smoke.

*But I don't want to go on writing for ever. If you put all your questions into one letter then I'll do my best to reply. I'll be as honest as I can. Then that'll be it. No more after that. Would you like a photo? Perhaps I'll send you a photo of us all, when Dad was still alive. I'll ask my mother if she has one. I'll send it when I reply to your questions, if you have any.*

She thought about tearing up the letter and starting again but she did not quite have the energy for this.

*I used to think about you sometimes when I was little.*

This was harder. She did not want to have to write about herself. And the nun she had thought of as a child was a distraction, a beautiful young girl with golden hair and soft doe eyes, with the voice of angels and the ear of God, her lost grandmother.

*I used to see nuns in church and it would remind me. I wondered what it would be like to be a nun. Once, at school, I told my teacher I had three grandmothers (they were all alive then, of course, the real two and you) and I got told off. It was the first time I'd ever really been told off. That's why I remember it. It felt unfair. I tried to tell them about you. I said one of my grandmothers was a nun who had had a baby and given it away. But they were furious. They sent me home. My mother said it was best not to mention it again. And after that, as I got older, I suppose, I understood that it wasn't the best thing to go around saying.*

The bohemian charm of the third grandmother had simply eroded; it had not been enough to keep her interest. It was merely an odd family fact, an unimportant quirk of history, something she had grown out of. She had never been told Bernard's name nor what Bernard looked like. She had no idea what kind of age Bernard might be and chose not to work it out. She knew nothing at all about the old nun. This seemed right.

*I'm sure if we'd had the chance to know each other, it would have been nice. But now I think it's best left. Anyway, that's all I have to say. I hope you enjoy reading my letter. I hope you are settled in well now at Les Cèdres. I hear it is a good place. If you are going to write, with your questions, please do it soon. I don't want this to drag on.*

Veronique took a deep breath and read back slowly through the whole of her letter. In the end, she was pleased with it. It was exactly what she wanted, firm and reasonably friendly, opaque. She offered her best wishes, signed the final sheet, folded the letter neatly and put it in an envelope. She knew the address of Les Cèdres by heart, but, oddly, was not sure of the nun's name. She could not quite remember now how she had been introduced. At the time, she hadn't been paying attention. She put the letter to one side until she could check the name somehow.

At half past eleven, the postman called. He had a package. She saw him through the pocked glass of her office window and came to the threshold to meet him, holding back the open door with one foot.

'You have to sign,' he said. He held the slim parcel out to her with both hands, an offering, and smiled at a point somewhere near her knees.

'I'll find a pen.'

Veronique stood for a moment without moving, then she turned back into her office. The door swung closed softly. The postman waited on the other side and when she came back out to him, he put the parcel gently and neatly on the seat of the chair that was pulled up by the door to her office, standing back when the short ceremony was finished and pushing his hands hard into his pockets. They both looked at the parcel for a while.

'It looks like stationery,' she said. 'The usual order.'

His reply came too quickly.

'I thought you might like to know that I've got a new job. A better job.'

He had his eyes on her face for a moment, almost smiling. She held the pen up in front of her, as though showing him something marvellous.

'I thought you might like to know,' he said again, when she didn't answer.

Veronique did not like to look at him. She felt that he had let her down somehow. She had assumed that he would always be there, bringing the post, making the air of the nursing home bristle around his unspectacular youth. She liked the way he wrapped her delivery separately in an elastic band, as if it were important, putting it straight onto her desk if he got the chance.

The postman shuffled and then he crouched down by the chair, putting a hand on the parcel, wrinkling the smooth surface of the paper wrapping.

Veronique was brisk. 'I'll not be seeing you again, in that case?' It was not what she wanted to say.

He had to look up at her, making his answer an appeal.

'I'm not moving away. I'm going to work for the town. I'm going to be in charge of post, internal and external, at the town hall.' He patted the parcel, proud.

'But you'll not be coming here.'

He nodded, as though she had said something wise. Then there was a long quiet, filled with the low buzz of office electronics and the old-fashioned hum of the nursing home, damp and thick around them. This was the moment. They both knew it.

'If you'd like, if you'd be interested, we could perhaps... bump into each other sometime,' he suggested, straightening up and stepping away from her. 'Maybe.'

'That would be nice.' Veronique heard the sharpness still in her words. Then she looked at him, the way his head was turned away, and she smiled, feeling the blush warm her through. 'Really, I'd like that,' she said, softer, as though beginning again. 'It would be nice to see you outside of work.'

'Without my uniform.'

'Yes.' She laughed and clipped the pen onto her pocket. Nothing had been signed.

'We could start on Friday. I wanted to celebrate my new job. If you'd like, we could have a meal somewhere.' His shyness folded the words one upon the other so that they came to her unready.

'That would be nice,' said Veronique. 'You'll be celebrating with your friends?'

'No. Just us. Just you and me.'

It was a relief. It settled everything.

'I'll take your phone number,' said the postman.

Veronique did very little work for the rest of the day. Something about the postman's lean uneven features disconcerted her, and when she thought of him, she thought instead of his wide palm laid flat on the parcel,

217

the skin clean and supple. She looked at herself many times in the small mirror that hung behind the door of her office, tracing what it was he might be thinking of, what it might be he had seen there. She put her fingers softly to her stinging eyes, feeling too old for the effort of romance. She could not imagine falling in love.

She did not post the letter to Bernard. It lay on her desk for several days gradually getting pushed further to the edge. Veronique knew it was there. She used it once or twice to rest her water glass on, although she was careful not to leave a ring on the envelope. Otherwise, she tried to ignore it. She did nothing to investigate Bernard's name. On Friday afternoon, her date with the postman almost upon her, she spent several hours pacing circuits of the corridor at extraordinary speed, everything a whirl of yellow carpet and dense smells. She stopped on one of these circuits to tear the envelope in half and put the pieces in the bin.

'Better off that way,' she said out loud. She was used to the raw inevitable sadness of the old. Just at that moment she could not bring herself to worry about it.

Thérèse, on her knees at the side of her bed, her hands joined in front of her, cried out that morning to her God as she tried to explain how unfamiliar the world was beginning to feel. But there was no comfort. Even God had begun to sound different to her. The unequivocally patient and consoling tone she had heard all her life at the convent seemed now to have an edge to it, something jaunty, sarcastic even. It further confused and disorientated her; she dipped her head to the counterpane and her tears came fast.

They picked Bernard up from Les Cèdres shortly after eleven. She was waiting outside the front door, stamping her feet gently to keep warm, her huge dark coat leaving nothing of her. A light snow was falling, tiny indeterminate flakes that did not settle but that, for a brief moment, made her veil glitter. When she heard the car come up the drive, she thought of Veronique. There was a lurch of disappointment when she saw it was only Corinne and Thérèse, even though she was expecting them. As soon as she was in the car, she noticed that Thérèse was wearing a new jumper, a soft grey, the kind of grey that would have been considered too resonant in the old convent days.

'It's most kind of you to take me like this,' she said politely to Corinne, who was backing uncertainly out of the closed loop in front of the entrance.

'Oh, it was Thérèse's idea,' said Corinne. 'She was missing you.'

They all liked the idea of this. It hung in the air for the rest of the day, clinging like perfume.

They did not go far. Corinne drove slowly. In the car, they hardly spoke. Once or twice, Corinne complained about the state of the road, or pointed out a turreted farmhouse or a wide barn, a landmark. Thérèse nodded in reply. She kept the map open on her knees and traced the route with her finger, though Corinne never seemed unsure about which turn to take and all the villages were well signposted.

Bernard was silent. Everything was new to her. It was as though the world had suddenly been rent open, laying bare great stretches of unfamiliar land, strange villages,

219

like her own but wretched and deformed. There were no edges to things; they kept on, as if to go for ever, taking no account of horizons, pushing the road out in front of them on and on, things shifting round every bend, unimaginable. She could not speak, even had she wanted to.

They ate lunch in a restaurant overlooking the river which ran black and slow under the winter branches. It was an uninspiring dish of flabby meat. When Corinne closed her hands over her plate and began a short grace, the other diners turned briefly to look at them and the waitress, heading their way with a basket of sliced baguette, strolled purposefully to the other side of the room until the prayer was finished. Thérèse noticed all this with alarm. She could not say the words of the grace out. Her tongue was dry and her cheeks hot. The mundane declaration of prayer, the public avowal of God, was embarrassing her. She did not know what was happening.

After lunch they headed for an abbey and parked as directed by small wooden signs. There was a printed board in the car park laying out the essential historical facts about the church and its grounds and Corinne put on her coat to stand out and read it, even though she knew the information already. Thérèse and Bernard waited in the car. The snow was faster around them now, the flakes thicker. They both watched the steady fall of it.

'They send letters on automatically,' said Bernard, suddenly. 'They send them on from the convent somehow. A letter came a few days ago – about Sister Marie. I had to sign something.'

'*You* did?' Thérèse could not help but sound scathing. 'Why you?'

'I don't know. Someone showed me where to sign. At Les Cèdres. They told me what to do. But it came from the convent, the letter. That was the address it had on it, underneath.'

'I wouldn't have thought it would have come to you. I thought the diocese dealt with everything.'

'I don't know,' said Bernard again.

'Perhaps it was a mistake,' said Thérèse.

They did not say anything more. They watched the fall of the snow and the long slide of the flakes down the windscreen. In this strange place it seemed something shared, the repetition of many winters.

'It was kind of you to think of me,' Bernard said, quietly. 'It was kind of you to bring me out.'

Thérèse did not hear. She turned her head to watch as Corinne walked across the far end of the car park, her figure blotted by the snow, and she pulled a word puzzle book from her bag. It sat unopened on her lap.

'Are they treating you well at Les Cèdres?' she asked after a pause.

'It's warm,' said Bernard, speaking up. 'The rooms are always warm.'

'God always seems to know what's best for us, don't you think, Sister? Even when we don't know ourselves.' Thérèse flipped open her book. 'Especially when we don't know ourselves.'

Bernard had not yet worked out what God had to do with Les Cèdres. She thought He might have sent her there as a trick.

'Yes, Sister,' she said.

Thérèse nodded. Corinne moved through the snow, strolling around the car park before coming back to the driver's door. She opened it and poked her head inside.

'I can see someone opening up the ticket hut,' she said. 'But it's a bit chilly. We should wait a moment or two. You'll get cold hanging around out here.'

She closed the door, not quite tightly, and left them again. Thérèse found her page in the puzzle book and tried to cross off the answers in her head. But even this felt awkward, impolite, and she closed the book again, folding her hands over it.

'We're off on holiday in a short while,' she said. 'Corinne and I. We've booked something at the coast. Nothing much, just a few nights in a small hotel. We got a special deal.' She spoke too quickly, already excusing herself. 'They call it a winter break. I'm looking forward to it. I've never had a holiday. I know the weather might not be up to much, but still…'

Her sentence hung unfinished while they both thought about the enormity of this. Bernard had never heard of a nun taking a holiday that didn't involve ministering to sick pilgrims or making a retreat. She presumed such pleasure-seeking would be sinful. She presumed someone would put a stop to it.

'Was this Corinne's idea?' was all she asked, however, her tone flat.

'No. Mine. I wanted to see the sea.' She felt she had given herself away to the old nun. 'Anyway, as I say, it's nothing much.' She wanted to change the subject. 'Do you have outings from Les Cèdres?'

'A minibus comes sometimes, some days,' said Bernard. 'I don't know what it's for.'

'Haven't you asked someone? Perhaps it goes to the market. Or around and about, you know, on outings. You should ask, Sister. You could go.'

Bernard could not bring her mind back. She had a picture in her head of Thérèse and Corinne, arm in arm, strolling along a sunlit promenade, the breeze skipping in their hair and brushing their cheeks red, Thérèse eating a coloured ice cream from a large cone, licking at the drips. The picture glowed and flickered, something taken from the television, undeniable. It made her think of the warmth of Corinne's hand closed around her own, their communion in the graveyard after Marie's funeral, and she shut her fist tight, squeezing her flaked nails deep into her palm.

Corinne hurried across to the car and opened the door again, surprising Bernard with where she was. The snow had eased, and the flap of the ticket hut was propped open.

'I think they're ready for us,' said Corinne. 'Look, there's more people coming.'

Another small car pulled down the driveway and parked at the far corner of the car park. Two elderly men got out and headed slowly for the ticket booth, one walking gingerly with a stick.

Bernard and Thérèse got out, too. They fetched their coats from the boot and muffled themselves against the cold they expected in the abbey. Bernard pretended not to notice when Thérèse offered her an arm for support so they crossed the car park separately, scuffing faint prints into the thin layer of wet snow. Corinne was already at the office, buying their tickets and talking to the young man who was serving her. He turned out also to be the guide, and less than ten minutes later he shut up the ticket booth again and came out to give them an official welcome.

Corinne kept up with the guide. She had been to the abbey many times in the past; twice she had come on pilgrimage.

'You'll like it,' she promised, as they all turned at the end of the path into the square that fronted the church. 'It's beautiful, really.'

'I remember it,' said Thérèse. 'I brought a class of girls one day on retreat. Ages ago now, of course – years. But I can't imagine it's changed.'

They waited for Bernard as they began the climb up the long flight of unevenly worn stone steps.

'It stank of varnish.'

Thérèse remembered the peace of it, even with visitors coming and going and workmen clanking tins on the hard floor. She remembered now, suddenly, the strips of red and white tape that had closed off the pews while they were refurbished, the tiny flick of them in the breeze from the door.

She shook her head. 'It was a good day. When the monks had finished talking to the girls, they all came back out here, into the square and went up the stairs again, on their knees. It's what the pilgrims used to do, apparently.'

No one laughed at the idea. The guide took it as a cue, and explained some more about the old-fashioned habits of worship. One of the men asked a question. Thérèse stood apart, looking back down the steps, remembering the face of every girl that had come with her that day, seeing them there, their knees grazed and bloody, their tights ruined, their eyes shining. Sitting afterwards on the daisied lawn in the cloisters, three of them had declared their firm intention to become nuns. None of them had fulfilled their vocation.

The guide held the heavy door for them to pass through into the church. Bernard was last, puffing with the cold and the climb, unable to understand why they had come here. The guide smiled at her and the door sprang shut with a soft clank. It was, for a moment, dark.

At one end the church was built straight into the cliff, like some kind of cave. Squat white candles were banked up against the rough-hewn wall, hundreds of them, perhaps thousands, Bernard could not be sure. This was all she saw at first, the immense glow of them, like a winter moon, and each individual blink of flame a promise of something.

She started as Corinne took her arm.

'It's better further in. Come further in, Sister,' said Corinne, tugging gently. She didn't like this part of the church, too much like the ancient dolmens and menhirs that intruded everywhere in the countryside, inexplicable and godless. 'The guide's gone up towards the altar.'

Bernard followed tentatively up the wide nave, the church opening around her, no longer a cave but something crafted, sculpted, the stones in clean neat lines and the vaulted roof glistening with colour. The soaring arches, the delicate chiselled decoration, the faces of the saints peering, grinning and glowering from above and behind, the purity of light filtering through the high windows, all this struck her with a dense physicality which made it impossible to stand. Her knees shook as she began to understand how the God who presided over this gloriously elegant temple, its massive heavenly spaces and its sheltered nooks of intense

225

prayer, could be so impatient and demanding with her poor efforts. She began to understand why He had cajoled and pushed and punished her so fiercely; how He was, finally, so disgusted and disillusioned with her weakness that He could not find it in Himself to talk to her.

She stumbled. 'I can't...' she whispered.

They came and helped her, Corinne and the guide, Thérèse just behind them and one of the men doubling back from a side chapel. She was not sure if she had fallen. It felt like falling. But they had her held up in the end, and the guide unlocked a side door so that they could take her straight through to the cloisters. They put a coat on the stone benches that ran under the arches and helped her to sit. It was gently done.

'I think you'll be fine in a minute or two, Sister,' said the guide. Visitors had been overcome with the greatness of God before. He was not surprised. 'We'll carry on through the church, the rest of us, and come back to you here. It'll give you a minute to yourself, to get your breath back.'

And they must have gone away again, back through the little door, because it was unflinchingly silent.

Bernard sat still. She felt the intense cold of the old stone even through the coat and her thick habit but she did not move. She could not be sure if time was passing. It seemed to her as if this might be eternity, in this motionless silence.

But Corinne came back to fetch her. She linked an arm through Bernard's, trying to raise her; Bernard was rooted to the seat.

'You'll be cold, Sister.'

Bernard's voice was tiny. 'Why was the convent never like this?'

Corinne thought the convent had been like this in many ways.

'So quiet,' Bernard said.

Corinne looked around. 'Perhaps it's something to do with the valley. You know, the dip of it… or, or the weather.'

'It seems so holy. The quiet here is so beautiful,' Bernard said. 'A thing from God.'

A figure in a habit moved rapidly across the far corner of the cloisters, like the dart of a shadow.

'We'll have to go soon, Sister,' said Corinne. 'They don't let you stay on, after the tour. It's only for the monks, most of the time.'

'God stopped talking to me,' said Bernard. 'It made things seem very quiet. I liked it, at first. Just at first. Then I… this is quite different.'

Corinne placed an arm on Bernard's shoulder.

'At first,' repeated Bernard, 'the quiet was a relief. Everything seemed better for it. Calmer.'

'Perhaps it was God's way of bringing you peace.'

Bernard shook her head.

'He just went away,' she said. 'It's not peace. This here – this is God's peace. This is Him not having to say anything, like He's smiling, you know – smiling so widely that He can't talk.' She looked at Corinne, and smiled too, but biting her lip until the smile faded. 'What I have is… not holy. It's like having nothing.'

Corinne rubbed her cold hands together. She did not know where to begin.

'God spoke to you, Sister? You mean when you prayed you felt something, His presence? You mean He offered you signs?'

'No,' said Bernard sadly. 'He spoke to me all the time. He told me everything.'

'But that can't be true.'

'Not any more,' said Bernard.

Corinne crouched, facing Bernard, seeing the nun's head and veil as if cut out against the dark stone behind. Bernard did not move. She let Corinne stare at her.

'Tell me again, Sister, about God, about hearing God,' pressed Corinne, her eyes fixed on Bernard's flat face. 'It could be a mistake, in the way we talk about it. I don't think God is the same for everyone.' She was alarmed by the fleeting sense that this was radical theology. 'I mean, hearing Him is probably not the same for everyone. He speaks differently to all of us, I'm sure. It could just be that.'

She wanted this to be right.

'It seems so long ago,' said Bernard.

'But what was it like?'

'Like you talking to me now, I suppose.'

'Clear, like that – and close, and personal?'

'Oh yes, very clear,' said Bernard. 'Very close.' She looked back at the crouching woman in front of her for the first time. 'Do you think it was something particular I did that made Him stop?' she asked. 'One thing? Or everything? Just Him getting tired of me?'

Corinne groaned. She slid onto one knee, balancing herself, letting her head drop.

'Oh, Sister Bernard,' she said quietly.

Bernard did not answer. She watched a robin flit along the edge of the cloister wall, tripping through the pillared stripes of light and dark. It came up close to them before flying off.

'I'm sorry, Sister – about the fuss at Armistice.' Corinne looked up as she spoke, but her eyes would not settle on Bernard's face. 'About making you go to the service like that. I really am. I'm sorry. About Les Cèdres, too… about everything.'

She shook her head, trying to clear the confusion. Everything she had thought about Bernard was muddled. She looked finally at the foolish face of the old nun, its wrinkles expressionless, and she wondered whether she had made a mistake, after all.

'Perhaps it's just age,' she said, doubting.

Bernard was not listening. She was seeing again the splendour of the abbey church. Over and over, all her life, she had been surrounded by the God of harvests, of fields meshed with hedges, of the birth and sickness and fear and death of small people, the God of everyday deeds. What she saw now was the huge, silent, unhuman proof of His towering, timeless divinity.

'The quiet here is not like my quiet,' she said, making it final.

'No, Sister.' Corinne felt she had no choice but to agree. She stood up stiffly and pulled away, looking out across the cloisters. She realized that they did not know each other.

'We have to go out through the garden,' said Corinne. 'And double back to the car.'

Bernard knew that if she had come here sooner, her life would have been different. It was too late now and she pulled herself from the cold stone, defeated.

'It's such a beautiful church,' she said.

*

On the third day after the trip, Bernard still had not taken her place at any meal except breakfast where she had steadfastly refused everything except one portion of bread, taken with a small cup of coffee. The staff felt obliged to intervene.

'I'm on a diet,' Bernard explained to the duty matron. Sitting in the bright office, she was confused for a moment. It could have been the Mother Superior's study. It could have been a warmer, brighter day with the sun edging round the ill-fitting shutters and the scrape of crickets in the grass outside.

'At your age,' explained the duty matron patiently, 'it is generally thought that dieting is not necessary. In fact, not healthy. Did you know that, Sister Bernard?'

Bernard did not reply.

'Is there any particular reason why you wanted to diet?' She tried to skim read the small folder of Bernard's notes which was open on her desk. There was nothing much there, a few matter-of-fact lines reporting Bernard's arrival and blood pressure levels, and a note about her tendency to wander, especially at night. There was no medical history.

'I don't want to eat too much.'

'You're hardly eating anything at all, Sister.'

'The Lord ate nothing for forty days and forty nights,' pointed out Bernard.

'He was not ninety-three.'

Bernard ignored this. 'It clears the mind,' she explained. 'Jesus went into the desert to find God. To be alone with God. And he fasted.' Bernard knew this for sure because she had checked it a few days previously in her Bible.

'I hope you're not comparing Les Cèdres to the desert!'

said the duty matron without smiling, only her tone scrubbed bright.

Bernard said nothing.

The duty matron sighed.

'Well then, how about we make a deal?' she said. 'How about we work out a diet sheet for you, so that you can diet and we can be reassured that you're getting all the nutritional values you need?'

Bernard wanted to try living on bread and coffee. When she had mastered this she would fast entirely. That way God would come back to her. She shrugged.

'OK then,' said the duty matron, undeterred. 'I'll speak to someone and get back to you. In the meantime, I think you should come to every meal. Just eat what you can. The food's very good, you know.'

Later that evening, Bernard was hungry. She offered her hunger up to God, who accepted it without comment. At supper she sat at her usual place, silently, and prayed while those around her ate. When the fruit tray was served, she was tempted by a ripe, red pear. She even took it off the tray and held it for a moment, warm, in her hand. A tiny drop of juice, thick with sugar, glinted in the dip where the stem sank into the fruit.

'A beauty, that,' said the man next to her.

'A temptation from the devil,' said Bernard, putting the pear on the floor and crushing it as best she could beneath her shoe. The man blinked and looked away, beginning to peel his apple slowly.

The next day, Bernard felt weak. Things about her were hazy and unbalanced, they would not stay still. But it felt as though sin was draining from her, leaching away, and she was glad. It was also Saturday, the day she had marked down for Veronique's visit. Now her granddaughter would come. As the early light sank through Bernard's window and the cars started outside, taking the night staff home, Bernard tidied her room, wiping round with wet tissue; she brushed every crease of her old habit with care. She wanted to be ready.

But Veronique was lying in bed with her left arm trapped uncomfortably beneath the stomach of the postman, thinking of their walk together the evening before under the chilled unerring stars, the grip of their gloved hands and their kiss by the freezing river.

Her tears came undemonstratively, because she could not explain them to the postman, and she concentrated on tracing the twining patterns in her curtains, seeing, for the first time, how the print was lined up incorrectly at one edge. When the postman stirred, she looked across at him, wiping her arm against her eyes to smudge the signs of her weeping. The squashed particularity of his face seemed a comfort to her, and she leant across to stroke his cheek. Sleepily he took hold of her and rolled her towards him, pulling her close, and they lay together for a long time, waking to each other, before he let the temptation of her overwhelm him. They giggled during sex, unsure of how else to be together. Veronique never dreamt it was the kind of loving that would leave her pregnant.

Bernard sat on the edge of her bed, trying not to crease the cover. She prayed for Veronique. She tried every prayer she knew several times. She spent a long time in conversation with her own Saint Bernard who beamed at her a toothless smile. She called on the intervention of the Virgin. She even, for good measure, recited in a quiet steady monotone the words of the Mass, as far as she could remember them. She took a pin from a fold in the hem of her handkerchief and pushed it hard many times into the scarred pad at the tip of her thumb, sucking the blood when it came so that it would not smudge on any of her clothes. By the time she had finished her devotions, the morning was well advanced and someone was knocking hard on her door, trying to rouse her.

After several fruitless knocks the young staff nurse entered. Bernard had never seen him before.

'Are you all right, Sister? We thought it might be time for you to be up and about,' he said gently.

Bernard turned to look at him. The room swayed unsteadily. She jammed her hands hard on the bed and peered. He was slender, but less drawn than most of the young people who scuttled about the corridors.

'Are you all right?' he asked again.

'I'm praying.'

'I see. Would you like to come downstairs and pray? You could use the chapel.'

He did not wait for an answer, but stepped forwards and took Bernard by the arm. She thought he was going to lift her right up. She yelped.

'Don't worry.' He was laughing. 'I'm just giving you a hand. I won't hurt you.' He stepped back. The old nun was dishevelled and slightly bloody, her habit skewed and her veil grubby. He smiled at her. 'Look, how about I run some water for you, and you can have a wash and sort yourself out and I'll come back in a few minutes to check you're OK?'

'I can do it all myself,' said Bernard.

'Of course you can. Think of it as a Saturday treat.'

Less than ten minutes later, the knocking was repeated. The young man came in as Bernard began to invite him. She had washed her face and hands and straightened her clothes. She was sitting again on the edge of the bed.

'I feel a bit dizzy,' she said.

'They tell me you've not been eating much.'

'I've been praying,' said Bernard.

'So you say. But you can pray and eat, you know.'

'Not really. Not for this kind of prayer.'

'Are you sure?' The nurse tidied the towel from the floor so she would not trip.

'It wouldn't be the same.' Bernard could not begin to explain everything.

'Would you like some breakfast?'

'What time is it?' asked Bernard.

'Time for lunch.'

The nurse came and sat on the bed next to her. Then he reached across and took one of the hands that were folded in her lap.

'What's this?' he said, unpeeling her fingers.

Bernard did not know what he meant.

'Sister?' He held something up to her face, shrunken and brown.

'Oh,' she said.

'What have you been... is it...?' He peered more closely at the parched string but could not make anything of it. 'You've got yourself a bit of old rope or something,' he said. 'We'd better dispose of it, I think. It doesn't look, you know... in much of a good state. If you want something to

234

hold, for comfort, we can find you something, I'm sure.' He looked around. 'Here,' he said, giving her something from the bedside table in exchange. 'Here's your rosary. That'll be better.'

Bernard did not see where he put the old umbilical cord. But she did not take the rosary from him, letting it fall beside her on the cover. It was not what she wanted. He took her hand again. She thought he would want to check her pulse, or perhaps examine her nails or the warts that crawled down the side of her middle finger. But he just held her hand. She liked the warmth of it and would have kept him there if she could.

The staff nurse held Bernard's hand for a few minutes and afterwards was brisk again.

'You need to have some breakfast. As a favour – for me,' he said. 'Please have something. I'll bring you something here. You needn't come down.'

Bernard was years away and only half-heard what he said. He wanted her to eat, she knew that. But her fast was bringing her closer to God, eliding the past, burnishing her memories until their colours sang, making them exhilaratingly real. She was trembling at the edge of the desert, believing, her trepidation mingled with hope, the expanse before her stretching away beyond sight. There was a journey ahead of her, a trial. But once she had crossed the wastelands, God would be on the other side waiting for her, speaking to her.

She agreed to a croissant and a peeled orange. She ate neither. The staff nurse brought them to her on a tray nicely dressed with a folded napkin. She smiled at him and promised to eat. Then, when he had left, she unfolded the napkin and replaced it untidily, crumbled the croissant to create crumbs on the tray and, for good measure, crushed out a small puddle of juice from the orange. Then she took the sludge that remained, barely edible now anyway, and put it carefully under the bed, washed her hands and placed the tray on the floor by the door.

'Thank you, Sister,' said the staff nurse when he came to take it away.

'It was very good,' lied Bernard, because she liked him.

'Perhaps later you will join the others for supper?'

'Perhaps.'

'And, Sister,' he said as he turned with the tray before moving on down the corridor, 'pray for me.'

If she had had time, Bernard would have liked to.


The night before their holiday, Thérèse and Corinne ate early to leave themselves time to finish packing. As they were washing their plates after supper, Corinne heard the telephone ring. She went into the small square hallway to speak. Thérèse guessed it might be a call, but not having heard the ring, wanted to make sure. She strained to see around the kitchen door and, once satisfied, went back to the task of removing dried rice from the bottom of the pan. Corinne came back with a pink spot in the centre of each cheek.

'It was Les Cèdres. They rang to say that Sister Bernard isn't very well,' she said, picking up a tea towel from the rail and making sure she spoke clearly.

'Why have they rung *us*?'

'I'd given them my name, and yours. Our details here. In case of problems. I didn't think it right that she had nobody,' said Corinne.

Thérèse scrubbed hard at the pan.

'What did they say, exactly?'

'Not a great deal. Just that she's not well. She's not been eating, apparently, and... well, they said she was depressed,' said Corinne, still speaking up.

'Not really sick, then?'

'I don't know. You can never tell on the phone.'

'But they said we should visit?' asked Thérèse.

'Yes, they said we should.'

Thérèse poured away the washing-up water and wiped the kitchen surfaces. She stacked the clean dishes on their shelves. She swept the floor meticulously and tied the neck of the bin bag in a neat double knot. But she could not calm the fear of going to Les Cèdres and seeing Bernard there, a judgment. In the end something had to be said.

'If we call in the morning, on the way, it'll not be a delay. It'll be all right. We'll still be at the hotel before dark, in time for supper.'

She wiped her wet hands.

'I know,' said Corinne. 'That's what I thought.'

'It seems odd though, when I should have been there anyway, looking after her.' Thérèse's voice trailed away.

She thought Corinne would contradict her somehow, as a comfort, but her friend simply nodded slowly, as though the proof of something had finally been given.

'She told me that she could hear God, speaking to her,' said Corinne. 'At the abbey – she said it plainly, as though it was any old thing. She wasn't pretending or boasting.

It was just, you know – a fact.' She looked for a moment at Thérèse but she could not keep her gaze steady.

'Do you think she might be holy?' Corinne said.

'Holy?'

'Yes. You know – blessed.'

'She's a nun. She's…' Suddenly Thérèse's voice glittered with spite. 'I said, didn't I? I said she was good. I told you that. You're the one who dragged her into the past – you're the one who raked up all that stuff, who had her there in the village, like it was some kind of trial.'

'I'm sorry about that, I really am,' said Corinne. 'It was a mistake.' She ran her fingers down her throat, stroking at the thick contours of skin there. 'You don't think, though, do you, that she does hear God? Did anyone ever mention it – before – at the convent? I can't believe… you don't think she really does, do you – not really?'

Thérèse did not quite turn to her friend. 'No,' she said. 'I don't think she's particularly special – not like that.'

'It's funny though, isn't it? You can't be sure. You can never know. I shouldn't have – well, the war thing, that seemed clear. And it seemed like everyone knew.'

'May God forgive you,' said Thérèse, the lightness of it bitter.

She hung the tea towel to dry and turned out the light.

When they arrived at Les Cèdres the following morning, they were asked to wait. They took one of the low bench seats in the entrance hall. The dry heat pressed around them and the drum of some kind of equipment rumbled into Thérèse's deafness.

'I couldn't have come, could I, to a place like this? I couldn't have suffered it,' she said.

Corinne shook her head, but did not reply. 'Do you think we should tell Bernard about her granddaughter?' she asked instead. 'Do you think she'd like to know?'

'I'll think about it,' said Thérèse. 'Perhaps she wouldn't want to know – perhaps not at the moment. It might be too much for her. We can tell her when she recovers.'

'But what if she doesn't?'

The nurse in charge, a warm, round woman with a great deal of hair, appeared from outside, tapping her hands lightly together to warm them. She sat down next to them and talked without referring to notes.

'Sister Bernard is quite poorly. We had the doctor out last night before we called you and he's coming back this evening. It's hard to be sure what it might be at this stage. There's general weakness, certainly, and she seems low. We've had some trouble getting her to eat. But he seems to think there's probably something else, something more, well, medical. He's going to do some tests.'

'She's an old woman,' said Thérèse.

'That of course makes a difference. It can be hard, at her age, to have much resistance to things.'

'Is she dying?' asked Thérèse.

'Is she in bed?' asked Corinne almost simultaneously, allowing the nurse to ignore Thérèse's more difficult question.

'We've got her up and about just now. We thought it best. But we'll have to see how it goes. As I said, she's weak,' said the nurse. 'I understand that you are also sisters, from her convent.'

239

'I am,' said Thérèse. 'And this is my friend, a lay friend. We've lived together since the convent closed. Sister Bernard has no one, no family.'

The nurse nodded a series of small nods.

'Can I ask how she was before the move? Did she seem well?'

Thérèse thought of Bernard's incessant work on small tasks.

'She was always energetic, always busy,' she said. 'I'm sure she was well enough, for her age.'

'Perhaps that's what she misses,' suggested Corinne. 'Being busy.'

'There's always a period of transition,' admitted the nurse. 'But usually, by now, things are beginning to settle down. She never complained of any pain? She never took any pills?'

Thérèse could be sure about that. 'Never.'

'She never got bad headaches that you know of? Never struggled with her breathing? It will be helpful if I can give the doctor some information. He seemed to think there might have been a long-term condition of some kind.'

'She was always just normal,' said Thérèse, knowing how inadequate this sounded. 'She never seemed ill.'

'Nuns don't complain much, you know,' chipped in Corinne, smiling.

The nurse smiled back.

'What about depression? She's never been treated for depression?'

Surely Thérèse would have heard. 'I don't think so,' she said. 'Would I have known?'

'Well, no, not necessarily. I just wondered. It usually shows up, one way or another. It can be physical as well as

240

mental. I thought you might have noticed something. But the symptoms can be confusing.'

'I didn't know her that well,' said Thérèse, and was sorry, immediately, that she had admitted this.

The nurse stood up.

'Well, if you think of anything, you could let me know. Any little thing might be helpful. Sister Bernard's not really talking to us. We can't discover much about her past, her medical past.'

'I'll ask her now, if you like, when I see her. I can ask if she remembers anything,' said Thérèse.

'You can try. She's in the chapel. Go down the corridor and it's right at the end, facing the garden.'

'Thank you. I visited once before. I remember it being a lovely chapel.'

'It's very well used,' said the nurse. She got up to go. 'I'll talk to you later, perhaps,' she said.

Corinne leant back against the wall and looked at Thérèse. 'She'll be better if it's only you. She'll be more comfortable. She'll talk more,' she said. 'I'll wait.'

'No, it's all right. Come with me.'

Corinne picked a magazine at random from the small pile scattered across the table.

'I don't think I can,' she said.

Thérèse did not press it. She moved away. The corridor was darker and narrower than she remembered, the small circles of the floor tiles more insistent. The air was too thick, the sticky loneliness too palpable. She walked slowly, as if nothing else were possible.

The chapel door was made of glass, coloured at the top and edges but with a clear panel in the middle. Thérèse looked through it for a long time, watching Bernard's veiled head, waiting for some movement which might suggest a good moment to disturb her. But the head was still. Thérèse looked back the way she had come, imagining Corinne there, waiting for her, their holiday almost begun, and she took a couple of steps away from the chapel before she closed her eyes, offering a desperate prayer that seemed to swirl back to her on the dense rest home air. When she opened her eyes, she still was not ready but she pushed the chapel door as quietly as she could, and stepped into the invitation of lilac light.

She genuflected quickly at the back of the short aisle and moved up to Bernard's side, where she stood with one hand on the end of the pew. She hoped Bernard would sense her there and look towards her. But Bernard continued to look straight ahead. Thérèse could see her lips moving in prayer. Ignoring the nag of impatience and not wanting to interrupt, she sat down directly across the aisle and waited.

For a few minutes Thérèse attempted to pray. She bent her head in her hands and tried not to think about Bernard. But she was strangely distracted by the stillness of the head alongside her. She closed her eyes, meaning to concentrate, but her thoughts were heavy with regret; she saw in glimpses, unwilling, the night walk down the unlit corridor that had ended in Bernard's cell and the blood radiant there. She recited the Lord's Prayer twice. Its familiar rhythms helped calm her. She rested her forehead gently in her hands.

Then she heard Bernard cry out. Echoing from the concave wall behind the altar, the sound was clear, hollow, returning stronger. Even in her deafness, Thérèse heard it plainly and started. She opened her eyes, expecting something to have happened. She looked over her shoulder for other people, intruders even. She could feel her heart flicker. But everything was still. Bernard was kneeling, her eyes fixed on the altar, and the rest of the chapel was empty.

Before Thérèse had time to say anything or to reach across the aisle to Bernard, even before the reverberations of the first cry had quite died away into the soft carpet and long curtains, there came another, and then, quickly, another and another. They poured out of Bernard as though out of a much larger and younger woman. They had nothing of the frailty of age about them. They echoed around the altar, not now as single cries, not involuntary yelps of pain or triumph, but as a conversation held at full volume, a slanging match, a full-blown row. Bernard was shouting at God.

She was gripping hard at the pew in front of her, and her face was knotted by each cry, but otherwise she hardly moved. All her energy was in her voice. Thérèse found it difficult to make out what was being said. The volume and tone wavered. Her damaged hearing caught sometimes single words, sometimes parts of phrases slung at the altar, sometimes only the shell of sounds. In between there were short silences, stuffed full of Bernard's anger. It was these which shocked Thérèse most.

The noise seemed everywhere. Thérèse could not believe that all the staff had not been brought running, that the lavender glass in the windows had not shattered, the roof come tumbling down to bury them all. Bernard got louder, shrieking her fury and despair, stony-faced and dry-eyed, her gaze fixed on the crucifix above the altar. Thérèse held back; she did not know how she could begin to interrupt. She was no part of this. All she could do was watch as Bernard yelled, hearing in her head the reassurance she would give when she had the chance, the beautiful texts that bore the timeless comfort of God, how He had formed Bernard in the warmth of her mother's womb, chosen her as a child, called her with joy to be His servant.

Thérèse felt the slide of tears. Her grip, too, was tight on the pew now, and she dipped her head away from Bernard. The flurry of verses had faltered to an end; she could not think of any more. And they were not enough. As Bernard's rage began to subside, her voice growling, the words coming wearily, Thérèse knew that she could find nothing to say to the old nun. The passion she had seen there in the chapel, hurled at the altar with such rage, was unassailable. It was something sublime; something she could not understand and could barely imagine. Thérèse remembered, as she always would, the intimidating grandeur of it, and knew that anything she said to Bernard was too slight and equivocal. She had never known God as Bernard must know Him; she had never felt Him so real. She pushed herself up from the pew and turned to leave.

Bernard's head swayed and her chin dropped. Thérèse's sudden movement finally distracted her and she looked across, unsurprised and unquestioning. Thérèse, not quite out of her pew, begrudged Bernard the exhaustion she saw on her face and could only go on as if nothing unusual had happened.

'We're off on our holiday, Corinne and I,' she said. 'We just wanted to call by on our way.'

Bernard nodded.

'Are you well, Sister?'

'They say I'm not,' said Bernard. 'But I feel well enough.'

'But they're worried?'

'They sent the doctor.'

'What did he say?'

'Nothing,' said Bernard.

Thérèse was supposed to ask about symptoms and report back, she knew that. But it seemed unimportant now. The old nun had prevailed. Thérèse had seen from her how to call out to God, how to battle with Him, flaunting the rawness of need. She could hardly breathe at the thought of it. What she had was frail beside it, a life of whispered prayer, inconspicuous and peaceable, a compromise.

'How do you feel, though, in yourself, Sister?' she said, the words tight and flat.

'You mean am I miserable? They say I am. They say I'm depressed.' Bernard pulled herself from her knees and sat on the pew.

Thérèse breathed long and low, trying to still the way her thoughts rushed.

'Yes, Sister,' was all she said at first.

Bernard dropped her head. 'He has forsaken me,' she said, matter-of-factly.

It was all confusion, a clamour of disappointment and longing. Thérèse wanted to hug Bernard, and to shake her, to cling to her in some way, letting the tremors of those echoed cries vibrate through her, too. But she stood back.

'You're very close to God, Sister, I'm sure,' she said.

Bernard looked hard at her deaf friend. She noticed that Thérèse's lipstick was slightly smudged above her top lip, that she was wearing an elegantly buttoned blue coat and that she was smiling too benignly, as if they were strangers. But she could not tell whether or not she was lying.

'How can you be sure?'

Thérèse drew her hands together, as if to begin a prayer. 'It's just something you have…' There was no way of explaining it. 'You have the look of it, I suppose,' she said. 'Of someone blessed.'

To both of them, this was ridiculous. Bernard got up unsteadily, moving out into the aisle where she genuflected uncomfortably, with the pop of cracking bones. Slowly they walked together back towards the glass door; Thérèse felt so much that she had failed.

'Did you know you have a granddaughter, a woman who lives here in town, the young woman who came that one afternoon when we were moving and took Sister Marie's bag away to the nursing home?'

It came out in a rush, breathless, a solution to something, but Bernard did not pause, nor turn to look at Thérèse.

'Yes, I know,' she said.

Thérèse had not expected this. She didn't believe it.

'I thought it might be a comfort to you to have some family, to know of someone. I thought if you were unwell, perhaps you would like us to let her know. Perhaps she could come here and visit you. No one need know who she is. She could be a friend. She could come with me – as a friend.'

'I'm not unwell,' said Bernard. 'I'm seeing the doctor again tonight they say, and I shall tell him not to come again after that.'

She pulled open the glass door and they passed out into the corridor.

'And anyway,' she said, 'she's due to visit in a day or two. I'd expected her before now. I've been waiting.'

Thérèse sighed. 'Well, you should think about, you know, having someone close to you. Since I didn't come with you; since I'm not here.'

Bernard was too dazed to hear the apology. 'She's coming – I'm expecting her soon.'

Thérèse bent and kissed Bernard lightly. 'God bless you, Sister,' she said quietly, not hearing her own words.

As she walked away towards the entrance hall, she saw Corinne sitting idly swinging her feet by the door and it came back to her, their journey together and the idea of the hotel, the promise of the sea. But her excitement was dented. She felt a craving to stay, to sit with Bernard in the lavendered chapel and learn how to pray with her, to rest there. She felt that the past might be retrievable somehow, unspoilt. She stopped for a moment, almost turned. But Corinne looked up. She waved, hardly smiling. Thérèse lifted one hand to signal back and went on.

Bernard left the chapel the other way to return to her room. Her throat was strained and chafed, prickling sore. She put her hand to it, surprised. She could not think how it could have happened. She thought it might be some kind of punishment, but without God to tell her, she did not know.

*

They reached the coast about an hour after dark. They had kept the heater on in the car all the way and were startled by the cold when they stepped out into the quiet street behind the park. Thérèse was immediately disappointed.

'I can't smell it,' she said.

Corinne, who was trying to take their bags out of the boot with one hand while rewinding her scarf closer to her neck with the other, was momentarily puzzled.

'You can't smell what?'

'The sea, of course. I can't smell the sea.'

All Thérèse could smell was greasy drains and her own sweat, the hot metal of the car exhaling into the dark. Somewhere, perhaps, a hint of pine but she could not be sure if this was natural.

'Perhaps the tide's out,' suggested Corinne reasonably. 'And there's no wind. That might make a difference.'

She was tired with driving and wanted to go inside.

'Perhaps there's no smell, after all,' said Thérèse.

Corinne ignored this. She finished with the bags and they made the short walk along back streets to the hotel. It was neat and clean and the proprietor friendly as he showed them up the narrow stairs to their room. The curtains were still open and Thérèse threw her bag on the bed and went to look out. Mostly she could see streetlights, house roofs and parked cars. Here and there were the darker masses of trees or the bright lights of unshuttered windows. There was a deep blackness beyond that could have been the sea.

'What can you see?' asked Corinne.

'Nothing much.'

Corinne came alongside her and they both stood for several minutes looking out at the strange-familiar view.

'Dinner?' asked Corinne.

'I think so. Just let me freshen up.'

They both had a glass of wine before their meal, to celebrate the start of their holiday, and another when the main course was served. The hotel dining room had been divided in half for the quieter winter season and one part of it closed off with heavy curtains. Thérèse and Corinne were given a table between the curtains and a large palm. The waitress came and lit a small candle in a jar. A sprinkling of Christmas lights sparkled across the doorway to the adjacent bar and a single foil snowflake hung orange from the lampshade over the homemade desserts. There was something fragile and exotic about it.

They were both hungry. They ate energetically and quietly. The food was good.

'I bet,' said Corinne, as they were coming to the end of their main course, 'I bet that a year ago, even half a year ago, you would never have thought you would be here, doing this, with me. You see, getting thrown out of the convent was a good thing.'

'It's certainly changed things.'

'God knows best,' said Corinne.

There was a pause.

'The trouble is,' said Thérèse, as she mopped up the last of her sauce with bread, 'I don't feel quite like a nun any more.'

Corinne smiled. She looked at the almost glamorous woman across the table from her. Thérèse's cardigan, though discreet, was not any shade of grey.

'You don't look like a nun, either. Does that matter?'

Thérèse was beginning to think it might. It might all be part of the same thing.

'I think so,' she said.

'It's only nerves,' said Corinne, 'your first holiday. You'll be fine. Tomorrow we'll walk along the seafront before breakfast and you'll be fine. You're just on holiday. It doesn't change who you are. Not for long, anyway.'

She pushed her empty plate away from the edge of the table and sat back.

'My first holiday without my parents was a weekend's fishing with a boyfriend I had when I was nineteen. He was rich. Nobody had holidays then. Certainly not in hotels. I thought it was the most thrilling thing. I thought I was in love. Then after half a day I thought I'd die of boredom. Sitting there with him in the cold while he fished, the worms and the maggots, everything damp. I hated the way he skewed the hook out of the fishes' mouths, and the way they lay there, gasping, as though they wanted to say something.' She shivered. 'He lost his glamour.'

Thérèse could not respond as she was supposed to.

'It's not only the holiday,' she said. 'I don't feel like a nun now anywhere, not at home with you, not here, not in church even. It doesn't matter whether I wear my veil or not. I say my prayers, I follow the offices, I make the penance I've always made. But I feel different.'

She took a sip of wine, and another quickly after it, almost draining her glass.

'You're not unhappy?' asked Corinne as quietly as she could. She was aware that Thérèse's deafness was making their discussion louder than either of them might have liked. She thought the other diners might be listening.

'It's funny,' said Thérèse. 'I was so excited at the thought of moving. I've enjoyed so much being with you. It's been such a relief to spend my own money after all these years.'

To both of them this sounded like an apology.

The waitress came and took their plates. They turned down the offer of cheese and chose dessert. Thérèse's chocolate mousse was dark and rich, worth a week of prayer.

'I miss my God,' she said suddenly when she had cleaned the bowl.

'He didn't come with you from the convent?'

'I don't think He did. Not really.'

'That's not what you'd expect,' said Corinne.

'No.'

Thérèse struggled to fold her napkin precisely. They ordered coffee.

'Perhaps you should give Him time. It's only been a few weeks,' said Corinne.

'There is no time with God,' said Thérèse, not smiling.

'But give yourself time. Breathing space. To find Him again.' Corinne leant forwards. 'Can't you feel Him at all?'

The waitress brought their coffee hesitantly. She knew she had interrupted.

'I don't know. I'm not sure any more. I always used to be sure.'

They both concentrated on stirring sugar slowly into their coffee.

'Would you go back? If you could? If they hadn't closed it?' asked Corinne.

There was the slightest of pauses.

'I think I would.'

Corinne had been rejected many times for many reasons. She recognized the lump stuck in her chest as something other than the crisp heat of the coffee. Thérèse realized for the first time that she would not die as happily as she had always supposed. There was nothing either of them could say.

'We'll take a walk in the morning, before breakfast, and find the smell of the sea,' said Corinne.

'I'd like that. If there is one. Perhaps we've come all this way for nothing.'

They both laughed. The waitress smiled at them broadly as they left the dining room.

Corinne yawned as they made their way up the stairs to the first floor. Unused to sharing a bedroom, they were unexpectedly embarrassed when they came to undress. In the end, Thérèse took her nightclothes with her into the bathroom and changed there. When she came back into the room Corinne was already in bed.

'I think I'm going to start collecting again,' she said, folding her clothes onto a chair. 'If you don't mind – it'll only be in my own room. I'm going to... I don't know – make it religious somehow, this time. Little statues and things – the stuff that they sell at the back of cathedrals. I can make it a project.'

Corinne pulled the bed clothes closer.

'I'll never have it like it was before,' Thérèse went on. 'I don't have time. But... but it'll be something, won't it?'

'It'll be a dust trap,' said Corinne.

'I can make it something – an act of praise.'

They prayed together, out loud, so that Thérèse could hear clearly, reciting at first the familiar lines of old prayers and then each focussing on their special intentions. They both thanked God for His wonderful kindness in granting them this special holiday together. They both praised Him for the beauties of the natural world they had seen on their journey. They both offered prayers for those less fortunate than themselves. Thérèse asked God to look kindly on Sister Bernard in her time of need and sorrow. Corinne remembered more generally those who consecrated their lives to the service of the Church. They did not pray for themselves because they did not know how to.

They agreed that they were weary enough to turn the light out immediately. Despite the strangeness of the room and the occasional thud of doors along the corridor, Corinne went to sleep almost straight away. Thérèse did not sleep. She turned to the window where she could see the light from the street clearly through the thin curtains. She thought about seeing and smelling the sea the next day. It didn't quite excite her. If it was an expression of God, after all, it was a God she did not recognize, too immense and unrestrained, too foreign. There was no reason to have come this far.

She could taste the chocolate mousse in the back of her throat as it repeated in her digestion, its bitterness metallic now and cloying. She listened to the dull buzz in her head, the distinctive hum of her deafness, familiar and comforting, sacred. She closed her eyes to stop the tears.

# Eleven

Several hours after the commandant had raped her, Bernard was found by the henhouse, weeping, her hands thrust through the sharp wire. Her habit was ripped and her veil missing and there were great gashes of blood in profane places. Her violent shaking and blank expression alarmed the nuns; Mother Catherine ordered them to wash her from the butt that they kept outside for the animals, but neither the shock of the cold water nor the chafe of their stiff brushes succeeded in bringing her round.

They found her a new habit, unshapely and worn, and she was sent to the town surgery with a sealed envelope. The doctor was thoroughly disgusted by what he read there, and carried out his examination through a series of questions rather than touch the defiled body of the damned. He quickly concluded that although the rape had certainly occurred, no major injury had resulted. Bernard relayed his diagnosis faithfully to the convent and was sent immediately back to work. For some time afterwards, she was spoken to only during prayer.

As soon as she could, she went in search of the soldier. She left chores undone; all around her there were things unwashed, undug, unpeeled, unclean. There were prayers unsaid. It did not seem to matter. Instead, Bernard walked to the church and back. She went slowly, ignoring her pains, the summer morning stretched over the cut fields and the dry stubble like short flames in the early light. She took as long as she dared to cross the square, keeping away from the shadows, making herself visible. She did not flinch when the villagers looked at her. She loitered by the well, standing aside from the line of buckets, and she paused on the flattened ground in front of each of the small shops. At one point she saw a group of soldiers emerging from one of the houses and she set off towards them quickly; they glanced at her and stopped, stiffening themselves into a line, a barricade. But she saw that he was not there, among them, and she turned away.

When she had finished the route, and there was still no sign of him, she went back again, retracing her steps. She did this many times, the day passing too quickly, as if it barely existed. As dusk approached, she stood by the open convent gates, where anyone could see her, looking down the hill to the road. The ache of her injuries was insistent and sharp, but she barely noticed it. She thought only about the soldier. Twice she pulled her sack from under the hedge, pressed at it and put it back, ready. But mostly she was still, waiting.

He did not come. God explained that she was repellent to the soldier now, soiled and damaged and foul. He laughed at her. He told her that she would be abandoned as she deserved. But she could not believe this. It did not seem right.

After almost a week, Mother Catherine sent for her. It was late; evening prayer was already finished and the nuns were preparing for bed, queuing quietly at the row of stone basins in the bathroom. There were no mirrors, and Bernard, staring at the wall above the dipped head of the nun in front, did not notice anyone behind her until she was touched briefly on the shoulder. When she turned it was Sister Assumpta, beckoning. Bernard did not move. Sister Assumpta screwed her face into some kind of sign that Bernard did not recognize, and beckoned again. Just as the basin became free, Bernard followed.

'Mother Catherine wants to speak to you, Sister, in her study,' said Sister Assumpta, so much under her breath that Bernard was not sure for a moment what she had heard. For a few steps Sister Assumpta hurried ahead, but then she turned abruptly into her cell and by the time Bernard had reached the top of the stairs, she was alone.

The study was bright with strip lights, the heat of the day trapped inside it. Mother Catherine was seated carefully behind her desk, the Sacred Heart impressive to one side of her. Uneasy reflections pulsed across the raised heart, making it glow, alive and fleshy. Bernard paused at the threshold, thinking she could hear its solemn beat in the convent's curdled quiet, and even when Mother Catherine looked up, she did not enter.

'Come in, Sister, quickly. And close the door,' said Mother Catherine impatiently. 'Quickly.'

Her tone made Bernard look behind her, but there was only the empty corridor. She went into the study. Her thick misery did not allow for anything else. She stood in the middle of the floor and looked at her Mother Superior with tired eyes. God pointed out that she still had her wash flannel in one hand, and she held this out limply as though it might explain something.

Mother Catherine shook her head.

'No, Sister,' she said. 'Put it away.'

Bernard could not think what to do with it, and let her arm drop loosely by her side. Mother Catherine shook her head again but her voice was flat and steady, without irritation.

'We want you to help us, Sister,' she said, leaning forwards across the desk. 'We have something we want you to do. A small thing.'

She waited, but Bernard just looked at her, not moving. The pulse of the Sacred Heart had faded with a change in the light; it was no longer a distraction.

'Yes, Sister. Well. Well, you see...' Mother Catherine stopped herself and began again, more firmly and clearly, placing her palms flat on the desk. 'I have been watching you, Sister. I have been watching many of my sisters. It is a time for vigilance. We cannot be sure of those around us. Even our neighbours, our friends – even those here, in this holy community – we cannot be sure. It is our duty, in these troubled times, to do what we can to maintain order and authority, to keep things under control, to watch.' Mother Catherine paused and leant back. 'You agree, don't you, Sister?'

Bernard nodded, guessing this was expected of her.

257

'Yes. Good. So I thought. So I thought.'

Mother Catherine sat back now and looked hard at Bernard. Bernard looked back, undisturbed. God chattered, unremarkably. And for a moment Mother Catherine frowned, confused, as though something she saw in her young nun was unexpected. Then she smiled, and began again.

'There has been some... discontent,' she said. 'So I hear. Some discontent about events that happened recently in the village. There are rumours.' Her voice was suddenly sharp. 'That cannot be. That will not do, Sister. You understand?'

Bernard caught her tone, and assumed she was in trouble. She dropped her head.

'I need our situation here to be correct. Unimpeachable. It's most important that for us to be here – to do God's work here – we are... respected – righteous. I need you to help, Sister.'

Mother Catherine paused for a moment. Then she pushed back her heavy chair and came around the desk to where Bernard was standing. Bernard raised her head, and the Mother Superior put one arm gently across her shoulder.

'You will go to confession tomorrow, Sister,' she said. 'In the village.'

'Father comes here, to the convent, to hear confession,' said Bernard simply, knowing how it had always been.

'This time you will go to the village, Sister. You will join the people in the church and Father Raymond will hear your confession there. That will be better. You know where the confessionals are, Sister?'

Bernard nodded.

'Good. Then you will be fine. The important thing is that you confess what you have done, Sister.'

'With the soldier?'

Mother Catherine took her arm from Bernard's shoulder and stepped back slightly.

'Well yes, Sister, with the soldier. Of course. Everything. Everything about that. But particularly how you betrayed Sister Jean with the soldier. Particularly how you gave away secrets to the soldier.'

Bernard was hardly listening. 'What's happened to him, Mother?' she said. 'I can't find him.'

She felt Mother Catherine start, and she watched her walk away towards the bookshelves that lined the far wall.

'You can't find him.' Mother Catherine repeated the words as though they might be amusing.

'No.'

'But of course you can't find him, Sister. Do you not know…' She was about to explain, but all of a sudden she drew her hands across her body and stopped. 'No,' she said then, more tightly. 'You can't find him.'

'No,' said Bernard again.

'But if you could help us with this – if you could make a full confession, might that not bring the soldier back, Sister? Might it not help you regain your place in his affections? Might he not come then and find you?'

Bernard held onto the questions as though they were promises. She screwed the wash cloth tightly in both hands and ignored the God that was beginning to rail at her. She felt she could do anything.

'I will see him again,' she said.

Mother Catherine nodded. 'When you have confessed, Sister.'

'But won't you—?'

'Let's see what happens, shall we?'

Bernard took it as another promise. She smiled. Mother Catherine smiled back, and made her way slowly behind the desk.

'Good. Then you'll help us clear up this little affair, Sister? You'll go to Father tomorrow in the church and confess yourself fully to God?'

Bernard was still smiling. 'Yes, Mother,' she said. And she remembered suddenly what it was that she wanted to say; her smile faded. 'I didn't think... when I told him about Sister Jean, I didn't think – I didn't want people to die. I didn't want Severine to die, Mother.'

Mother Catherine sighed. 'It would have happened anyway, Sister. You can be sure of that. There are many of us who are tempted by sin.'

Bernard did not understand. 'But when I told him—'

'You will simply do what we're asking, Sister? That will be enough.'

'Yes, Mother,' said Bernard, disappointed.

'Good. Then you may go.'

The following evening, the church was busy, as it always was when the confessional boxes were open. Candles were lit everywhere, making the dark dance, and the nave was filled with the soft silence of shared purpose. Kneeling on the floor in front of the Lady chapel, in the front row of pews by the altar and here and there down the side of the aisle, those who had already spoken to the priest were reciting their penances, their heads bowed and their hands clasped tight. At the back of the church, where the confessionals were tucked into a corner, four or five rows of pews were filled with those waiting their turn, praying quietly, unhurried. When Sister Bernard came to take her place at the end of this queue there was hardly a ripple of movement. No one spoke. No one seemed to notice.

The penitents were admitted at brisk intervals of two or three minutes, each leaving the door of the confessional ajar as they left to signal to the next that the priest was ready. One or two exchanged a nod as they passed, or even a word; mostly it was choreographed as though from ancient memory, without need of prompts or signs. Bernard moved up the pews steadily towards the front of the queue, her mind on the soldier and how he would look after their time apart, his blue eyes shining on her finally, everything forgiven. She did not notice those coming and going around her; she hardly knew where she was. God's grumble seemed distant to her, nothing more than noise. Everything was suspended in the promise of love. When her turn finally came to confess – when she knelt on the soft cushion and leant towards the pricked grille to begin her prayer – she did not notice that Father Raymond had stepped outside of his confessional for the briefest of moments, looked around him blankly at the cold church and then left his door open so that the stories of Bernard's sins would seep out to the faithful gathered close to listen.

Bernard confessed everything as she had been told to, trusting the priest to absolve her. She recited her trespasses steadily to the trefoiled screen in front of her, and she bent her head for the blessing. When it was finished, she said her penance by the candles at the side of the Lady chapel. The other penitents moved apart for her. Behind her, the queue had ended and Father Raymond came to stand by the confessional door, the villagers clotting towards him, watching her, waiting for her to finish her prayers. But Bernard did not notice. The priest had been stern with her, unusually relentless in his battle for her soul, and she had been given several rosaries to recite before she could leave the church. She edged the beads slowly through her fingers, her head low and her breathing tight. She lost count several times and had to begin again.

By the time the penance was said and she was finally back outside in the village, it was dusk – the hour when the soldier might come. She hardly glanced at the villagers still clustered by the confessionals; she did not think it strange that they should be gossiping there, so long after the sacrament was concluded. All she felt was the skip of expectancy. She could not believe it would be long now.

But he still did not come to her. There was no sign of any of the soldiers in the village. And yet it was not how it had been before they came. It was all new. What she had known before seemed faded and forgotten. Instead, there was the unshakeable sense of them, the constraint of occupation somehow knotted into everything, the unmoving branches in the breeze, the moss gathering on the shadowed corner of a roof, the silence of her footsteps on the stone square. Bernard felt all of the Germans, close about her. She knew they were there. But although she walked again to the places where she had met her soldier, he did not yet appear. And in the end she had no choice but to go back to the convent, making her way up the hill, the village receding behind her, the church sinking into the dusk.

At the gates she watched the last of the light fade turquoise behind the high oaks and again she waited. A night wind blew up, bristling with the smell of summer, and a slim crescent of moon hung low behind the trees. Bernard swayed gently from side to side, relieving the pain and tiredness in her legs. She kept watch in the dark for as long as she could. But there was just the tumbling song of the nightingales and the burr of the crickets and the wretched twitter of God, unstoppable.

The footsteps, when they came, were brisk and heavy, unfamiliar, and when the figure emerged from the night, it was the commandant. Bernard heard her breath come more quickly but she was so confused by the sight of him that she did not move. He did not greet her.

'Ah, Sister. You have confessed,' he said. His French, as always, was impeccable but his tone was coarse and unsteady.

She nodded.

Shuffling in the dark, he took something from his pocket. Bernard stepped back. But it was only a loose packet of cigarettes which he tapped on his palm. The flare of the match illuminated him for a moment.

'Good,' he said. 'You are very good.'

He turned his heel rhythmically in the dusty ground at the end of the drive and looked about him, the soft summer dark somehow inviting. Bernard was thinking of the soldier.

'Your Mother Catherine is a wise woman,' said the commandant. 'An honourable woman. The stupid peasants should be grateful for her.' He grinned. 'I am grateful for her.'

'She said the soldier would come again, once I'd confessed,' explained Bernard.

The commandant laughed, too loud and raucous for the falling night. Birds fluttered up from the trees nearby, alarmed, their wings panicked; a dog barked in the village.

Bernard knew then that something had happened.

'Oh,' she said.

And there was such dread clawing at her throat and stomach, such a darkness sinking upon her, that she could not think of anything else to say. She looked up into the commandant's face, silent, but the plea was there, begging him, of all people, to make things right.

The longing in Bernard's eyes confounded him.

'She didn't tell you? The boy's dead, you know.' He said it quickly, fiercely, so that there could be no mistake. 'He did not die honourably.'

He had curled in the corner of the damp cellar, gripping a small bronze crucifix and weeping. They had called the priest to give the last rites, but the soldier had found a final furious anger from somewhere, and had pushed him away, spitting and kicking, uncontrollable. They had had to tie him up in his own filth like an animal and cut out his tongue to silence him. The commandant had carried out the execution himself, disgusted.

'Schwanz?' asked Bernard quietly, but the name came too heavy and abrupt, too strange. It felt like a blasphemy.

The commandant smiled.

'Jens Aden was his name.'

For a moment, delighted, Bernard thought they might have killed another man.

'Not Schwanz?' she said, and she tried to describe him as she would see him in her dreams. 'The fair one. Tall and fair, with gentle hands and the straight back of a man and the beautiful—'

'The skinny one. That's him. But his name is – was – Jens Aden,' said the commandant again, with some impatience.

The darkness closed in on Bernard. They had not killed a different man. They had killed her soldier. To be without him in this way, even now, to be without hope of him, crushed her. She felt faint. There was a whimpering in her head that might not be God and it felt like she was in a storm again, encircled by a tumult she did not grasp.

She sat back on the low wall that ran out from the gates. The commandant took a step towards her, perhaps to help, but thought better of it and just stood watching her, fascinated by her grief. Then, even though she did not want to know that the soldier had been lying to her, even though she could not bear the half-thought that he had tricked her into believing in him, Bernard asked, 'Schwanz? Is that… a nickname?'

That would have been merciful, fond and intimate, somehow innocent. But even his name would not be left to her. The commandant shook his head, smiling.

'You French are all so stupid,' he said, chortling at his platoon's vulgar joke and rather proud of its success. 'Schwanz is not a name. It's a thing. *Der Schwanz*.' He grinned and tapped at the flies of his uniform trousers with a wink. 'Sometimes,' he said, 'a big thing, juicy and satisfying – is that not so, Sister?'

A barn owl screeched and a moment later its pale wings cut through the night to one side of them. The commandant let his hand drop, and found he could not quite look at the nun now. He frowned, dropping his cigarette end to the ground and stamping it hard into the dry earth. They both smelt the cloying summer of the soil.

'I thought I would love him for ever,' said Bernard simply.

'Did you?' He had never been so respectful.

'What shall I do?'

The commandant shrugged. He straightened his uniform jacket.

'I have an appointment, Sister,' he said. 'I'm sorry.'

He saluted her neatly.

'God have mercy on us sinners, eh?'

And he walked away up the hill towards the convent, dissolving into the shadow of the clenched oaks that lined the drive.

Bernard watched him as far as she could and then listened for all sound of him to die away. She got up from the wall. She was unsteady, stumbling slightly as she stood. The air seemed suddenly too cold, and she clasped her arms around her, drawing the warmth from her body. Her injuries throbbed. Schwanz then was a part of a man, the shameful, brutal, unholy part that is hidden from God. Not a lover; not a fit name to be treasuring. She was sorry it was too late to do anything about this. Schwanz was the name she would carry with her through the despair of her mourning, and the terrible sorrow that replaced it. For the rest of her life, she knew, she would cling to it, to the radiance of her weeks with him and the frantic desire to do penance for his death. Jens Aden would mean nothing to her.

She breathed deeply, coughing, and went back inside for evening prayer. The sickle of the moon continued to rise over the convent, but its light was faint.

# Twelve

At Les Cèdres the Christmas party fell on the feast of Saint Lucy. In the bustle, the saint was mostly unremembered. The uneven strings of blinking lights were a distraction, and those who thought to offer a prayer to Lucy that day were less concerned with the cult of her virginity than with a persistent pagan craving for more light to keep back the winter dark.

Immediately after breakfast, the tables were laid with bright napkins, paper plates and sprigs of cedar. A haphazard dance of skinny nativity figures and fat foil snowmen was stuck to the windows by lunch. Some of the residents enjoyed watching the preparations. One or two helped with the decorations. There was a loosening of routine, a sense of holiday. But Bernard was confined to her bed with a drip in her arm and knew nothing at all about it. For an hour or so in the afternoon she was faintly aware of unfamiliar activity in the corridor, more noise and footsteps than usual, an unaccustomed smell of spice, but she did not care to think what it might all be about.

The staff left Bernard to herself. Now and again they looked in on her, conscientiously filling up the blank lines in her medical sheet, the changes of handwriting marking the changes in shift. But there was plenty to do for the party, and the nurses took their readings briskly and left. Bernard did not move. By the time the celebration began and the buffet was irrevocably muddled, she had been lying for so long on her back with her eyes fixed to a spot in the ceiling that the bones in her hips, shoulders and ankles screamed with pain even through the fog of her medication.

Veronique heard the sound of brittle singing dribbling along the corridor. She did not recognize the tune. Two nurses hurried past her flapping something between them, a sheet or a sack, perhaps part of the fun, and she stepped aside too quickly, knocking her ankle against a sharp angle of the wall. She rubbed at it, bewildered. The bustle confused her. She had been expecting a familiar institutional hush, the permanent whisper of age. She had pictured her grandmother dozing in the corner of some deserted day room, everything about it predictable, the sticky magazines and the plastic covers and the colourless light. She had thought it would be quietly done, a secret. But now there was the sparkle of Christmas breaking through here and there, and the song. The thought of joining a festive party unsettled her.

She followed the noise and watched through the open door for a long time. All the staff and residents had their backs to her. The man who played piano was twisting bright balloons as an interlude to the music, making a series of bulging dogs. Veronique looked hard at the backs of heads, the matted and thinning hair, the skewed tufts pushed hard against the stiff antimacassars. She knew Sister Bernard would be effectively disguised if for some reason she had decided not to wear her veil, but still Veronique was quite sure that her grandmother was not in the room. She looked again, to be sure. It was very hot. She felt the bruise on her ankle throb. She had brought an extravagant selection of chocolates, piled in a gold box and tied round many times with metallic ribbon. She feared they would melt.

The show with the balloons was brief, and when the next song started up, one of the staff sidled along behind the row of chairs. She glanced at Veronique's stylish chocolate box and pulled back, wary of some kind of trick.

'Yes?' She was haughty. 'You have come to see someone?'

Veronique was not put off. 'Yes, I have,' she said, and paused. 'I've come to see Sister Bernard.'

The nurse could feel her unlit cigarette in her pocket. She fingered the butt end, pleased by its softness. She too was hot and craved the relief of standing outside by the deliveries door in the smoky chill.

'*Sister* Bernard?' she said. 'I think you must be wrong.'

Veronique looked at her without replying, daring her to say something else.

'Bernard,' said the nurse, 'is a man's name.'

'It's her name,' said Veronique.

The nurse shrugged. She looked again at the glitzy chocolate box.

'Ask at the desk,' she said. She pushed past Veronique into the corridor and took the cigarette from her pocket,

lodging it between her stained fingers. Then she turned.
'Is it *Sister* Bernardette or *Father* Bernard?'

'Neither. It's Sister Bernard.'

There was a rumble of uneven applause from behind.

'You're sure?'

Veronique nodded, already doubting.

The nurse gave a half-smile. 'Beautiful chocolates,' she said, and she turned away sharply, cutting across the corridor and pushing through a blank door.

The slop of the nurse's shoes on the hard floor faded quickly, there was a pause in the singing; no one else joined or left the party. It was as though everything was waiting for her decision. Veronique leant against the door frame. The heat was terrible, stifling, impossible. She could not shake the grasp of it. She closed her eyes.

Where had she got the name from, anyway? There had been a brief introduction one hurried afternoon at the old convent, nothing more. She could have misheard. At the time, it hadn't been of any importance. There had been no reason to pay attention or remember. Perhaps she was mistaken. She tried to think back to the funeral. She thought she had heard the name again there, something the other nun had said, but it was hard to be sure. It would be an odd name to have, for a woman. She saw that. Bernadette was more likely. Veronique had heard of Bernadette. Given time, she could have remembered her visions at Lourdes. It was a genuinely religious name.

The piano began again with a soft tune, a lullaby. Veronique could not bear its melancholy. She slipped further down the corridor and found a glass door wedged open with a table. It led outside, to the back of the building. A narrow concrete path sliced down through the bins to the gas cylinders, and turned at right angles towards a square of tarmacked car park and some kind of shed, its corrugated iron roof hanging loose at one end. Veronique did not take the path. Instead, she set off across the short grass, skirting the gas cylinders and following a sparse line of shrubs, winter bare and gnarled. The ground was chill through the thin soles of her shoes. In the unwarmed shadows, frost lay, not quite silver any more. Veronique breathed in the cold. Her skin tingled. It felt like an escape.

She walked along the length of the building until she came to the back of the chapel, extending from the far corner, its long windows a break in the monotony of plain wall. She could not see in. There was just the muted colour of the glass, unspectacular from this side, dense violets pressed into fragmented frames. A ragged length of chicken wire ran from top to bottom, some kind of protection against hail or wind or boys with stones. It was the pattern of this she noticed, the loose hexagons somehow pleasing and the rusts and lichens mysterious. She stood for a while, tracing lines up and down through the wire and wondering about her grandmother's name. Could it be a nickname? Something shortened over the years, or a tease of some kind? Did nuns do that? She did not know enough.

She looked along the back of the building. Regular rows of small windows marked the layout of the rooms inside. Each was the same, uncurtained, the winter light stifling reflections and making the glass too dark.

Veronique looked at every window, but there was nothing in any of them, no clue. She shivered. The cold in her feet was damp now and almost painful. She heard a car pull up somewhere, its tyres noisy on the gravel. She knew she would have to decide. But the decision had been taken, long ago, before she even knew of it, in a time that had passed. It was perfectly made already, encrusted with age, crystalline, complete; it did not need her. Veronique realized this, too. She pulled her collar tight across her neck and walked back quickly to the party, shaking the cold from her legs, seeing the footprints she had left on the way out, pressed like bruises into the grass.

The song was one she knew. Her father had sung it with gusto every Christmas, standing on a chair at the head of the table, his arms flung wide and his head back, an enormous glass of eau de vie sloshing in his hand and tears streaming down his face, the agony of it making his voice coarse. Veronique heard it through to the end. The audience around her warbled, the high notes slipping away. At the end there was silence. Veronique edged her way forwards through the close armchairs and clutter of furniture. She put the glistening box of chocolates on the low glass table under the window, and someone nearby gasped in quiet admiration. Then she left.

When the nurse came in, she found Sister Bernard out of bed, leaning hard on the window frame, her stuttered breathing too loud in the room. Bernard turned at the noise. Her face was unsettled, so many questions there that it would not be still.

'Sister?'

'I can hear God again.'

The nurse smiled. 'You should be back in bed, Sister.'

She came forwards, but Bernard batted her away weakly.

'I'd been waiting,' Bernard said. 'I'd been waiting to hear God.'

'Then it is a blessing, Sister,' said the nurse, starting to rearrange the covers on the bed and wiping the end of the loose drip tube with a cloth.

Bernard clutched at the sill.

'I've been waiting,' she said again. 'All this time...'

The nurse filled the glass by Bernard's bed with water from a small bottle and snapped two white pills from their foil wrapper.

'You'll get cold, Sister. You should come back to bed.'

'It's different. It's not what I remember.' Bernard turned away and looked out of the window. 'I think perhaps I might have been confused. I might have been wrong.'

She spoke quietly to a point somewhere beyond the green gas cylinders and she pushed her flat hands against the glass.

'I wish... I wish I'd known. I wish someone had told me. I wish I'd known what God was. Do you think it's too late?'

Blood dripped fast from the purple gash where she had wrenched the drip from the soft skin of her arm. Below her, a figure moved across the grass, but she hardly saw it. Everything was murky.

The nurse came to her and pulled her gently towards the bed, making her sit on the edge and handing her the glass of water and the pills.

'It'll be all right, Sister,' she said. 'Come on – we just need to put you back to bed. We need to get you fixed up again.'

She reached for something on the table and then pulled the drip tube across, letting it hang loose across Bernard's shoulder for a moment.

'I'll pop downstairs and find someone to help me, Sister. You'll be all right. You just lie down for me, you make yourself comfortable. And I'll be back to sort you right out. I'll only be a minute.'

She left the door ajar. The music pressed up from the party below. But Bernard was undisturbed by the tuneless singing and unmoved by the song of memories. She could hear nothing except the voice of God. Clear and soft, no longer strident in His scolding, He filled her with the balm of His conversation. He spoke to her without ceasing, called to her gently, intoned His love for her. The fasting had been worthwhile. The waiting had ended. He had come back to her. Her head was full of Him again, blotting everything, making sense of her. Bernard lay back on the bed. She could not feel her pains. There were only the unsteady shadows of the room, dim to her sight, and the voice, undeniable.

That God was, for some reason, speaking in an impenetrable dialect, with the rhythms of a language that sounded to her like Chinese and with a deluge of slippery phrases which made no more sense than birdsong did not, just at that moment, matter to her. She hardly noticed. The relief of an ending was warm inside her, a comfort. It was enough to know that she was again important to God and that He spoke to her in Schwanz's familiar tones, her life dissolving in its aging melody, everything else forgotten. It was enough that her passion had not been wasted.

# Note on the Author

Jacqueline Yallop read English at Oxford and did her PhD in nineteenth-century literature at Sheffield University. She has worked as the Curator for the John Ruskin Museum in Sheffield and writes on the Victorians. She is the author of the non-fiction work *Magpies, Squirrels and Thieves* and the novel *Kissing Alice*. She currently lives in France.